THE

SAMURAI'S

SOUL

Other Titles by Walt Mussell

The Samurai's Heart (The Heart of the Samurai Book 1)

The Samurai's Honor (The Heart of the Samurai Book 0)

A Second Chance

THE

SAMURAI'S

SOUL

Walt Mussell

ISBN: 978-0-9992910-7-8
Published by Chrysanthemum Cross Press

Please Note

This is a work of fiction. Names, characters, places, and incidents either are the product of the author's imagination or are used fictitiously, and any resemblance to actual persons, living or dead, business establishments, events or locales is entirely coincidental.

Cover Design by Killion Publishing. Sword picture on cover provided by RVA Katana of Richmond, Virginia.

DEDICATION

For Mom – Because I was nearly 11.5 lbs. at birth.

For both my parents – Because I've remained a huge pain.

Dad, I'm glad you're still around. Mom, I wish you were.

CAST OF CHARACTERS

In 16th century Japan, commoners only had one name. Surnames were reserved for the upper levels of society, though famous artisans might "earn" the name of their location. In the case where more than one name is shown, the name is given Japanese style with the surname first.

The Cloth Merchant Family (No surname)

Mori – The head of a family.

Futsu – Mori's wife. Calligraphy teacher.

Genta – Eldest of six children and will inherit the family business. His wife is Sadayo.

Natsu - Child #2 and eldest daughter. First Husband passed. Married to a tatami mat merchant. Two kids.

Shuji - Child #3 and the only other boy. His wife is Ogin. Lives and works at home.

Kiku - Child #4. Married to an oil presser. Childless. Husband not named.

Hoshi - Child #5: Married to cotton merchant. With child. Husband not named.

Aki – Child #6 and the only unmarried one.

Riku – Mori's older brother. Runs the business he and Mori grew up in.

Osaka Police Office

Nishioji Tsuneomi (Tomi) – Samurai from Himeji. Works with police in Osaka. Seeking a clandestine group of anti-Christian samurai.

Matsubara Kiitai (Matsu) – Fellow samurai from Himeji. Works with Tomi.

Yori – Teenage samurai and Osaka native. Supports Tomi and Matsu. Yori has a last name, but it is not stated in the book as he is trying to earn his name.

Oeda, Tanaka – Constables. These are surnames. Oeda is the direct superior to Nishioji, Matsubara, and Yori. Tanaka

oversees a separate department.
Goto, Ishii, Arai, Shoichi – Officers in Osaka's police department. The first three are surnames. The last one is a first name.

The Tokoda Family

Tokoda Shigehiro – Deceased patriarch and former high-ranking samurai at Himeji Castle.

Tokoda Ujihiro – Eldest son. Assumed his father's role at Himeji Castle. Coordinating the search for anti-Christian samurai.

Tokoda Toshihiro – Middle son. Seeking the group of anti-Christian samurai in Kyoto.

Tokoda Nobuhiro – Youngest son and swordsmith. Bullied as a child by Tomi.

Catholic Missionaries

Padre Alvares – Portuguese priest who runs a Catholic mission in Osaka. His parishioners call him *Arubaresu* or "padre" with a Japanese accent.

Hisa, Ruka – *Dōjuku* (Japanese Jesuit laity who assist with church activities). First name as well as variations on Baptismal names.

Kazu – Preteen boy who assists Padre Alvares. He was homeless on the streets and adopted by the church.

The Family From The Undersirable/Outcast Village

Father – Addressed as "Father". Referred to by others using such words as outcast, undesirable, and by a pejorative.

Shio – Outcast's daughter

Hachiro – Outcast's son. Goes by "Hachi". He is married and his wife (no name) is pregnant.

Other Characters

Wakizashi – A Japanese word that refers to the shorter of the two swords worn by samurai and the nickname the main villain uses in self-referral. He oversees smuggling in Osaka.

Tantō – A Japanese word that also refers to a short sword and another villain's nickname.

The Captain – Captain of ship that brings smuggled silk into Osaka

Soru – First mate on the smuggling ship.

Lord Eijiro – Figure in the capital who oversees all anti-Christian operations

Akagi, Fukuhara – Retainers of Lord Eijiro

Ruri – A young boy

Special Japanese Terms Used In This Book

Iesu – The Japanese word for Jesus.

Kirishitan – The Japanese word for Christian. If spoken by a Japanese person, this term is used along with synonyms such as "believer". If unspoken, the word Christian is used.

Bateren – The Japanese word for foreign missionaries. It approximates "padre".

Eta – A generic societal name used for "undesirables", denoting those who work with dead bodies, leather tanning, sanitation, etc. It is in line with the 16th century but inappropriate and cringe-inducing in modern Japan.

Koshikakae – Title given to elderly woman who assists with local births. Forerunner of midwife. A typical koshikakae would serve a specific neighborhood or district. One resident in a district would also have a special building that a koshikakae uses for all births in the aera.

Yūjo – prostitute. There are three prostitutes in the book, but none of their names are mentioned.

Kaizoku – pirate, though there were multiple terns.

Referenced Historical Figures

Toyotomi Hideyoshi – Current ruler of Japan and the second of Japan's three great unifiers, he was referred to as "the Regent". His nickname was "Saru" or "Monkey".

Oda Nobunaga – The first of Japan's three great unifiers. Assassinated (took his own life after being surrounded) by one of his generals, Akechi Mitsuhide, in June 1582.

Ishida Mitsunari – One of the *go-bugyō*, Hideyoshi's five administrators who assisted Hideyoshi in running Japan. Mitsunari oversaw justice for Japan. He was likely the magistrate of Sakai, or else served as magistrate of Sakai and Osaka with Mashita Nagamori, another *go-bugyō*.

Takayama Ukon – A daimyo and Japan's most famous male Christian. He lost his fief in 1587 for refusing to renounce his faith. The Jesuits referred to him as "Uçondono".

Padre Organtino (Gnecchi-Soldo Organtino) – Italian Jesuit missionary. His compassion made him popular in Japan.

Padre Frois (Luis Frois) – Portuguese Jesuit missionary. Wrote well-known historical records of his time in Asia and was the official translator in Japan for many years.

PREFACE

This book is a work of historical fiction, but it attempts to project realistic images from history. Because of this, it uses a Japanese term that was appropriate for the time but is unacceptable in modern Japanese. The term is discussed in more detail in the Author's Historical Notes, along with other items. The author is working on a complete historical explanation. Please check his website for details. The items below are suggested for reading before starting the story.

City Place Names

Kyoto – The city of Kyoto was the capital of Japan for over 1000 years, and the word means "capital city". It had several names during that time. At the time of this book, the term "Miyako" may be the most appropriate name. However, the author uses Kyoto. European documents from the time record the name as both "Miaco" and "Kioto" as well as other titles.

Nakajima – Modern-day Osaka has a section called "Nakanoshima". In the 16th century, the few maps available say "Nakajima".

The Layout of Osaka

Osaka has a long history of re-routing its waterways and creating new ones to make commerce more efficient. Maps of that time are speculative and conflict with current perception. In addition, Osaka underwent substantial growth beginning in the 1580s as Hideyoshi, the second of Japan's three unifiers, embarked on a massive building campaign, ordering others to move into the city and making it a time of great change.

In 1587, Regent Toyotomi Hideyoshi issued a series of edicts ordering the Jesuit missionaries out of Japan. The edicts were a bluff. Hideyoshi feared a loss of trade with Europe, but he wanted the Jesuits to downplay their proselytization and adapt more to Japanese society. He looked the other way while most Jesuits remained in Japan, but he ordered over sixty of the 250 Christian places in Japan destroyed as an example to keep the missionaries in line.

Some people believed he didn't go far enough.

CHAPTER ONE

Osaka, Japan—February 1590 (A Few Days After the Lunar New Year)

Aki blew on her chilled fingers and then stuck her hands under her *kosode*, scrunching the sleeves of her garment. She shivered in the pre-dawn air and eyed her eldest brother, Genta, who stoked the fire in the floor hearth in the center of the room. The charcoal crackled as he spread it through the pit. She could have worn a long-sleeve garment to ward off the cold but found it restricted her movements when she practiced calligraphy. Her father added more charcoal to the hearth. The room would warm before the family cloth shop opened.

She examined the kanji she had written. Even with all her practice, her characters remained bland, not flowery like those of her sisters. *One more attempt.* She dabbed her brush into the ink and drew the first character again, making sure every stroke was in the correct order and possessed appropriate depth, as her mother had taught her.

Mother taught calligraphy classes to children at one of the nearby temples. Some samurai even paid her to give private lessons to their daughters, despite her mother's merchant status. Aki's two oldest sisters taught calligraphy to the daughters of high-ranking samurai. Her other sister likely would do so soon.

Aki's sisters were more than talented. They were beautiful, too, each with the round face and long hair of their mother. Aki's face was squarish, like her father's. When she was younger and her grandparents were alive, her grandmother had mentioned Aki reminded her of her sister. Father said her great-aunt was beautiful. It hadn't helped.

"All fathers say such to their daughters," she murmured.

Her father approached her. "All fathers say what to their daughters, Aki?"

She looked away, her face warm. Had she spoken out loud? "Nothing, Father."

Aki returned to her morning practice. A light breeze brushed her cheeks. She glanced at the window, which was open a crack to allow smoke to waft outside, and listened for Shuji, her other brother, but heard nothing. Father had said Shuji was assisting their uncle this morning and should return soon. She again looked at her paper and shook her head. If she didn't improve, no one would pay her to teach calligraphy.

"Daughter, you work too hard on that," her father said. "Why trouble yourself about it?"

Aki laid her brush on the bench. "I will *never* be the equal of my sisters."

"You are *my* daughter. That makes you equal. Do not forget that. You also have a gift for numbers. Genta will need your help when he inherits. Without you," her father said with a shudder, "without you, this could be the last generation of our family business."

Aki stifled a chuckle. "Father, one day I will marry. What will Genta do then? My sisters are married. I am not even promised." She looked him in the eyes. "Are you asking me to remain unmarried to support Genta?"

Her father shook his head. "No, you will marry one day. My only concern is to avoid a . . . avoid a . . ."

"An overbearing mother-in-law?" Aki offered, thinking of Kiku, her second sister. Kiku's mother-in-law was so tight she could squeeze a rope from discarded hemp fibers. Kiku taught calligraphy as an excuse to get out of the house.

Her father's expression grew soft. "Yes, but maybe someone else, as well."

Aki nodded in shared sympathy. Her father could only mean Genta's wife, Sadayo. Forget making a hemp fiber rope. Sadayo could weave cloth from beard shavings. "I understand."

Her father put his hand on her shoulder. "Do not worry, Aki. I will make the arrangements. Genta will need your support, but you'll marry someday. Soon."

Soon? The word hung in the air like the nasal chant of a temple priest begging for funds. Should she ask her father what he meant?

No. Remain silent. Father will tell you in time.

Her father sidled next to her at the desk and studied her characters. "Your efforts are improving. You would find a position if time allowed. I know you yearn to be like your sisters, but embrace the talent you have. We'll always need you here." He flashed a supportive smile. "Finish your practice. It will be light soon. We have work to do."

Her father squeezed her shoulder and headed toward Genta, Aki's thoughts trailing in his wake. *Need? Here?* Something else was happening. Something Father did not wish to discuss.

Chirping sounds through the window crack made Aki smile. Nature was rising to work, as well. Aki rubbed her palms together and reviewed her prior effort. *Improving?* Father's kind words were just words. Her brush strokes lacked definition the same way her weaving lacked firmness. She lacked the talents her sisters inherited. The family traded silk, cotton, linen, and hemp in all variations. Silk brought the largest profits, but cotton was growing, and her father said it was the future. Osaka continued to grow, and they could sell more if they had the space for more cloth.

Dogs barked nearby. Was Shuji coming home?

Her father returned to her side. "Do not brood any longer. You've a talent for money and good business sense. I've seen it. Customers respect your opinion. Genta may be older, but he will learn from you. Grab tea." His voice now carried an edge. "We've a busy day."

"Yes, Father." She stowed her paper and brush. *Genta. Genta. Everything for Genta.* When she was younger, Genta had tormented her, saying a demon had dropped her off during the night. Back then, he lived to make her life miserable. Then, one day he put a bee in her bedding as a prank. The bee stung her and turned her skin red. When Genta saw the doctor arrive, he apologized and rarely troubled her again unless he was in trouble himself. Aki forgave him.

Now Genta was married to a shrew, so Aki pitied him.

His wife seemed nice enough when Uncle arranged the marriage. She came from a family Uncle knew. Father had agreed with the match.

Father always agreed. His duty as the younger brother demanded it.

Uncle viewed her sisters as products. Marry them off and grow the business. Uncle had adopted Natsu, Aki's oldest sister, and married her into another family, but then Natsu's husband died. The family blamed Natsu for their son's death and the lack of children. Uncle declared Natsu a bad omen and sent her home to Father. Natsu remarried and now had two children. Uncle's return of Natsu was never mentioned in family conversation. Fortunately, Natsu's shame lasted only a short time.

The door slid open. Shuji entered, followed by his

wife, Ogin. Uncle sauntered in after them, his walk declaring him in charge. His gaze lingered on Aki before he motioned to Father, wanting to talk with him.

"Father, you have two appointments today," Aki reminded him.

"We'll talk later. Help Genta get ready."

Aki moved toward her brother, and Shuji joined them. Ogin flashed Aki a sympathetic glance and then went to the kitchen. At least Father had Shuji. Genta would oversee the family one day, and Shuji was there, if he was needed. Uncle had tried to adopt Shuji. For once, Father had refused.

A few minutes later, the door slid open. Uncle departed, again looking at Aki before he left. Her stomach churned as if she had eaten foul fish.

"Aki, a minute. Now," her father said.

Aki hurried to him. "Father, about the appointments, two merchants are visiting from—"

"We can discuss that later."

Later? Father's tone chilled her like the morning wind.

"What is it?" Her voice trilled like the bird songs outside.

Her father rubbed a hand across his mouth as if afraid to speak. "Uncle has a request."

Nishioji Tomi rubbed the wooden railing of the bridge, feeling the smooth finish against his fingers as he eyed the figure retreating from a visit to the cloth merchant, a connection to investigate after Tomi reported the morning activities to the constable. The man headed in the direction of Osaka Castle, but nearly everyone did if they headed east. A crescent sliver of moonlight glimmered against the gold plating along the eaves of the castle, illuminating the two golden *shachihoko*, the mythical fish with a tiger head at each end of the ridge. The black castle was more silhouette than shadow at night, but the plates reflected available light.

Little time remained before daylight. Darkness was

fading against the soon-rising sun. Icy wind sped through the streets, billowing through the layers of Tomi's clothes. The sharp air cut his cheeks, driving away the scant sleep left in his eyes. Tomi had been up over two hours already. No samurai slept well when duty beckoned.

Murmurs from shops preparing behind closed storefronts disturbed the solemn, pre-dawn setting. Birds chirped and cawed about him, an ensemble of high and low pitches like lutes fighting for supremacy. His fellow samurai, Matsu, would know which songs belonged to which birds. He'd learned about them from his parents while growing up. He claimed the bird songs appealed to his personality. Tomi's own mother would know the songs, too. When Tomi was younger, his mother had tried to teach him the song of the tit bird as a warning for snakes, but snakes slept in winter, and bird sounds merged in dissonance. Tomi remembered little of those lessons. Mother would be disappointed in him.

May she wake well this morning. If it warmed up, they could sit outside and enjoy nature when he had a few minutes to rest at home, if he had a few minutes.

Every morning, it felt like he rose earlier to work and returned home later. He should try for an early evening. She would enjoy that. If only he could build a place for the sick here. The padres had built one in Kyushu. They called it a hospital. Unfortunately, people like his mother had few options.

Tomi focused on the shop that was the target of the morning activities, a large trader in the cloth district, a merchant who handled a good quantity of silk. Was it too much? Rumors abounded of silk smugglers who traded directly with merchants from China instead of obeying the required trade controls. Some fabric businesses always seemed to have silk available. The question was which ones were getting it illegally. Tomi sighed. His gut said this was probably not the place, but they had a tip and had to search.

They would take the owner to jail for nonpayment of taxes and then search the business for excess silk. Tomi did not like lying about his intentions, but the constable had given orders.

Were they ready to move?

Shadows flickered from the stone oil lamps that lined the street, catching a subtle movement near a building two shops away from the place Tomi watched.

Matsu.

Tomi would chide him later. His friend, Matsubara Kiitai, was supposed to remain hidden, keeping watch for surprises. Granted, Matsu would retort it was intentional, that he'd allowed Tomi to see him to confirm his position, a signal that it was time to move.

He again studied the storefront. The low knocks and thuds from inside suggested a family preparing for the day. He glanced back toward Matsu. Nothing. His friend had disappeared into the remaining darkness to hide.

Pressure slammed on Tomi's shoulders, pushing him toward the ground. He struggled to maintain his balance. Stepping back, he jabbed his elbow down.

Bone met bone. The pressure released. Tomi turned.

A figure fell backward and hit the ground. Tomi grabbed his sword, drawing it halfway out before recognizing his friend's face in the scant light. He heaved a sigh and shoved his sword back into the scabbard.

Always with his jokes. "Matsu, what are you doing?"

Matsu rose and rubbed his right forearm with his left hand. "Catching you unaware, it appears."

Tomi shook his head. "I drew my sword. I could have killed you."

Matsu rolled his eyes. "You were distracted. Admit it." He waved his arms upward. "You were looking about. Enjoying the scenery for a change?" He paused for a second to allow for a few chirps. "This morning's symphony is stellar for winter."

"I'll never understand your fascination with pigeons."

"*Hato?*" Matsu shook his head. "More than pigeons out there." He paused, likely to make a point. He joked the same way. "Don't forget the crows."

"They're black and hard to see in the dark."

Matsu stared as if annoyed. "Not important. What's important is this." He slowed his speech. "Had I been an assassin, you'd be dead."

Matsu's words hung in the air as if waiting for a challenge.

"You overestimate yourself," Tomi whispered. "You're not that good."

"Snuck up on *you*. Not alert this morning."

Tomi huffed and broke a smile. "I'm always alert. Birds or no birds."

More chirps sounded. "Appreciate the birds as I do. They help one keep life in place. When they change their song, the situation has changed. Notice they just started chirping a few minutes ago?"

Tomi thought hard. "No. Why?"

"They just woke up. They sleep later than we do. Try it. It'll help you focus."

"My focus is fine," Tomi huffed. "It's always fine."

Matsu eyed him. "Then how did you misplace your sword?"

"I'll have revenge for that prank one day." Tomi gritted his teeth and stared. "Uji always said you were like him, somber. But you're nothing like that. You have more in common with Toshi."

Matsu chuckled, and Tomi bit back a smile as fond memories of the Tokoda family surfaced. He missed all three of the Tokoda brothers. Ujihiro, or Uji, the eldest of three, took command of the samurai guarding Himeji Castle upon the death of his father, the famed Tokoda Shigehiro. Uji's search for a conspiracy of clandestine anti-Christian groups had prompted Tomi and Matsu's move to Osaka for a covert investigation. Uji sent his middle brother Toshihiro, or Toshi, to Kyoto for the same reason. Nobuhiro, the youngest, was a swordsmith in Himeji. Given how often Tomi had bullied Nobuhiro when they were children, earning Uji's respect and Nobuhiro's forgiveness were the most important honors Tomi had ever earned.

"Uji was right," Matsu said. "Like him, I prefer silence. It's the reason we get along. In silence, you can hear the birds. However, Uji rarely broods, which is why I never pranked him."

"That, and he is your superior."

"Yes, but he has a sense of humor."

"Uji? Really?"

"If we were in a horse race, I could claim his saddle was loose and cause him to lose focus. He'd find it funny."

The fabled wager of the samurai who lost a race and his horse for believing his opponent when he pointed out a loose saddle was a lesson in preparation and vigilance. "As long as he didn't lose the horse."

"Never take it from him. Besides, he's Toshi's brother. Hard to be Toshi's brother and not have a sense of humor. Therefore, he rarely broods. You brood a lot. If you weren't a *Kirishitan,* you'd make a good temple priest. Most of them seldom laugh."

Tomi relaxed. Matsu was one of the few in Osaka who knew Tomi's faith, not that Tomi kept it hidden. The nationwide Christian ban remained in effect, but enforcement was another matter. The churches left were allowed or overlooked. In Himeji, there were no churches, but there never had been. In Osaka and nearby Sakai, authorities destroyed the churches and missionary residences there. The padres, the foreign holy men, established fresh places amid old ruins. The authorities allowed it, provided the missionaries remained discreet.

Tomi reached below the fabric on his left side, fingered his rosary beads, and uttered a quick, silent prayer. No enforcement for now. The time might come when they must hide. "I wouldn't make a good Buddhist priest," he said. "I have warred against them too much."

"Rub those juzu beads of yours all the time."

"They're not juzu beads."

"Look like the beads Buddhist priests carry."

"I'll teach you the difference one day."

Matsu opened his mouth to respond, but Tomi silenced him with an open palm. Both men had fought at Negoro-ji. The warrior monks fleeing that blazing temple had had no chance, but it wasn't the time to relive that bloody battle and why such killing filled him with remorse.

Seeing the destruction then, seeing more death in later battles fought with his soul. Was there not a life beyond killing and those who took their own lives out of duty?

"We can discuss my religious future later," Tomi said. "Did you see the man who left? I couldn't see his face."

"Yes," Matsu said. "Riku, the silk merchant."

"The ward leader who lives near the castle?"

"The same. Know him?"

"I wouldn't recognize him." A light flickered in the corner of Tomi's eye. He glanced at the merchant's storefront. More light emanated from a cracked window. The house was awake. "We need to understand why he was here later. Our target stirs. Time to summon Yori."

Matsu cupped his hands and placed them in front of his mouth, making the low-pitch warble of a wren. Matsu had picked the bird, saying it would be rare this early in the year. He blew a second time and listened.

A similar call returned. One tweet.

A tall, thin shadow emerged from the darkness to the left of the business. The light revealed a gangly young man with his hair tied behind him. He darted toward them, closing the distance to the bridge to reveal a face mixed with eagerness and servitude. He bowed to Tomi. "I am ready, Nishioji-sama."

Tomi eyed the 15-year-old samurai called only Yori for now as the family petitioned for a new last name. He was talented. By age thirteen, he'd earned the right to test his sword. Last year, the constable assigned the young man to Tomi and Matsu to assist in their investigations. Though a low-ranking samurai like most officers, Yori possessed the lineage to be a constable himself. Tomi and Matsu had been wary of adding the young man, but Yori had served well.

"Seen anything that gives you concern?" Tomi asked.

"Nothing. Think the merchant will be suspicious when we explain?"

A dog barked in the distance, a sign of activity nearby but not close. Nothing to worry about yet.

"They'll be intimidated by the sight of us," Matsu said.

"Agreed," Tomi said. "Are you ready, Yori?"

The young man nodded, his gaze turning to steel.

"Then," Tomi said, "it's time to meet them."

Uncle has a request.

Aki's father's words pounded inside her head like a temple bell on New Year's Eve. She pressed her palm against her chest. The nearby voices of her brothers faded into silence. "What does Uncle want?"

"He . . . has requested a marriage for you. The youngest son of another fabric dealer. The family just moved to Osaka. They have relatives in Kyoto who handle only silk. Through this marriage, Uncle will expand his business."

His business? Aki's breathing grew labored. She wanted to throw up, but her stomach was empty. She wiped her hands on her sleeves but couldn't eliminate the sweat that permeated her fingers. "How would my marriage expand *his* business?"

Her father coughed and avoided her gaze, but his lips trembled. Not a good sign. Poor Father. Aki knew what was coming but could see how difficult it was for him.

"Father, I know my responsibility." She forced a smile to cheer his mood. "I will do my duty."

Her father nodded at her, at last making eye contact. "I know, Aki, I know. Uncle will . . . adopt you. You will become his daughter."

Daughter? Though Father's request matched her expectations, hearing it stung like a swarm of angry *hachi* protecting their honey. "*His* daughter? Father, tell Uncle to adopt the younger son. There are many women who would marry for money. How will I serve Genta if I am Uncle's daughter?"

"We'll find a way."

Aki lowered her hands to her sides and gazed at the wooden floor where her stomach now resided. Soft thuds echoed in the background with the crackle of fire as Genta and Shuji added more charcoal to the floor hearth. The yellow-orange sparks from the center of the room flashed as the wood hissed and then burned away like Father's request burned away her life.

Uncle's daughter. It was not Aki's place to voice her disapproval. As the youngest of four daughters, Aki's life was always marriage fodder. Had Father requested she marry, she would for love and respect as much as duty.

With Uncle making the request, she complied only from duty.

"Don't worry, Aki. Whatever your uncle is planning, I will ensure that you spend time here. We need you." He glanced toward Genta. "We will *always* need you."

Father's tone reassured her. Fighting to hold back tears, she raised her gaze to his glistening eyes. "Father, I will do whatever you think is best."

The door slid open, interrupting her thoughts. *Who would be here at this hour? A pre-morning delivery? Not likely. Uncle?*

No. Aki's breath caught in her throat. *Not uncle.*

Three samurai stepped into the genkan, their faces

hidden in shadows.

Aki knelt, bowing deep. Her family did the same.

"Osamurai-sama." Her father kept his voice low and measured, showing respect. "Welcome. Please enter. How may we serve you?"

Two of the three men removed their shoes and grunted as they crossed the threshold. "Stand," one of them said.

Aki rose but maintained a respectful gaze toward the floor. Of the two men, one was older, in his mid-20s, with muscular heft on his frame. The other one was younger, close to Aki's age, with long hair tied behind his back. The man in the genkan matched the older one, but the darkness made it difficult to tell. The men wore beige-colored *kosode*, cinched with an obi at the waist, and a darker *yono-bakama* that bunched at their knees. They also wore two swords, the mark of a samurai. Oddly, no crest decorated the kosode, but these men were higher than most police. Most police carried a club with curved blades.

What brought them here at this hour? Did a prominent official's wife need an early escort to shop? It had happened before. Who were these men?

Her father stepped forward. "How may we assist you?"

The young samurai maintained a flat expression as the older man approached her father. "We have reports of tax evasion from this business. We need to see confirmation of frontage tax, revenues, trade duties, plus the new temple tax."

Taxes? Samurai were here to discuss taxes? This was a neighborhood matter handled by guild wardens like her uncle.

"Yes." Her father nodded and glanced in her direction, his eyes perplexed. "My daughter will fetch them for you."

"I will help you." Genta moved to follow.

"You will stay put," the young samurai asserted. His tone raised the hair on Aki's arms. He would not be disobeyed. None of these men would.

Aki headed to the back of the shop, her heart pounding like a large *taiko* drum. Samurai checking taxes and asking for their records? It made no sense. The family paid the temple tax when it was authorized. The penalty for nonpayment was severe.

Whatever the concern, it must be sizable for samurai to be involved. Father could go to jail or worse. Aki helped Father with the records. What could they have done wrong?

Nothing. It was not possible. She'd measured the front of the property several times, including once with her father. She'd then checked the measurements against the payment stamp from the prior year. No discrepancies. There could be no excess frontage tax that they missed. There must be another reason. Other taxes, like the fees on imported silk? She worked with Genta since Father insisted Genta learn the financial aspects of the business. Father had reviewed everything and pronounced it acceptable. Could they have made an error?

Why did the young samurai forbid Genta to help?

Because he didn't fear a woman. *If he knew Genta better, the samurai wouldn't fear him, either.*

The lantern light in the back room cast a yellowish glow on the darkened records area. This section of the storage room was small, but father maintained the books in an ordered stack. She saw the table and hesitated. Today, the books appeared askew. Had Genta done something? She would ask him at her first opportunity.

Aki located the three record books she needed. Their faded black covers were tied at the top and bent from wear. She scanned both to ensure the information was complete. The calculations were right. The stamps were correct and properly notated for payment. Aki hurried back to the main room, slowing as she entered, to appear respectful, and approached the older samurai. The younger one stepped forward and blocked her approach. As he did, the samurai in the genkan stepped into the house. Aki bowed and held out the records to the young samurai, extending her arms to their limit.

The young man grunted, his voice dropping as if to suggest he was older. "Deliver them to the Justice Office yourself. Give them to Constable Oeda. I'm not a messenger."

Take them myself? To a Constable? Constables manage groups of officers. "Understood," she said, her voice high and meek in respect.

Aki stepped back as the older samurai stepped forward and gestured to Father. "You will come with us."

No. Do not take him. Aki stepped between her father and the samurai.

"Aki," her father ordered, "back to your place."

Conviction held her feet to the floor. "I do the records, Father. It should be me. If there is a mistake, it is my fault."

The young samurai glared at her, his face the hue of crimson after the third dye.

Aki's frame tightened and she trembled all over. "I meant no—"

"Silence," the young man thundered, his hand raised toward her. "How dare—"

A hand reached out and caught his wrist. The young man's face twisted in surprise.

"Stay your hand, Yori," a deep voice said.

The samurai from the shadows stepped into the light. He was half-a-head taller than her father, with a scar on his right cheek. His hair was tied in a topknot and folded toward the bald pate of his forehead. He wore a brown kosode like the other two, but muscles rippled in the arm that gripped the young samurai's wrist. His face brooked no argument. His figure stoked fear.

Why did he stop the younger samurai, who was within his right to strike me?

"She defies us." The young man's face remained intractable.

"She exhibits duty to her family. Do not mistake love for insolence."

The young man relaxed, and the tension ebbed from his frame. Aki was fortunate to be spared. The samurai with the scar released the wrist of the one called Yori. "Yes, Nishioji-sama," the young man said.

The samurai from the shadows, the one called Nishioji, stepped toward Aki. "Do not concern yourself. Your father won't be harmed. You have my word."

Aki's mouth quivered, but no words emerged. She looked in his brown eyes long seconds and knew she could trust him. She then glanced away, unfit to gaze into the eyes of a samurai. The warmth from the floor hearth behind her failed to stop the ice needles that danced across her skin. "Yes, Osamurai-sama," she said. She mustered a bow, the name Nishioji streaming through her thoughts.

Her father moved to stand next to the samurai. "I will return soon," he said. "Genta makes decisions until then."

Samurai Nishioji addressed Genta. "Several officers will be here shortly. Yori"—he nodded toward the young samurai—"will remain here until they arrive. The officers will search the premises. You and your family will answer the questions they have. You're not to open for business until they leave."

Genta's face resembled a nocturnal animal surprised by a torch. "We will obey your orders."

The one called Nishioji grunted then signaled to the one called Yori. Hand signals only. Nothing was said, but orders were given and understood.

Both older samurai scanned the room. Were they gauging the family? Mother kept their home neat and organized. Would the samurai find them insufficient? This Nishioji turned to her. His gaze softened, once again showing the mercy that had stifled the young samurai's anger. "Search your records again. Ensure you have everything. Bring them to the Justice Office as instructed."

"Yes, Osamurai-sama."

"Do you know the building?"

"I know the area. My father has shown me the new building."

"Not the new building. That is for land and population concerns. The Justice building is the remodeled temple next to it."

"I understand."

"Do not leave until full light. Brigands are out at this hour. It also creates improper impressions."

"I understand." Aki's breathing grew heavy. She was nervous about the visit to the Justice office. Samurai Nishioji held her gaze and released it with a nod.

A nod?

A show of respect from the samurai?

The back of her neck tingled. Honor to someone beneath him? Even the scar on his cheek relaxed, as if to convey that message. Had her defense of her father impressed him?

Maybe.

Samurai Nishioji-sama leaned aside and whispered to the young samurai, and then he and the silent one departed, her father trailing a few steps behind. The young one, Samurai Yori-sama, maintained a rocklike position at the door. Stoic. In charge. If Aki offended him again, she would not survive.

She glanced over his shoulder and watched as her father and the two samurai reached the street. The morning light was growing, and the road was coming alive, though people outside stepped back to give the samurai room.

The young samurai closed the door on her curiosity. Best she search the back room again to ensure she had everything, whatever she could provide. Appearing at the Justice Office without complete records would delay her father's release. The samurai indicated the family could eat while they waited. Food should help, but Aki wasn't hungry. The situation made no sense. Why samurai? This was a neighborhood issue.

Unless they are here for a greater reason.

The samurai were looking for something. Aki yearned to know the answer, but it was not her place to ask.

She did her best to avoid looking again at the young man. Everything would be known in time. This Nishioji-sama had said Father would return today. The thought calmed her. Something about the man's face, including his scar, made her believe him. His face was the kindest face she had ever seen.

For that reason, she knew she could trust him.

CHAPTER TWO

Tomi and Matsu left the cloth dealer with another officer and then departed for a break. It had been a long morning. They ducked into an alley a few streets away, finding a spot to talk between a dry goods shop with a stone wall and a lacquer products store. The spot provided relief from the wind. The day had warmed but remained chilly.

The alley was tidy and private. Given the proximity to Osaka Castle, the street crews maintained it well. No one would enter and approach them. If anyone did, then Tomi and Matsu would place a hand on their swords

Tomi chewed on a toothpick, a bad habit his mother chastised him for. Though that habit allowed him to focus, today his thoughts remained muddled. He leaned against the stone wall. A tingle on his back remained, like a spark igniting into flame. That tingle had taunted him all morning, ever since he'd glimpsed the cloth merchant's daughter.

Aki. A common word meaning "autumn" but not a common girl. As beautiful as the *kōyō* at Tōfukuji in Kyoto, a mix of leaf colors unequaled at any temple he'd ever seen. Tomi stared at his feet and recalled the morning, but the bitterness remained. He'd marred that girl's beauty when he took her father away.

For questioning. For useless questioning.

This wasn't a family of criminals. There were minor rumors of smuggling silk and silk threads but no leads on who was handling the goods. Rumors were not enough. They needed to jostle the district and make the fabric merchants nervous. Nervous men make mistakes. The police would be ready when the true criminals moved. Best to force something. Waiting reeked of desperation.

A small white dog galloped through the alley, glancing at Tomi like an old friend. The dog stopped and flashed his teeth. Tomi matched the display.

"Good to see there's one thing you like," Matsu said.

"He reminds me of a neighborhood dog I remember from Himeji. Go, my friend," he said, pointing to the other side. "We have work to do."

The dog barked and galloped away. Wafting scents of a nearby food stall, likely the dog's next destination, reached Tomi.

Matsu's stomach growled in response, like a bear waking from a winter sleep.

"I said yesterday we're going to get hungry," Tomi said, his chest puffed up. "I told you we'd be busy this morning. Did you listen? Follow the dog and beg for his scraps."

Matsu shot Tomi a silencing glare and then reached under his own garment, withdrawing a small pouch with two seaweed-wrapped rice balls. "Think me unprepared? Always ready."

Tomi relaxed. "I should've known."

"You should eat, as well. Much work to do."

"I ate before we started." Tomi glanced at the knots in the lacquer shop's walls. Muffled sounds of hard work inside mixed with the quiet steps from the streets. Could anyone inside hear them? "I'm not hungry."

"Doesn't matter," Matsu said, his gaze serious. "Better to keep your strength than your appearance. That toothpick you chew doesn't fool me. You have something."

Tomi smiled at Matsu's mention of the proverb of the hungry samurai gnawing on a toothpick, giving the impression he'd eaten. That wasn't Tomi. He reached under his coat and withdrew a rice ball himself. "Yes, I'm prepared," he said in a flat tone.

"Not bad." Matsu eyed Tomi while he downed his food. "That it?"

Tomi reached again under his clothing and withdrew a piece of sponge cake wrapped in leaves. He broke off a piece and allowed his mouth to absorb the honey flavor.

"What's that?" Matsu asked, looking confused.

"*Kasutera*," Tomi said, breaking off another small bite.

"Oh"—Matsu paused as if thinking—"that dish your...whatever makes. You've mentioned it before."

"Padre. His title is padre."

"Ask your *padre* to make some for me. When you fought in Kyushu, you came back with that new faith of yours. Converted for that sponge cake."

"It's offered to visitors. You're welcome to visit."

"Have my own deities."

"Yes, I know your deities." Tomi shook his head and sighed. "They have wonderful personalities, dance well, and play the koto."

"Such sarcasm, my friend, but my deities have other talents. Some are also skilled in tea ceremony. I know one that's good on the *sanshin*. Impress even you." Matsu curled his lips. "I worship my way."

"Well, you are fortunate." Tomi broke the remaining portion in half and offered it to Matsu. "The padre made extra this week. Try it."

Matsu took the proffered cake and nodded in gratitude. "You are generous. May you be blessed with their favor."

Tomi chuckled. "I'll pass."

"Your misfortune." Matsu took a bite. "Better than rice

balls. I should consider this faith if this is how you eat."

Tomi ignored him. "Did you think about something to drink?"

Matsu withdrew a gourd. "Of course."

"I should've known."

"Yes, you should."

Tomi laughed. Matsu grinned as he passed the gourd to Tomi, who took a swallow. Water. He would ignore Matsu's comment about tea ceremony with his deities, but tea would taste better. If only Tomi could convince Matsu to give them up.

The morning sun rose higher and breathed fire into the gold plating on the castle, the grandest anywhere in the world. It was the biggest Tomi had ever seen. According to Uji, Osaka Castle was even larger than Nobunaga's palace at Azuchi.

More passersby flittered on both sides, glancing in and then looking away. No person would enter, other than someone from the Justice office.

Not that Tomi was concerned. He'd left Yori at the home of the fabric merchant to watch things until other officers arrived. They must be searching the place for proof. How would one prove that a quantity of silk was more than normal? How would searching the house show that the family had paid their taxes? Only the young woman with the finances could show that.

What about her? Aki. Would she have an escort? Robbers might impede her at an early hour. That would not do. He'd guaranteed her father's safety. He needed to keep her safe, as well. Time would pass before they could free her father. *How can I keep my promise to her when the father's care is out of my control?* He bit his lower lip. He must maintain his word.

Matsu's face grew grim as clouds above them shaded the sun. His fingers tapped on the hilt of his short sword. "You view this duty as I?"

Tomi wiped flecks of sponge cake from his mouth with his finger. "A waste of time? Yes, activities like this morning distract us from our mission."

"Didn't mean that," Matsu said, a thoughtful expression on his face. "We've been here over a year. We're no closer to finding the clandestine group in Osaka than when we started."

"What are you saying?"

"Maybe there isn't one."

"I don't believe that," Tomi said with more force than he'd intended. "They're here. Those here have a special purpose."

Matsu avoided Tomi's gaze as he locked his hands behind his head. "Like you, I heard about Omi's rant before she died. The raving of someone who laughed at death to strike at life."

"Meaning?"

"She was possessed by the fox. A death poem with no truth."

"They're here. I feel it. We will find them."

Matsu looked at him. "Then we search elsewhere."

The suggestion struck Tomi like a winter plunge in the Dojima River. "Where?"

Matsu rubbed his palms together, a sign he was speculating out loud to hear himself talk. "Original plan was sound. You meet all the Kirishitan here. We work with the police. Know the city. Lower status, but better than a castle assignment."

"Maybe the castle would have been better. Actual decisions are made there. In Himeji, the criminals were samurai. It's probably the same here."

"Have you forgotten?" Matsu stared as he tilted his head. "Your status was reduced for your actions in Himeji. We're no longer worthy of the castle. This position is more plausible."

"In Himeji, the—"

"Listen to me," Matsu said, his voice heavy. "This. Is. Not. Himeji. In Himeji, the church was hidden. Here, the church is in the open. A violation but open."

"It feels like a secret."

"You go there every few days. Complaining?"

"No." Tomi's head throbbed as a prickliness streamed down his neck. "I want to make progress. We've accomplished nothing."

Matsu took a deep breath. "Patience, my friend. Criminals attract criminals. In our year here, we've brought many criminals to justice. Catching silk smugglers is a good use of time."

"Yes, but I crave—"

"What is it your philosopher says?"

Tomi cleared his throat but could not remove his embarrassment. He should preach to Matsu, not the other way around. "'Ask, and it will be given you?'"

"Was thinking 'have faith.'"

"Have faith?"

"Yes. Have faith. You're frustrated. Will pass."

Soft noises drew Tomi's attention. More onlookers stared at him and Matsu from both ends of the side street. A man dressed in a short coat that reached his thighs hefted a pole laden with umbrellas that hung down. How was he not cold? Tomi glared at him. The man's gaze widened, and he retreated.

"I crave progress." Tomi bit his lip. "I didn't see any purpose to this morning. This family? They're not criminals. No reason to put them through this."

Matsu opened his palms in agreement. "And no reason to leave them with a temperamental Yori."

"That, too." Tomi paused, recalling the early morning. "He's rash. Unpredictable."

"He's learning." Matsu rubbed his forehead. "Admires you. Follows your example. That's good most of the time."

"Most of the time?" Was Matsu serious or having

another joke at Tomi's expense? "What do you mean?"

"Know the story of the rich man and the poor man?"

Tomi searched his memory. "No."

"A poor man's wife convinced him that he should become a disciple of a rich neighbor and copy his artistic abilities."

"A sound strategy."

"Yes," Matsu replied, "except that the rich man's art was using a medicinal recipe to pass gas on command. Eager for riches, the poor man's wife pushed her husband to perform without practice. Did not go well."

Tomi pressed his lips together. "How does that affect Yori?"

"Be thankful that we have different talents, and that Yori practices what we teach him." Matsu smiled then turned serious. "He's grown this year, though he showed anger toward a girl who didn't deserve it."

Tomi brushed the light stubble on his chin. "Yori will do nothing further. I made sure of that."

"What did you say to him when you whispered in his ear?"

"I told him I'd received a sword from a renowned artisan and that I would test the blade on him if he did anything that brought grief to the merchant's family."

Matsu laughed. "What renowned artisan?"

"Nobuhiro."

"Nobuhiro? Uji's brother, who you *bullied* when we were younger. He made you a sword? You never told me."

"His first after completing his apprenticeship. A gift for saving his wife's life."

Matsu shook his head in amazement. "Never imagined that new sword of yours was a gift from Nobuhiro. No wonder you were upset when I hid it. Must mean a lot."

"Yes," Tomi's chest swelled. He'd healed his childhood wounds but had yet to salve his failure in Himeji. Several of his fellow believers had died. He was responsible. He should have foreseen the treachery. Forgiveness was a promise, but he did not deserve it. The sword Nobuhiro crafted contained the sun symbol of the foreign holy men in the sword guard, a reminder to Tomi of his faith. "I've atoned for the sins of my youth, but there are more to address."

"You protected the merchant's family"—he paused and bit his lower lip while nodding—"especially his daughter."

Tomi chuckled. "You are seeing things, my friend."

"The young lady is provocative. In several ways."

Tomi glared at Matsu. "Women are more than beauty."

"Not that you notice."

Tomi rubbed the back of his neck. A sign of trouble he'd learned never to ignore. He looked at the sun's position. It was time to free the fabric merchant. He must ignore it for now. Time to keep his promise.

Wakizashi eyed the young man before him. Devoted. Eager. Capable. One of the many who assisted with smuggling and supplied Wakizashi with information. "Any trouble with this morning's arrest at the fabric shop?"

"None, master," the man responded. "They arrested the father for tax evasion. A ruse. Sufficient to keep the police busy and away from us."

"Did they search the place?"

"They did." The man beamed. "We transferred our shipment of silk thread without notice."

Wakizashi nodded. "As I knew you would."

The young man studied him. "Master, how did you know?

"I know the man in charge." Wakizashi's chest swelled. "Constable Oeda is foolish and predictable. His actions were easy to foresee once it was suggested to him. Who knows? Perhaps they will find something."

"You believe the merchant a thief?"

"'Merchants are as crooked as screens,' as the proverb states. *Our* merchant fits that."

"Do you want something to be found?" The man hesitated, as if worried he'd forgotten something.

"No. That merchant is clean, but our operations are connected. I need Oeda to leave this family alone after today."

"Very good. What next, my lord?"

"Check the status of the jade shipment. We must ensure it's on its way to the capital. No mistakes."

"Yes, my lord."

Filled with pride, Wakizashi nodded at the man. "You're a capable apprentice, always seeking to provide service. You need a name that befits you."

"I have chosen one. *Tantō*."

"Good. Resume your searches of the remaining abandoned temples. If a place is promising, tell me. I'll search it myself. The riches of Settsu are someplace."

His servant smiled, conveying his agreement. "It will be done, my lord. Anything else."

"Continue studying those infernal Kirishitan. They are responsible for our master's troubles. They must suffer."

The man bowed, straightened, then departed. All movements were sharp, all executed with precision. He served well.

All would soon learn to serve well.

CHAPTER THREE

Aki checked the records she carried for the fifth time as she walked along the street that led to Osaka's Administration Buildings. There *had* been a new temple tax enacted last year to support the rebuilding of two temples in the district. The family had paid fees for both, and she had the temple stamps showing the payments.

She'd measured the frontage twice and compared it to last year. The figures were correct. She also had a record of the street and ward duties paid. Nothing was missed.

She pressed her hand against her middle. Mother had given her something to eat before she left. She had hoped the food would soothe her, but her stomach churned like a heavy wind. She needed to calm herself. Getting sick would not help her father.

Clouds crossed the morning sun, preventing warmth from easing the bitter breeze that blew through the streets. Shop walls were a mixture of betel-nut shades, waiting for the brightly-colored signs that would bring life to the day. Some *matcha*-hued banners were already on display as people moved in the street.

She took two deep breaths to warm herself. It was not necessary. Her blood churned from what had happened at home. *Seeing my father taken away and officials search my family's home. Seeing the young samurai grasp his sword.*

Seeing the older samurai save me.

She recalled his face, the brown eyes that whispered passion and the cheek scar that carried a memory. Had he received that scar in battle? Whatever the reason, it added to his appearance. Many samurai wore the scars of battle. It made them as frightening as their swords.

Not this one. Nishioji-*sama*. His presence made him imposing. His scar marked him as humane.

A bump from the left broke Aki's thoughts. More people moved about her, a mixture of browns, blues, and grays, getting the workday started. The air swam with scents of sweat from arduous early-morning labors. Lightly dressed men brought deliveries and talked with shopkeepers. At other places, doorways stood cracked open to allow air and activity.

Aki walked a few more blocks, bringing the city's administration buildings into view. The thought of taxes still troubled her. Ward committees collected most taxes and then reported the collection to the city, whoever that was. Did the ward not pass along their information? Why were the police asking? The police handle actual crime.

Loud knocks drew her attention. Carpenters worked to repair a temple down a side street on her left. Was that from the temple tax? Hard to know. Two monks dressed in yellowish-red, lighter than the usual colors, directed carpenters that swarmed the side of the building. Like the deliverymen, the carpenters wore light clothing, a mix of short gray trousers that reached their knees with shirts the color of unhusked rice. *Hard work must keep the men warm.*

She passed by the monks, who did not acknowledge her. Most everyone wore dull shades at this hour, except for the monks, whose faith required a greater show of color. The monks wore robes of hemp fabric with a touch of silk for the sash. They lived their vows. Other monks wore silk robes. They lived their vanities.

Beyond the monks, a lone figure moved as if trying to stay out of sight.

An *eta*.

One of society's undesirables. They worked as butchers, leather tanners, and dug graves: the jobs considered unclean as they dealt with death. Some executed criminals. They also came to her neighborhood and performed dirty jobs. Father always said they had their place, but Aki didn't know how she felt about them. They were friendly and at least kept their distance.

This one glanced toward her. He stepped into the light and smiled. She knew this man. He'd been to the neighborhood before.

How odd her solace on this walk was a man she must avoid.

In another block, the building where her father was being held came into view. As the samurai had stated, the Justice building was the remodeled temple next to the new building that handled land. Crowds milled about. How long had people been waiting? Since before the hour of the rabbit? Father had shown her the buildings before. Until today, she'd never imagined she would enter any of them. She dodged the people in front of her and hurried toward the building that resembled an old temple. The place looked half-depleted, with a storehouse attached on its right. An expanded stone foundation and dark timbers connected it to a building next door. Father often mentioned Osaka's growth, a push by the regent to expand the city. Many fresh places could be seen throughout the city.

What kind of people would she meet at the Justice building? Would they assist her or ignore a person of her meek status?

She again recalled the morning. Nishioji-sama said he would be here. What if he was not? What if that young samurai appeared instead? He had departed as soon as other officers showed up to search their home. He was within his rights to end her life for her affront. If not for Nishioji-sama, Aki could be dead.

Breathe. She must show respect and then show the proof. That would bring Father home.

Her chest tightened as she climbed the worn yet solid steps. Two officers positioned on each side stood guard at the front entrance. They wore hemp garments a darker shade of brown than the samurai, with a single weapon in their obi. One man was in his twenties, while the other was in his teens like she was. Both men, their faces impassive, had their hair tied in the back.

The one on the left, the older one, fisted one hand into his palm.

The other one held out his right hand, stopping her. "State your purpose," he said, his voice trembling as if he was new.

She took a deep breath and then held up the books she had brought. "My father was brought here this morning. The officer commanded me to bring additional information here. I have it with me."

The older one stared as if in doubt. "Information? What's the charge?"

"Taxes."

The man's expression grew puzzled, and he shook his head. "That's a matter for your village or guild." He pointed to the main building. "We don't address tax matters here. You are mistaken."

Aki trembled in her shoes, fearing to challenge the officer. The door behind them slid aside, revealing another man who was dressed in brown clothes that matched the samurai, except his were cotton. He was likely in his thirties. A receding hairline exposed his scalp. A thin mustache disappeared into minor scratches on his face. The fabric of his clothes was better than the fabric of the clothes of the men at the door and matched the quality of the samurai's clothes. This man was richer and more important.

"What's this girl's purpose?" He directed the question at the guards, not even glancing at her.

The one on the right responded. "Tanaka-sama, she claims she is here to see her father. Something about missing tax payments. She says she was told to bring documents."

The older man turned his gaze toward Aki and studied her. "I am Constable Tanaka. Who's your father?" His tone conveyed annoyance. He did not like being bothered.

Constable? The same title as the man she was ordered to find. This man could send her home. Aki bowed low, hoping her respect would soothe the reason for his terse speech. "Constable Tanaka, my father is Mori, the fabric merchant. Two samurai brought him here this morning. Those men told my family to bring records of frontage measurements, stamps, and our other guild and temple requirements. They told me to present them to Constable Oeda." She held up the books. "I am complying with their order."

"Unnh," he said, sighing as he shook his head. He was a busy man, but the mention of Constable Oeda's name sparked interest in his eyes. Did he believe her? Would he tell her to leave? Her heartbeat sounded in her ears. She kept her gaze down. Respect. Respect.

She inched lower, holding her papers tight against her chest. "I apologize for this imposition on your time."

The man grunted and motioned her to follow him inside.

She stepped across the threshold, hearing one guard mumble and then slide the door behind her closed. A flash of heat greeted her from a nearby hearth fire, along with rank scents of moldy soot. Pots for water hung over the hearth. The man directed her toward the side wall at the right of the room, showing where she should wait and then turned without a response.

Aki bowed toward the constable's back as he headed out the door, then she removed her straw shoes and placed them to the side, lining them up with others on the shelves. Men waited against the wall, most in silence and kneeling on the backs of their feet in a show of resignation to the ropes that bound them. Two more men sat with their backs to the wall, their hands behind them and tied by ropes that crossed their chests and kept their arms at their sides. One officer stood guard over them. Given their bonds, that was all that was needed.

Officers led more men through the main area. The place was crowded, like vegetable stands an hour after opening. The murmuring in the room grew quiet. Men stared in her direction. Her breath caught in her throat. She was the only woman there.

The office was cold, though better than the outside. The floor hearth provided modest relief. Two braziers in the room appeared active, but the one near her was not lit.

Aki moved toward the wall, acknowledging the stare of the guard but avoiding the gaze of the men waiting there, their faces dirty and unshaven. One man's face was pockmarked, like Shuji's wife Ogin, a sign of smallpox as a child. None of them looked familiar. For that, she thanked the gods. She moved as far away as possible and sat on the backs of her feet, trying to show respect while holding the books to her chest. The dank, unwashed mixture of dirt and perspiration of the prisoners filled her nose. If she were fortunate, the Constable would be quick.

The candle clock near the wall burned, emitting a thin line of smoke that drifted toward the ceiling. It kept her attention, but her gaze did little to speed the flame. Two overweight men sat across the room talking in hushed tones as they sipped drink and glanced at her. They appeared to be of higher rank than the ones at the door. Were they discussing her father's situation?

Was her father even here? Was she wasting her time?

She twirled the ribbon that held the books together around her fingers. People entered and left through the front door several times, allowing a breeze each time, yet the breeze did little to freshen the air in the room that reeked like years of accumulated dust.

Three men seated near her were called over and then escorted under guard toward the other side of the building, their arms held by ropes. Another guard pushed them forward with a nudge from the curved club. Were they really criminals, or were they like her father and accused of a crime?

When would her matter be addressed? She stood ready to prove her father's innocence but could do nothing until called. She rubbed the back of her neck. *Nothing to do but wait.*

Two more men sitting near her were called and escorted out. Still no call for her. Aki fidgeted where she sat. Time drew out like a castle procession of the regent, the bowing interminable. Would that she had a cushion. She glanced around. No cushions. Not surprising. The people waiting lacked importance.

An officer brought another man to the group near Aki. Hands tied behind his back, he wore a blue coat with black streaks. Dark streaks lined his face. Something about his glance seared her with fear. She craved to flee. That would not help her father.

Would it be acceptable to stand for a second? She placed her books by her right side, away from the other prisoners. Then she pushed herself to her knees and stood, rubbing her hands against her kosode, which stuck to her thighs.

A guard for the waiting prisoners moved to accost her, the look on his face sterner than her uncle's. "What are you doing?"

A chill ran across her neck. "My apologies. I wanted to stand for a second. I have been sitting for a while."

"Not my concern." He sneered as he bobbed his head back toward the wall.

She bowed. "I understand. I beg your forgiveness. I only want to help my father. The officers instructed me to bring information here for him. I have the proof they—"

"Quiet," the man said, his voice rising. "Follow my instructions and wait. Do you—"

"Hold your tongue," a strong voice ordered from the other side of the door. The person's voice commanded attention.

Aki's heart sped, sending warmth through her body. The tension in her frame receded, almost in a show of trust.

Nishioji-sama had arrived.

Tomi grasped his sword. The movement brought the office to hushed whispers, enough to silence the man's tongue. He had little use for self-important people who cared more about their positions than the service they provided. Most officers were hardworking. Unfortunately, there were demons.

"Nishioji-sama, the girl is of no consequence. She is here to see family. If they are criminals, so is she."

Tomi gritted his teeth and tightened his grip. The banging and hustling of the building resumed. *Lord, grant me the strength to stay my temper.* "Do you know why she's here?"

A cough from behind drew Tomi's attention. An older officer, Arai, stood there. His wide face sagged with age. "I know," he answered. "Constable Tanaka allowed her in earlier. He commanded she wait at the wall."

"Did he tell you why?"

"He mentioned her father was brought in this morning, and that she has information for Constable Oeda. That's all I know."

"I'm the one who brought her father in, but it was not an arrest." Tomi glanced at Aki, who had returned to kneeling on the floor. The fear in her eyes chilled him. She held three books tight to her chest. He turned back to the officer. "I see she brought something."

The man glanced in Aki's direction, pulling at his clothes as he did. After one long gaze, he swallowed hard. "Yes. I see that."

Tomi closed the distance between him and Arai. "Did you see it before? Why didn't you do something?"

Arai's face grew stern. "I support Constable Tanaka. It was not my responsibility."

"I know you support Tanaka-sama. Was Oeda informed she's here?"

The man retrieved the books from Aki and brought them to Tomi. "My apologies, Nishioji-sama. We have been busy."

Tomi got in the man's face. "In the future, treat a visitor different from an accused. See that a straw mat is brought for her if Oeda is detained."

"Understood," Arai said.

"Let Oeda know the woman is here."

The man bowed. "Yes, sir." His voice rose in pitch.

Tomi adjusted the thread that bound the papers together and opened the hard covers. One held records of official stamps showing neighborhood business payments. Another other showed tax payments to the temples. The third showed other payments. *Elegant writing. Like a court lady.* He motioned to Aki. "Come here."

Aki walked over and bowed low. "How may I serve you?"

Tomi averted his gaze. The merchant's daughter was attractive, with reddish lips and a short ponytail held tight with a clip. Her upturned eyes, which before had shown fear, now displayed flickers of cautious confidence. She also carried herself well. "I made a promise this morning. My promises are oaths. I don't forget them."

Arai returned with Constable Oeda and Ishii, an officer

who reported to Oeda. "Nishioji, you had a busy morning."

"Unnh," he grunted back. "Oeda-sama, these are from the house of the early morning raid." He tilted his head toward the young woman. "This is the merchant's daughter."

He handed over the documents. Oeda leafed through them, pausing at certain points. "Everything appears to be in order, but it will require a longer examination. That will take a few minutes." He looked at the young woman. "Wait where you were before. When I'm ready, you will know. Ishii, see that she's not disturbed."

"Yes, sir," Ishii said.

"Nishioji, my office," Oeda said. "We need to talk. Now."

Oeda put the books under his arm and walked toward his office. Tomi followed, maintaining a respectful distance. Oeda signaled a man Tomi didn't recognize and then turned by another floor hearth. The place still felt like a temple. The layout embraced meditation and the walls smelled of sandalwood and cypress.

They reached Oeda's office and stepped inside. "We need privacy," Oeda said.

Tomi slid the door closed. "That keeps out the heat."

"And everything else," Oeda responded.

A faint whiff of incense struck Tomi's nose. Ashes smoldered in the holding cup of a small memorial on the left side of the room. He walked over and glanced at the drawing behind the ashes. "Remembering your brother again?"

"Yes, it brings me comfort. Besides, it smells nice. You should try this for your mother."

Tomi thought of the sandalwood he burned at home to ease his mother's sickness. "What is it?"

"The finest camphor."

"Expensive?"

"My family runs a temple, remember, so not so much. This scent was my brother's favorite. My family uses the same merchant as Shitennōji. I'll get you a couple of sticks later."

"I don't want to trouble you."

"It's no trouble."

Tomi nodded his head, again glancing at the picture on the shrine. "Will you ever move it home one day?"

Oeda rubbed his fist against his arm. "When I retire. My wife never liked him. She questioned his integrity. Also says it takes up too much space."

"And you?"

"He was my brother, and I will maintain it in my lifetime. It's a sad day when the last memento of the dead vanishes."

Tomi tried to remember the Buddhist priest Oeda was quoting. Kenkō. Did Oeda utter Buddhist quotes to counter to Tomi's beliefs, or was he a follower? He was the only one who knew Tomi's and Matsu's true background. Several officers viewed him as a disgraced samurai.

The door slid open, revealing the man Oeda had signaled earlier. Oeda grunted his assent, and the man brought two cups and a pot of hot water, placed a cup before each of them and then left, closing the door behind him.

"Who is that?" Tomi asked. "Is he new?"

"Shoichi."

Tomi scratched his head. "No family name?"

"Not from a samurai family. He's part of the city's defense militia. Our numbers are depleted due to Hideyoshi's draws men to the capital. He likely has plans to attack Odawara. We pull from the neighborhood merchants and farmers, demanding their service, but the regent pulls them, too."

Odawara. The Hōjō, the only clan left that still resisted the regent's rule of Japan. "Is the defense militia really needed? Can we not operate without them?"

"The regent has some plan. Remember that last year he executed over one hundred in Nakajima for hiding the criminals who wrote defamatory statements about the regent's son on walls in the capital. Nakajima's magistrates are our magistrates. I don't argue with the regent's messengers."

Oeda opened the books and reviewed the documents. Tomi surveyed the room. He'd been in Oeda's office before but seldom examined it. Drawers filled with records stacked as high as the constable occupied much of the room. Sufficient space separated the shrine and drawers so stray ash wouldn't burn the paper. The picture of the constable's brother guarded the room.

Oeda kept his desk organized with ink and brushes set to the left and papers stacked on the right.

"Nishioji"—Oeda looked up at him—"you're tapping your foot. Are you nervous about something?"

Tomi glanced toward his foot, seeing it moving up and down as if setting a light taiko drumbeat. He sighed. "I am concerned about the merchant. There's always a possibility."

Oeda nodded. "You think him a thief?"

"No. I worry about his safety. The jail is a hard place. This family is honest."

He closed the books. "Good. I accept your opinion. Nothing here of concern."

Tomi exhaled louder than he expected. "I am gratified to hear it."

Oeda stared, a curious expression on his face. Tomi needed to control his emotions better in front of him. He knew the man well, but Oeda was still his superior.

"Now," Oeda said as he leaned forward and invited Tomi to sit, "the reason I wanted to speak with you in private. The search turned up nothing, as expected."

Tomi pressed his lips together. "You sound like it surprises you. You acknowledged the family was honest."

"Yes, but as you know, someone in the fabric district is importing silk around the entrance gates and avoiding transaction taxes. Crime between districts. It's the reason we're involved. The ship from Macao doesn't come every year. How is the silk getting here?"

"We should check the weaving district."

Oeda shook his head. "I have. None of them could afford to import it. It must be the clothing merchants."

"Maybe someone is using them."

"Meaning?"

"I've been in Kyushu and seen the cargo. Merchants come from everywhere to buy it. The foreigners bring silk thread as much as silk. You could bring in the thread and pay the weavers."

Oeda stared him into silence. "The magistrate in Nagasaki knows what comes in and who buys it. Unless the foreigners are hiding cargo."

"There is no silver in hiding it."

"Somebody's hiding something," Oeda said. "We have to find it."

"That's why I suggest searching for thread."

Oeda's look told him he had pushed too much. "There is more here than just silk."

More? Tension returned to Tomi's shoulders. "What else is there?"

"The men were searching for other items. Valuable ones. Precious goods stolen from elite families in Osaka. I agree the family is innocent, but we had to look. We had a report."

Tomi rubbed his chest. "A report? What items?"

"Jade."

The word surprised Tomi. That explained much. "Matsu and I weren't told. Was anything found?"

"Nothing."

Tomi rubbed his fingers. "Why didn't we know?"

Oeda rose from his chair and circled to face Tomi. Tomi had the constable by a few inches, but the man was skilled in battle as he. "It was a last-minute report. Another officer. We needed the three of you to play the part you did. No chance of a mistake."

"Who made the request?"

Oeda said nothing.

"Another constable?" Tomi asked.

"I cannot say, but it was a request I had to honor."

Only another constable could require Oeda's silence. "May I know why?"

"You forget how you're seen. I know what happened in Himeji, but I hide your mission."

Tomi sighed. He'd hidden his faith, and it had cost him. In Osaka, he and Matsu were now police, still samurai but a demotion considering his previous castle duties. Oeda was keeping their real reason for being here a secret. "I will endeavor to win them over."

"Give it more time. The respect will come."

"Can we release the merchant now?"

Oeda nodded and opened the door. Tomi grabbed the books and followed, standing back as he ordered Ishii to retrieve the merchant.

They headed back to the waiting area. The young woman, Aki, now sat on a mat, along the wall but away from the criminals. Tomi walked toward her. She rose to meet him. "An officer is retrieving your father. It will be a few minutes." Her face showed relief, but her body remained stiff. "Are you not pleased?"

She raised her gaze to him. "I am grateful for the news."

Tomi's heart pinched when he heard her words. The family had endured much this morning. The girl maintained her composure. "Your name is Aki, correct? That's what your father called you at your house."

She nodded with hesitation. "Yes."

"You serve your parents well, Aki." He handed her the books. "You also have spirit."

She brought the books up to hide her face. "I am

humbled by your praise."

"I saw the tax records. Your calligraphy is impressive."

Her face reddened. "My mother taught my sisters and me. They now teach calligraphy."

"In the Buddhist temple classes?"

"Yes, and private lessons. Their talent is greater than mine."

"Do they keep the records?"

"No. The markings are mine. Father says my sisters do not understand business like I do. Neither does Genta, my oldest brother, and he will inherit when my father retires."

"You have more siblings than I saw."

"There are six of us. I have three sisters. They live with their husbands."

"I saw two women this morning," Tomi said.

"The wives of my brothers. They live with us."

"Unnh," Tomi smiled, not knowing what to add. He had no siblings.

The young woman's eyes grew wide as she looked beyond Tomi and brought her hands to her mouth. "Father?"

Tomi wheeled. Seeing the merchant with Ishii on his left and an unknown officer on his right, a man older than Tomi, angered him. The merchant's clothing was ripped, and he was missing his outer garment. A bruise marked his forehead.

He stared at the man he didn't know, a man with a worn look but no weapon in sight. "Are you a guard?" Tomi's voice carried his disbelief.

"Yes, sir," the man answered.

Tomi drew himself to his full height and glared. "How do you treat the men there?" he asked, his voice rising.

The man quivered in place. "I follow orders, sir. They get their meals. Is more needed?" the man said, more a statement than a question.

"Why are his clothes ripped? Why is he bruised?"

"All prisoners must fend for themselves. It is cold in the holding area."

"Order must be maintained." Tomi turned to the Oeda. "Why does this happen?"

Oeda's face betrayed no remorse. "Most there are guilty. If something happens, it is no concern."

The merchant shook his head. "The head injury is my fault. I tripped over the threshold as I entered the waiting area."

"Your clothes are ripped," Tomi said.

The merchant nodded "I am grateful to be out. Aki, you do a father's heart well."

Tomi fought back a smile. It wouldn't do to show emotion here. "I'll escort you both home. I'll see nothing else happens."

The front door opened. One officer strode in and stepped to the right of the entrance. Three prisoners, their hands tied behind their backs, followed him, their heads down, their faces unshaven. Two more officers trailed behind them, shoving the hilts of their blades into the prisoners' backs. The prisoners smelled of dank water and sweat, despite the cold weather. Two were dressed in faded gray attire worn down from use. A third man wore a tattered blue garment. All three men had black marks on their faces and arms.

Tomi didn't recognize the officers trailing behind them, more men from the city defense without last names. He motioned for Aki and her father to stay back. The escort home would need to wait.

Oeda faced the prisoners. "What have we here?"

The leading officer, a good man called Goto, stepped forward. Hardworking and gaining responsibility is how Tomi knew him. He respected his insight and considered him a friend. "We caught these three breaking into a rice storehouse near the river."

"You caught them in the act? You could have disciplined them there."

"They were working on a coal ship docked nearby. They are not from here, so it went to the Administration building first to be recorded and then referred here."

"I see," Oeda said. He stared at the prisoners. "I'm Constable Oeda. What were you doing?"

The two men in gray said nothing. The man in the tattered blue clothes stepped forward. "Just celebrating the new year. Too much *sake*."

"The new year was three days ago."

The man smiled, displaying two missing teeth. "You must not be busy these days, Oeda, if you have time to greet me yourself."

"Constable Oeda to you," Tomi thundered.

"*Constable* Oeda. My apologies," he uttered the words in derision, then glanced at Tomi, tilting his gaze in a flash of recognition. "How difficult must be your shame. You now use disgraced samurai for your laborers."

Tomi searched his memory. This man knew him? From where? The ragged clothes and black streaks shielded his identity. He would have to return after the walk to the merchant's house.

"My men are not your concern," Oeda said. "Answer my question. What were you doing there?"

Hands still behind him, the man got into Oeda's face. "Drinking is not a crime. Why do you trouble us? You must have more important things to do."

Oeda slapped the man's face.

The man didn't flinch. "You're weak and foolish. You could work a year, and you would find nothing."

"Answer his question," Tomi said.

The man looked at Tomi. "Do what you will. Questioning us does not matter."

Tomi grimaced. "I'll keep my own counsel on what matters."

The man stepped toward Tomi. Aki and her father stepped back further.

"My hands are behind my back, girl," the man said. "I doubt my breath could kill you."

Tomi gripped the hilt of his sword. "Keep your attention on me."

The man's jaw dropped. "Defending a common girl?" He eyed her up and down. "I see why. One question for you. Why does the Constable use people who cannot even tie decent knots in rope?"

The man brought his arms forward and rope flew in Tomi's face. He produced a dagger and lunged at Tomi. Aki's gasp rang in Tomi's ears. Tomi deflected the ropes onto the dagger and then drew his sword. He punched the hilt in the man's face and then smashed a blow to his stomach.

The man doubled over and grabbed his midsection. The dagger clattered on the floor. Oeda kicked it away. The prisoner reached for Tomi, but two guards captured the man's arms. The prisoner struggled, but the guards held the man's hands behind his back. A bone snapped and pain streaked across the man's face.

"You should have killed me."

"Take them all away," Oeda said. "Make sure they are tied right this time."

Officers escorted them out of the main room.

"Do you know that man?" Oeda asked. "He knows you."

"Vague memories, but I don't know from where."

Oeda sighed. "Whoever he is, he was right about one thing. You should have killed him."

"Didn't your brother die in battle?" Tomi asked, recalling the shrine in Oeda's office.

Oeda appeared stunned by the reminder. "He did."

"That's why I left him alive. I need to know who he is and why he attacked me."

"His actions deserve a quick death."

"I want to question him. I need an answer."

Oeda eyed him and nodded. "Fine. I'll order his nose split later."

He left without another word. Tomi checked on Aki and her father, their faces frozen in stares. He knew his actions were a surprise to them. Had he killed the man, it would have given them nightmares. But there was more. Tomi's words to Oeda had been true.

Who was that man? Why the sudden attack?

"Thank you," the father said.

Tomi acknowledged his gratitude with a look. "It's been a long morning for you. Time to leave. I'll see you both home now."

Aki and her father expressed their gratitude. Tomi tried to tell himself that the walk would benefit him. He could learn about their business and family.

He could learn about her.

Tomi studied the bruises on the merchant's face, wounds because the police failed to protect them, because Tomi had failed in his promise.

Father, forgive me. My actions today put the merchant's family in harm's way. I must make amends for my fault.

CHAPTER FOUR

For the third time in the last few minutes, Aki wiped her hands on her kosode. Despite the chilly weather, the perspiration remained. So did the samurai who strode before her and her father.

He had offered to see them home from the Justice Building. Status required that she and her father trail him to convey the proper respect, but something about his manner suggested he wanted them closer. Silence marked most of the journey, while her insides screamed.

The criminal with the hidden knife had broken his bonds, drawn it, and tried to kill the samurai. Nishioji-sama had drawn his sword and disarmed the man. Recalling it made her shake her head. Constable Oeda said the man should have been killed, but Nishioji-sama had shown mercy. Had he not been there, she and her father might have been hurt or worse. He had saved them.

How could she repay him for saving her life? How could she forget he put her there in the first place?

The streets bustled with people milling about in clumps of activity. Crowds made the streets warmer. Osaka was always crowded, ever since the regent built a castle here. Father said the regent had ordered craftsmen and other artists to move here from Sakai, even filling in Sakai's moat to force the move. Did Sakai have this many people? Even when she had walked through the city as a little girl with her father, the streets had hummed with constant activity.

A low rumble drew her attention skyward. Dark clouds billowed, promising rain. She sniffed the air. Nothing. The scent of rain only appeared in summer. These clouds would open soon. Hopefully, she and her father would be home before then.

They walked in silence for several more minutes. Aki studied the samurai's gait, stealing glances so no one would think she was staring. He walked proudly, without fear, like the samurai she had seen often growing up, the ones who had made purchases at the shop. Father and Mother always handled those visits, and Father now trained Genta to work with these important customers. Father trained Aki to remain close and ensure Genta did well.

The shop eventually came into view. Genta and Shuji appeared out front and busy. Relief flowed through Aki. It was good to be home.

Nishioji-sama glanced back, holding her gaze before she looked away in deference. Aki froze, but what was she afraid of? She was home and she had maintained a respectful silence and distance.

It didn't matter. Something was on the samurai's mind.

Her father bowed low. "*Sumimasen,* Osamurai-sama. We are humbled by your kindness and are in your debt."

"There is no debt. No need for payment. I am responsible for your injury. You were there only a short time."

Her father inhaled slowly. He had stated he just wanted to get back to work. The look on his face said he needed more rest, but he would not take it.

"I appreciate your concern," her father answered. "I am well."

"And you," Nishioji-sama turned his gaze toward her.

"Are you well?"

Aki caught herself staring into his large brown eyes and lowered herself to hide. One should not look directly into the eyes of a samurai, but she could no longer avert her gaze. "I am honored by your concern. I am fine."

"That's good."

"Can we offer you some tea?" her father asked.

He shook his head. "I have duties. Another time. You should rest." It was a command, not a suggestion.

Father moved toward the open entrance. Genta and Shuji continued to serve customers, while Mother stepped out into the street and hastened toward Father. Aki moved to follow.

A grunt from behind brought all to a halt.

"I have one request." He directed the words to her father. "Of your daughter." He paused and allowed the request to linger. "Excuse us."

His request was a statement. Samurai understood their words were always followed. Trepidation swirled in her chest. What could he want of her?

Her father nodded and left them alone, barking out orders as he returned to his duties. Aki heard extra accents on comments to Genta, an indication he would follow the samurai's command to rest. Action from the shop drowned out his movements.

She turned back to the samurai. "How may I serve you?" Her lower lip quivered as she spoke.

"Your voice trembles. You've nothing to fear from me," he said. "I wanted to tell you that you're an impressive girl. You have your father's trust. Your attention to duty is laudable."

Aki's cheeks grew warm. "I am not good at selling. Father says I contribute in other ways."

"I don't doubt that. Your importance shows. It was you who made the trip to the Justice Building this morning. No one else."

Another compliment from the samurai on my caring for my father? Is this not the duty of any child? She tilted her head to hide her embarrassment. The discussions in the background from her family's store slowed. They must be staring in her direction. "Again, you honor me with your praise."

"There's more. I'm here to request your service."

Request her service? Did he have children in need of a teacher? "My calligraphy skills are not the equal of my sisters. My sister Hoshi is pregnant, but the baby is not due for some time. She is more talented than me and has time for students."

"It's not that."

Not calligraphy. Aki mulled it over. "How may I serve you?"

"I need you at my household."

A servant to the samurai? "Of what use could I be?"

"Of great use. My mother is"—he pursed his lips as if he feared the word—"ill. I have a servant who looks after her during the day. My father cares for her in the evening. My servant's daughter is pregnant, and the baby's time is near. She requested time to care for her daughter. I need someone to care for my mother. It will be three or four weeks."

Care for his mother? She had never thought of samurai having family. "I will discuss it with my father." *Father would never refuse the request of a samurai.*

"Good. I will return in three days for your answer. My servant says there is still a little time, but I must find a replacement by then."

Three days? His mother was ill, but there must be many people who could do this. *Why me?* They had only met this morning. *What kind of help could his mother need?*

"I understand, Osamurai-sama."

"Call me Nishioji-sama," he added.

"Yes, Nishioji-sama. I remember from today when

both the younger samurai and the Constable addressed you."

His expression conveyed a mixture of interest and annoyance. The scar on his face hardened it like stone.

"Have I displeased you?" Aki asked.

"No. I'm impressed. You're full of surprises. Now I must go. I must find Matsubara. He's the older samurai that was with me this morning. Do you remember him?"

"I do."

"Good. If you accept my request, you will see him again." His lips thinned. "Expect me in three days."

Nishioji-sama turned and strode away, pulling Aki's gaze in his wake. *A striking man, even the scar did not mar his handsome looks.*

He merged into the crowd, but it did not matter. His bearing stood out among everyone else.

Aki sighed. It would be a long three days.

###

Tomi stepped into the tea house in the Shinchi District, hoping no one would see him enter. He'd been searching for his friend, Matsu, since leaving the merchant and his daughter, visiting work and Matsu's home. After two hours of searching, Tomi realized there was only one place left.

"Yes, Matsubara-sama is here," the older woman confirmed. "He will not wish to be disturbed." She grinned and gestured toward the left side of the room. "Perhaps you would care for some entertainment."

Tomi saw two women waiting near the wall, one dressed in dark green and the other in a deep yellow. Both styled their hair the traditional way, and each wore a matching solid-colored *obi. Why does Matsu come to these places*?

"The girls are versed in the arts," the house mother continued, as the women sauntered toward him, playful smiles on their faces. "The one in green can teach dancing.

The one in yellow is one of my two girls from Ryukyu. She has talents on the *sanshin*. Matsubara-sama enjoys the sanshin and is with the other Ryukyu girl right now. I am certain you would find either woman stimulating."

Tomi gritted his teeth, recalling the few times he had heard someone play that three-string instrument. Matsubara might like the sound of it. To Tomi, it resembled a cat coughing up a hairball in mid-screech. His presence didn't intimidate the older woman, an indication that Matsu was not the only samurai who frequented these premises and that other visitors were likely of higher status. "That will not be necessary. Tell Matsubara that"—he hated giving out his name in a place like this—"Nishioji is here."

She shooed the two women back to their waiting area and then nodded, indicating the wall opposite from where the women had stood. "Would you please sit there? I will return shortly."

Tomi sighed and headed to the wall. There were three chairs available. A fourth one was occupied. Tomi didn't recognize the man. His clothing suggested he was a merchant. The dust on his clothes appeared to be straw, likely a tatami mat business or a maker of cloaks and hats.

Thankfully, no one knew he was here. What if an acquaintance saw him enter? What would they think? Tomi strove to live as an example to others.

Matsu, why do you make me find you here?

What did his padre say? *Iesu* met with yūjo. He allowed one to wash his feet, but Tomi struggled with contradiction. He consoled himself with one thought, waiting outside the place where people could see him would be worse.

He sat as far away from the merchant as he could. The man kept to himself, likely afraid of him. Tomi glanced at the two women across the way, tapping his foot as he did. Hopefully, Matsu would not be long. A man entered with a woman clothed in red, her tousled hair on his arm, and the two of them chatting and laughing. When the man saw Tomi, his smile disappeared. Did the man recognize him or just see the swords? *Best to avoid any eye contact.*

More minutes passed before Matsu entered. A woman wearing a deep yellow garment similar to the woman on the wall strode next to him. They laughed as they approached, both smiling and gazing into each other's eyes. They said their farewells, and the woman retreated to another room near the waiting area.

"Want to talk here?" Matsu asked.

Tomi knew Matsu was joking, but Tomi was not as jovial as he was this morning. He pointed to the exit where he and Matsu stepped out into the street.

A biting wind blasted their faces, reminiscent of the weeks only a month ago. Tomi pulled his clothes tighter. Passersby moved with purpose, likely afraid to get near two samurai. It was better this way, better for conversation. A side street would be nice, but this area lacked a place to hide. Tomi steered them in the closest direction to exit the district.

"Problem finding me?" Matsu asked.

"It wasn't hard. I wish you'd find a different vice. The woman in charge must see a lot of samurai. She wasn't intimidated by me."

"Husband's a samurai. Why would she be?"

"Are you serious?"

"Unnh," Matsu grunted. "Stays away to not frighten customers."

He looked Matsu in the eyes. "Sorry to interrupt your rest."

"Not a problem. Come here for tea, but the woman's sanshin playing is relaxing."

Tomi eyed his friend with what he knew was a gaze of disbelief. "You come here for tea ceremony? And the sanshin? Really?"

"Yes, often. Will do it again soon."

Tomi shook his head, seeing people enter the pleasure

district. His greatest fear remained: someone from the church might see him and lose faith, or someone who would see Tomi and doubt his reputation.

"No need to eye the district as if fearing leather tanners," Matsu said. "Further South of here. Someone sees us? I'll speak on your behalf."

Tension danced on Tomi's skin. "I don't find anything relaxing about the sanshin."

"You are too stiff. More than one way to relieve stress, and the woman doesn't touch you."

"Stiff? I am not stiff."

"Nishioji no Tsuneomi, stop by here some time. There are other ways to feel your strength renewed."

Matsu's use of his full name was his way of needling him. They could discuss it later. "We have work to do. We have no time."

"No time?" Matsubara asked, his tone rising with a chuckle. "I'll remember that the next time I hide your sword."

Tomi tried to smile back, but the effort proved for naught. "Another time."

The sun reached the hour of the ram, but clouds shielded the early afternoon heat. Things would improve by the end of the day.

"That prisoner who attacked you this morning was interesting."

"You could say that." Tomi scanned the area again, his nerves still jagged. Once out, no one would know he'd been there. "Where were you when the man attacked me?"

"Left to find Yori. Tried to tell you, but the only thing on your mind was the young woman. Heard about it from someone else. Nothing new for us."

Matsu was right. The incident this morning with the prisoner was not new, but the man knowing his name left him uneasy. He pointed toward a bridge that led out of the pleasure district and toward a street of carpenters. The two hustled over, and Tomi searched for a place to talk. He indicated a spot closer to the riverbank and shielded from the roads.

"Why the secrecy?" Matsu asked.

Tomi held a finger to his lips to hold Matsu's attention then drew a breath and confirmed again that no one was close. Small shallow vessels sailed toward the direction of the castle, their sharp bows cutting through the water. More vessels approached from the opposite way. One of the men on board stared in Tomi's direction but then returned to his work. No one else was close.

No worries.

Satisfied, Tomi related the full details of the prisoner incident, focusing on the man in black streaks who knew him and his conversation with Oeda.

"You defended the girl," Matsu said.

"*That's* the first thing you mention? This is *not* about the girl."

"Right." Matsu's tone indicated light sarcasm. "She's more important."

"She has nothing to do with this."

"The attack, no. You showing interest in a woman, yes."

"Can we stop talking about her? What about the man who attacked me?"

Matsu shook his head. "Agree with Oeda. Should have killed him."

"Kill him and I won't know who he is."

"There were two other prisoners. They likely know something. Don't make this personal."

Tomi fingered the hilt of his sword. "Sometimes I think before I end a man's life. Is it necessary? I spared the man."

"Mercy," Matsu said, "is not healthy. It should not be personal. Like your philosopher, mercy will get you killed."

Water sloshed against the bank, quick for a February

and noisy in Tomi's ears. *Just a little push. Knock Matsu into the water and wake him up. That would be personal.*

Another day. They had tasks. "It's not personal. Work is never personal."

"Work is personal in one place."

Tomi rubbed his hands under his clothes, fingering his rosary beads. "Where?"

Matsu smiled and glanced back at the district where Tomi had found him. "Over there."

"I'm serious."

"Yes, my friend, I know." Matsu turned around to watch the river flow. Tomi perked his ears, concerned that someone might approach from behind. "Just saying you need a zest for life. No pleasure in that religion of yours."

Tomi rubbed a bead between his fingers. "There is for me. One day, I will convince you. There is more in life than the pleasures of this world."

"Tea ceremony and the sanshin are pleasure. The more you spend, the less you receive. I spend much of my pay."

"You need to set an example for Yori. What if he goes there?"

Matsu laughed. "Our assistant has found me there before. The only time he ever chided me. You're the greater influence."

Tomi smiled inwardly. There was hope for Yori yet. "As long as we do our duty. Yori will be a constable one day. He has the lineage. With experience, particularly in battle, he will be a fair adjudicator. After working with us, his connections can request a position supporting Ishida in Sakai."

"Ishida?" Matsu laughed. "I thought you said you wanted him to gain experience in battle."

Tomi looked back. "He *is* the Commissioner of Police for the nation and one of the Regent's Council of Five."

"And has drawn only brushes, not swords. He keeps the regent organized…not in power."

Another boat, riding low, headed upriver. Whatever the cargo was, it was heavy. As it approached their side, Tomi noted black streaks on two of the men's faces. Like the previous boat, one or two men glanced in their direction, startled to see samurai, and then returned to their jobs. Wind whipped off the river, freezing Tomi's body. *Working on the river must make it hard to stay warm.*

Matsu interrupted Tomi's thoughts. "The man who attacked you this morning. He had black smudges?"

"Yes, like those men."

"Charcoal boat, is it not?"

"Yes, I plan to check with Oeda later. The storehouse is on the river next to the new rice warehouses."

"So?" Matsu asked.

Tomi watched the men fade in the distance. "The prisoners could be part of the coal guild. We should investigate the dock that the guild uses, the one near the warehouses."

"Are there others who can do that?"

More water gushed from the riverbank and splashed against Tomi's feet. He and Matsu stepped back from the ground, a mixture of soggy and frozen mud. He held his hands out slightly to maintain his balance. "Yes, not many. But since the one man knew me, I want to see what else is there. It's only a feeling, but one I should follow."

"Speaking of feelings," Matsu said, smiling, "what do you know about the family of cloth merchants, other than they have an attractive daughter?"

Tomi pressed his lips together before answering. "They appear to be honorable."

"Honorable enough to escort home. What else?"

"I felt responsible for the father's injuries."

Matsu stared at him. "Regrettable, but you've been responsible for many things. Is that the only reason?"

Tomi turned his head, hoping to avoid the question. He knew Matsu was needling him but had long found his counsel prescient. "For now, it is."

"Want to talk?"

"We can talk later. We need to find Yori and apprise him of Oeda's discussion."

Tomi waved them back toward the street. Matsu shook his head as if amused and then followed, catching up on his right.

Something told Tomi they had little time.

CHAPTER FIVE

"No message yet from the samurai?" her father asked. "He said three days, and it is the third day."

Aki reached for a cloth and wiped the bowls from dinner. The patter of rain hitting the roof sprinkled doubts in her thoughts. "Nothing, Father." Aki had eaten little, the pit in her stomach made every morsel she ate weigh like a rock. "If he had arrived by now, you would know."

"Today was busy, and I didn't see you until dinner. I thought maybe he came and you were keeping it a secret until you had time."

Aki smiled at her father. "I could never keep a secret from you. You know that. The samurai said he would return in three days. It is still early in the evening."

"You accept this position with your mother's and my approval. This is a wonderful opportunity for you. When you are working at home again, you will have much to teach us."

Aki bit her lip as she set the last of the bowls aside. She hoped she would teach. She hoped more that she would have time. She had spent much of the day in solitude, making sure everything was ready for Genta. She had explained things to Shuji, as well, but Shuji was like his older brother. Numbers were also his weakness.

The time alone had given her a chance to think.

The samurai had said her service was temporary, just until his servant returned from her own daughter's pregnancy. His mother was ill. What type of illness? Was she bedridden or was it something else?

Unless.

Certainly not that. The samurai was a handsome man, and women must fight for his attention. He did not need Aki for his own entertainment.

"Are you feeling weak, Aki?" Her father's voice broke her thoughts. "You're not saying anything."

Aki looked away. She always told Father the truth. Father always knew her thoughts. "Just thinking about the samurai. He says his mother is ill, but I do not see any way that I can be of service."

"He must disagree. Whatever help is needed, you will serve well. He is an honorable man. It is nothing to—"

"Father," Shuji said as he entered, his voice fluttering like he had seen a demon in the forest. "Uncle is here."

Uncle Riku? Aki's impression was correct. Shuji had seen a demon. She had been expecting Uncle ever since her father had mentioned the marriage the morning they met the samurai. Business had kept him away since then.

If only the samurai could show up now.

"It is late for Uncle to be here." Aki knew her voice trembled. She hoped Shuji would not notice.

"Agreed, it's late," her father said, "but fetch tea. There should be sufficient hot water on the hearth."

Aki watched Shuji leave then grabbed trays and cups, along with the tea and utensils.

"It is late for Uncle to be here," her father said with a grin, then leaned in closer, "but not late for the samurai."

Aki's chest tightened. He had heard her thoughts again. "It is unusual for Uncle Riku to be here at this hour."

Her father chuckled. "I agree."

The tension in Aki's body departed, and she sighed, nodding to Father, who stepped forward as Aki trailed behind. *Best not to wait.*

She carried the tray into the main room, avoiding eye contact but counting the number assembled. Only her uncle and her father remained. Everyone else, including Shuji, had left. Even Shuji's pleasant wife, Ogin, did not want to be around Uncle.

She placed trays in front of each of them and then knelt at the hearth to make tea. Her shoulders tensed under her uncle's gaze. She measured enough for two cups then poured the water. Her hands shook so much that the tea splattered.

Stay calm. Stay calm.

She rose and offered Uncle the first cup. "Here you are."

Her uncle smiled like a highway robber trying to lure a victim into security. "Ah, Aki, you are always so dutiful."

"It is good to see you."

He grunted his assent but said nothing else.

She handed the remaining cup to her father. "I will leave you two to discuss business."

"No, Aki, you should stay," her uncle said. "Sit."

Her stomach fluttered. "Uncle, I am certain you and Father have much to discuss, things beyond the concern of a young girl."

"Aki, my reason for being here involves you, as well."

Uncle's oily tone likely helped him with merchants. She sat back on her calves. "How may I serve you?"

He grunted then looked at them as if holding news of value, though Aki knew it had no worth. "I found a situation that can benefit both our families. Your father says that he has informed you of my request to adopt you."

The only benefit would be to her uncle. She had promised Father she would support Genta and intended to keep that promise. She was beyond the age when people married off their daughters, but she trusted all would be well. Aki tried to inch backwards. "He mentioned it three days ago. Then we were approached by the police about a tax problem. We have not discussed it since that morning."

"Ah, yes," her uncle said, attempting a soothing tone as he looked at her father. "That unfortunate business. Your father mentioned it. Well, nothing arose from it. Thank the gods."

"Why—?"

"As I said, I plan to adopt you," her uncle continued, cutting her off. Aki bristled at the interruption but remembered she needed to keep her place. "We have an opportunity to merge our family with a trading family that deals exclusively in silk. This family moved from Kyoto two months ago and is looking for a bride for their younger son."

Marry me off? What benefit to the family is that?

"Exclusively silk?" Concern crossed her father's face. "Are you sure that's wise?"

"They have connections in Gion in the heart of the silk guild. Why wouldn't it be?"

"Silk is not the future. We need to expand more to cotton. This is the reason Hoshi married into a cotton family. This is the reason Kiku married an oil seller. Even you agreed with these decisions."

"Yes." Uncle paused, as if acknowledging her father's strong point. "The city is growing," he finally said. "However, with the regent now in Kyoto and maintaining palaces there and Osaka, silk is more promising. Aki, do you not agree?"

Uncle's direct question sounded like a dishonest market seller. He had interrupted her earlier but now wanted to hear her talk. She took a deep breath. "I agree with Father. Cotton is the future. I only ask why the adoption?"

Aki knew the answer, but the hurt across her uncle's face exacted the reaction she desired. Would her father say something to make her uncle stop it, the same way when Uncle tried to adopt Shuji. "Uncle, if you need help, I will help you, but I must remain here and support my brothers."

Uncle tilted his head with a demonic grin, as if to chide her for her immaturity while imparting his own wisdom. "I've no children, and I need an heir." His gaze grew wide. "That is why I need you."

There it was. The real reason. He wanted a son to take over his business. The pit in Aki's stomach increased to the size of a temple gate. "You sent Natsu back."

Her father's eyes widened at Aki's defiance while Uncle's face turned crimson and then cooled to a shade of rose. Her rude mention of Natsu's return likely surprised them both.

"That was unfortunate," her uncle said. "The gods did not smile on us, but I made entreaties at temples, and I know you are suited. Aki, you'll become my daughter. The son of the family I am talking with will marry into our family, take my name, and become my heir. It is a good match."

Yes. A good match for her uncle and for the other family's son.

She craned her neck to look her uncle in the eyes. A disrespectful act, but the alternative was worse. "What would Father receive in return?" Her voice rose, along with her trepidation.

Her uncle's face reddened again, and his hands balled into fists at his side. "That is between your father and me." His sharp tone jabbed the air. "Your only concern is to follow my instructions. You're a woman. Obey my orders. *That* is your duty."

Father stuck out his hand and created a barrier between her uncle and her. "She's still my daughter." Anger coursed through his voice. "You will address her that way."

Aki forced herself not to smile at her father's defense. Her uncle shrank back and grew sheepish. "My apologies," he said, stumbling at a phrase he'd probably rarely uttered.

"I forgot myself. The match would be beneficial. We could increase our family business."

"Aki asks a good question. This benefits you, not us. You are my elder brother. I respect that. But Aki has special talents. She is a born merchant. She is capable and could manage this business if needed. Genta will need her when I am no longer fit for a full day of work."

Uncle's face tightened. "You're being stingy. It's your duty to do what I tell you. Ten years ago, when the typhoon struck and destroyed your property, I helped you rebuild."

"I thank you for that. I thanked you before." Her father paused. "And when the earthquake in Ise destroyed your investment there, I helped you rebuild."

Aki recalled the typhoon. Storms came every year, some worse than others, but this one had damaged her home. Earthquakes happened all the time, too. Uncle claimed one had destroyed a chance to make a lot of money, but she didn't trust her uncle. Father seldom trusted Uncle. If not for family ties, then Father would have nothing to do with him.

"I only ask," her uncle continued, his hands open in a plea, "so that I may have an heir…as Futsu's parents gained from your marriage to her."

For one moment, Aki experienced a twinge of sympathy. Uncle had been married. He had no children, and his wife had passed. He had never remarried or gotten over his lost love. It was the only thing about Uncle that called for feeling, but even doing so brought pain, like pulling hairs from one's head. One bit of feeling could move her father.

Now it was her problem.

"I am the elder brother," her uncle continued. "You married into a family with no sons and have been blessed with many children. This is about continuing our family line. Deny the adoption, and you deny your duty."

There it was. Aki understood obligation. Father's

actions in the past did not matter. Never would. Uncle would always be the elder brother. Father would always have that obligation.

Father's shoulders slumped as if carrying a load of cloth off a boat, but then he stiffened. "You are right, but now is not the time. A samurai who works for the police has requested Aki's services. He will return tonight to get her answer."

"We do not have time for this. Decline it. Tell the samurai you're betrothed."

"The job is temporary. The samurai's servant is returning home as her own daughter is with child. I will not decline his request. I can make no commitment to Aki's future at this time."

"This will not do. I must make plans."

The door slid open and brought the argument to a halt. Aki imagined Nishioji-sama standing at the door. His imposing figure would drive Uncle into the shadows.

The young one, the one called Yori-sama, stood there in the genkan, light rain and wind blowing behind him. He was clothed in a mixed-blue kosode and matching hakama, though much was covered by his straw rain jacket. A pointed hat hid most of his face, but his expression showed his disdain.

Aki bowed. "Osamurai-sama, welcome."

He grunted, as much of an acknowledgment as she expected. "Nishioji was delayed. I'm here for your answer."

She glanced back at her father and uncle before turning to the young man. "Please tell Nishioji-sama that I accept."

The young man's head jerked at her use of Nishioji-sama's name, but he showed no anger this time, unlike before. "Be ready in four days at the hour of the rabbit. You will be met and shown the way."

"Yes, sir." *Four days?* She had expected more time, more time to delay her uncle. *Something must have happened. What could it have been*? "I will be ready."

He grunted and then turned without further acknowledgment. She wished she knew his family name, at least to keep it in her head. Knowing only his first name meant the possibility of making a mistake. She watched him proceed down the street, the evening wind freezing her fingers. Light drops of rain fell. Hopefully, he would get home soon.

Aki closed the door and placed the wooden jamb at the base to lock it, then turned to face her father and uncle. She breathed deeply and readied herself for her uncle's ire.

Instead, her uncle appeared confused. "That is the samurai you will serve? I am impressed that such a young man would see your value. What is his name?"

Aki's mouth grew dry. "That is his assistant. The one I will serve is older. He is called Nishioji-sama."

Her uncle smiled like a greedy rodent. "I see."

"Good? Earlier you were unhappy about it. Now you approve?"

"As you were talking with the young man, I saw his clothes and had a chance to think. Samurai need silk." He looked at her father. "This is an opportunity for us. I already own a location close to the castle. A well-placed samurai offers possibilities."

Now she understood Uncle's change of mind. The young man's garments were finer than what he himself wore. Uncle realized the family had money. *Better not to let him know that Nishioji-sama wears only the required basics.* She opened her mouth, but her father gave her a slight tilt of his head, a signal that always meant no and silence. *Let him handle this.* Father knew best.

"Once her service is done," her uncle said, "we can hold the wedding. Aki's position is a sign."

"The biggest spenders are in the capital," her father said. "Osaka Castle is active, but the demand for silk is minimal. We must focus on cotton. That's the future."

"Brother, I know you mean well." Her uncle paused as

if savoring the moment. "Once Aki is my daughter, you will see the wisdom of my strategy. Moreover, the debt between you and me will be settled."

Until the next time Uncle needs something and reminds Father of his duty.

Her uncle rose. "I will start the adoption process tomorrow. A simple matter of filing and recognition." He headed toward the door. "Good night, brother. Good night, daughter."

Daughter. Aki gritted her teeth and kept her gaze down as she removed the jamb. "Good night...Uncle."

Uncle's murmur of disapproval rumbled in Aki's ears despite being smothered by the wind. He walked to the street and sidestepped the neighborhood fire caller without a glance. She had angered him, and people needed to stay out of his way. Likely, he had hoped to hear *Father* instead of *Uncle*. The words created a sour taste in her throat.

She closed the door and inserted the jamb with force.

"Calm yourself, Aki. No need to get angry. You'll have trouble sleeping. We've much work to do before your days are occupied."

"Father, please reconsider your promise to Uncle. I will go where you say, but I do not wish to leave our family. I would even accept marriage to a dealer of human waste. Is there no other way?"

He patted her shoulder. "Daughter, it is my fault. I should've married you off already. You passed the appropriate age. I know a fish merchant who has an eldest son your age."

"Fishing?"

"Yes, there will always be a need for food and bad fish makes good fertilizer. The river will always be active for business."

"Yes, father." Aki smiled inwardly. He was still thinking about survival and expanding the business. "I will do whatever you ask."

"Give me time. Your service to the samurai gives us a few weeks. I will find another way. For now, do as your uncle requests."

"He will start the adoption tomorrow."

"I will do everything I can."

"Thank you."

"If we are fortunate, the samurai's duties will take long enough to make your uncle seek elsewhere." He then flashed a proud smile. "Maybe the samurai will see your beauty and request a marriage."

Not likely. Aki's sisters had inherited their mother's moon face and gentle steps, while she resembled a relative long forgotten. Samurai wives stayed home, and she would be reduced to a life of menial tasks. Such tasks were still preferable to a life as Uncle's daughter.

Caring for the samurai's mother. What could that involve? She could assist other family members of samurai. She could find a way to make it long-term and support Genta in the evening.

Life would be busy and unexciting, but it would be preferable to her uncle and a lifetime of misery.

CHAPTER SIX

Tomi eyed the church in the pre-dawn darkness, wanting some privacy to pray before he started his morning duties. It had been two days since he'd sent Yori to get an answer from the merchant's daughter. The girl, Aki, had agreed to serve him. That was one concern resolved.

He yawned and tried to rouse himself but was tired. He and Matsu had worked late last night. It had poured the final few hours, so drenched and muddy roads made the morning footing uncertain. Thankfully, the skies were now clear. Constable Oeda had told them to rest themselves this morning. Tomi could not rest long. Yori had more to learn.

Tomi grabbed the main door to the church and tried to slide it open, but it wouldn't budge. He stepped back from the building to look for signs of activity. The light from the half-moon illuminated the cross nestled in the front, the only thing about the place that marked it as a Christian church. After Hideyoshi's edict in 1587, officials destroyed Osaka's main church and the seminary. Only the mission survived.

Tomi walked several steps in each direction, searching for signs of candlelight or lamps glowing against paper windows. Nothing. The church was an older building, a converted temple that had survived the siege of ten years ago when Osaka was a temple town. Had the structure been newer and more sound, it would have been designated for another use. Its dilapidated state was the reason it was given to the church.

The wind whistled through the street, breaking the silence. Should he ring the bell at the entrance? The padre would notice, but Tomi might wake neighbors. If he rang the one at the residence across the street, the effect would be the same.

Tomi closed his eyes, listening to the sounds in the air. The padre often rose early to pray. So did his assistant. Tomi sighed, wishing he had daily time for reflection.

"Nishioji-sama," a familiar, accented voice called out with authority, "what comes you here at this hour?"

Tomi turned. Padre Alvares stood before him grinning, his eyes sparkling and a ring of hair encircling his otherwise bald head. He wore a black robe cinched at the waist with a belt. A knee-length cape with the top turned up shielded his ears from the wind. A golden chain with Iesu on a cross hung from the man's neck. It was only color showing on his black outfit and it captured all the light it could, a testament to his faith.

Padre had spent a few years in Japan and spoke Japanese well. Said he'd studied first. Most of his pronunciations were fine, but he sometimes confused the grammar, and his sermons were stilted. After his first confession with the padre, Tomi had shaken his head in puzzlement. Things had improved, though the man still couldn't pronounce Osaka correctly. Only a believer attempted to say *padre*. Everyone else called the foreign holy men *bateren*.

Padre apparently learned how to walk with stealth. How did the man approach me? Was my attention so diverted?

Tomi grinned as the padre neared him. The man's

height always surprised him. Padre was about one *sun* taller than Tomi and about ten years older. Tomi was tall compared to his countrymen, but with the padre, he looked neither up nor down. "I needed to pray, Padre *Arubaresu*," he said. "The door won't open. Is it locked? I thought the church never closed."

"It's always open," the padre said, "especially for believers. But we maintain a watch on the building as best we can."

Tomi's stomach clenched. "Did someone damage the mission?"

"No, we've been fortunate. We see passersby staring, but nothing happens."

"Anywhere else?"

"Not recently."

"That is good. How was my pronunciation of your name?"

"Better, but I know Alvares is difficult for you to say. 'Padre' is fine."

"Yes, Padre-sama."

A stiff wind whipped through the street, blowing mist from the ground and on Tomi's clothes.

The padre shivered. "I'd like the benefit of your warrior training," he said, his teeth chattering, "when we're more awake. For now, we go inside."

"I tried to open it earlier."

"Hunh," Alvares said. "Sometimes, the door sticks. Let me try it."

The padre pressed on the door, attempting several places without success. He then pushed up and slid it open. "There we are."

The two of them entered the mission, and the padre shut the door behind them. Heat greeted Tomi's face. The brazier on the floor contained a few pieces of charcoal, not enough for comfort, but it did provide some light. Two more lined the short hallway.

Tomi held out his hands to warm himself. "Who is maintaining these?"

"Kazu."

"He's just a boy. Can he handle this alone?"

The padre nodded. "He is younger than your friend Yori-sama, but Kazu's vigilance does him credit. If there is a problem, we keep shells ready to sound any alarm at the street leader's insistence."

"Can he blow the shells loud enough?" Tomi asked.

"He can, but he has a child's enthusiasm. I fear he'll blow on the shells early."

Tomi laughed. Kazu was a devoted young follower with a gift for happiness. Homeless and living on the street, he found the padre and dedicated himself to this mission. He would make a good padre himself someday. "What about other places nearby? Has anything happened?"

Alvares shook his head. "No, but those places are more remote. Our donation to your officials saved this mission and the house." He looked at the building. "If we have one place to worship, we exist in Ozaka."

Tomi nodded. The mission was small but large enough to provide a presence in the community. "That is good to hear. Any other news?"

"Come with me to the office. We can talk about it there."

The spaced-out braziers threw off low light that made their shadows dance as they headed to the padre's office. They had reached the door when Tomi heard footsteps from a nearby corridor.

"Kazu, is that you?" Alvares called out.

"Padre-sama, it is me," a lantern-carrying figure cried out. "Hisa."

A few seconds later, Hisa, the *dōjuku* who assisted the padre with administering the mission, reached the door, his sheepish grin spread ear-to-ear in the lantern's shaded light. "Padre-sama, why are you here so early?"

"An early start. Where's Kazu?"

"On the roof. He was falling asleep on his feet. I told him to rest and said I would monitor the lights. He headed for the roof, instead, saying the cold air would keep him awake."

Hisa looked twice in Tomi's direction, then his eyes grew wide, and he bowed. "Nishioji-sama, welcome. It is good to see you."

Tomi returned the gesture. Hisa's mouth dropped open, revealing the gap between his two front teeth. "Nishioji-sama," Hisa's voice quaked, "you do me too much honor."

Tomi laughed. "My bow is for Iesu, not you. Padre doesn't understand the depths of bows like you do."

"Yes," Hisa said, his face turning another shade of embarrassment. He set the lantern high in the holding place on the wall, which gave an eerie yet bright glow to the section. "I should have known, Nishioji-sama."

"Call me by my baptismal name. Tomasu."

"I have always liked the name 'Tomasu'," Hisa said. "It sounds Kirishitan and Japanese."

Tomi smiled. He liked the name Tomasu, too, but he was jealous of the slender assistant. Hisa always said his baptismal name could be shortened to his real name of Hisa, so he got to use it anywhere. Tomi had heard the story once but had forgotten and was too embarrassed to ask again.

Hisa opened the door and then readjusted the lantern, lighting up the room as much as possible and illuminating the crucifix on the wall shelf where likely once had stood two Buddhist statues. His orange robe glowed in the light. Other than the color, the robe resembled the one worn by the padre, except it lacked a cape. The head of the padres allowed Japanese converts to wear the colors of the Buddhist priests but required their own people to remain in black.

Hisa added charcoal to the brazier in the room and then

headed to the door. "I will bring both of you some tea," he said, turning as he stepped out and then peeking back in. "One question, Tomasu-sama," Hisa said, his eyes flashing concern, "what if I err later? Someone"—he stopped and made a mock grab of his own neck—"may take my head out of duty."

"It would take more of an insult than that. Besides, I would defend you. If you died"—he smiled—"you would not die alone."

Hisa laughed. "Then may whoever he is find God before your sword finds him."

Alvares laughed. "Hisa, ensure the sanctuary is warm and lighted. Let's show that the mission is open. One more thing."

"Yes, Padre-sama."

"Get Kazu off the roof. He can freeze up there. Tell him to keep warm or assist you. The two of you can say prayers in the sanctuary."

Tomi imagined the roof. He hoped Kazu slept well during the day as the nights must wear on him.

Hisa departed, his footsteps echoing on the wooden walkways. Tomi always appreciated the man's smile. He wondered what Hisa would say if he knew the name Tomasu was based on Tomi, his nickname and a shortened version of his first name, Tsuneomi. Hisa would never say Tomasu if he knew.

Like the apostle, Tomi also carried his doubts. *Is showing respect for God the same as showing respect for one's own lord?* Tomi never doubted his own service. He gave his loyalty to the regent, as well as Uji and other samurai with whom he had fought.

He was also loyal to God, had been since his time in Kyushu three years ago when he first discovered his faith. The regent had issued an anti-Christian decree, but that edict had no hold on Tomi's heart. "How many places were destroyed in the country?"

"At last count," Alvares said, "we lost around sixty. Then the regent's anger subsided, and he left the other buildings standing, but we remain vigilant."

Tomi rubbed the spot on his clothes above his rosary. "You maintain watch on this building to protect it?"

"Yes, one man remains inside the mission. He's supposed to be awake to welcome others and sound an alarm if necessary."

"That sounds like a challenge. Especially for Kazu."

"He's resourceful. I have maintained the watch myself. I know the gods of the bonzes do not exist, but I jump at shadows, as if the spirits of former residents wish to debate my thoughts."

"No one should do it alone," Tomi said.

"We have only the three of us. Other missionaries in the city drop by to assist. However, we want our numbers to appear low."

Alvares added fuel to the brazier nearest in the hallway and then returned to the room. "Some members also assist." He motioned toward a chair. "Please sit, Tomasu-sama, so I can understand why you are here."

His warm words washed over Tomi. "I don't know how to begin."

"Then let's talk about your mother. How is she?"

Tomi breathed in deeply. "She is stronger on some days. She spends time outside and takes short walks when she can."

"Is that wise? The walks? Others might notice her condition."

"She's covered up. No one can see her. She hopes you will come by and hear her Confession."

"I will visit soon."

"Thank you.

Alvares leaned in close. "Now, what's troubling you? Remember that anything you tell me, I will tell no one else."

"I'm failing in my mission."

The padre paused. "Your search for the anti-Christian group in Ozaka?"

"Yes. I came to Osaka as we learned there was a group operating here. It's been a year. I've learned nothing."

"You could be stopping things and not realize it."

Tomi tapped his foot. "With my work?"

"Yes. Or your target is frightened of you."

The suggestion pleased Tomi, but he shook his head. "I doubt I could do everything. There must be another reason."

"Are you here to pray for guidance?"

"I hope the Lord will provide direction."

"In His time. But according to the wisdom of my mother, so will food and sleep. Are you getting either?"

"I have tried," Tomi said, sighing. "Nothing has come to me yet."

"It will come, my friend."

A loud knock resounded from outside, making the corner walls shake. Tomi rose, his hand atop his sword hilt. "It's an attack. I'll get you to safety then see what it is."

"It's not an attack, Tomasu-sama. The walls are thin in some parts, owing to pieces being taken for other buildings before we arrived. Strong winds stress the wall. We are shoring up the roof. Something must have fallen and struck the outside.

"Are you certain?"

"I am. At least we do not have to leave the building."

"Leave the building?" Tomi asked.

"Yes," Alvares laughed. "Padre Frois told me about our first mission in the capital. It was a former bonze temple. The walls were thin, and everyone fled outside during severe storms. This place is in better shape."

"Padre Frois? I have only heard stories. I hope to meet him."

"One day. Unfortunately, he is becoming old. He is passing his interpreter duties over to Brother Rodrigues.

The Society of Jesus could use men like you. You would make a fine member of our society and help us grow."

Tomi glowed within. "Padre-sama, my duties as only son to my parents take precedence. Catching criminals takes time."

"Maybe the challenge is that nothing will happen here."

"What do you mean?"

"What if Ozaka has a different purpose for you?"

Tomi thought hard. "What kind of purpose?"

"No idea, but my fellow padres tell me that Ozaka is a unique place. I agree with them. What does your intuition tell you?"

"Nothing. I am drawn to the garment area, but I do not know why."

"What are you doing about it?"

"My duty."

"Then you are doing everything you can. Allow our Lord to guide you."

The padre's words reassured Tomi, but he could not relax. *Not until I find whoever was operating here.* "Thank you."

"Anytime, my son. You said you are here to pray?"

"Yes." For once, Tomi felt sure of himself.

Alvares smiled as he raised his right hand, making the sign of the cross in front of him. Tomi bowed his head. "Pray," the man said. "You will find your way.

Tomi rose and opened the door. Hisa stood there waiting.

"Hisa," Padre said in a sharp tone, "were you listening to our conversation? That is inappropriate."

"Forgive me, padre," his speech sounded hurried, "but I needed to find Nishioji-sama, I mean Tomasu-sama."

Hisa's urgent tone placed Tomi's senses on alert. "What is it?"

"A messenger arrived," Hisa said with a hitch in his

voice. "A messenger for you."

Wakizashi studied the group of men before him. Riku, the cloth merchant, stood apart from the rest, as if he thought he was in charge. The sudden meeting at the abandoned temple had been Riku's request. They would get to the reason soon.

"Riku, how was it two nights ago?" Wakizashi asked. "Did your brother agree to let you adopt his daughter?"

Riku grunted then licked his lips. "He agreed, though he does not like it. I submitted the paperwork to make it official. It should be soon."

Wakizashi rubbed the sweat from his palms, amazed he could perspire in the temple's icy confines. "Then why did you want to meet?"

"There is one delay."

"A delay?" Anger rose within Wakizashi. "What delay?"

"My niece must work for a samurai for a short time, a few weeks as a servant, while another servant cares for a pregnant daughter."

"Our master, Lord Eijiro, is in the capital. I will need to inform him of the delay. Who is this samurai?"

"His name is Nishioji."

"Nishioji?" Wakizashi repeated, his voice rising. "This could be fortunate."

"You know this man?"

"I know one named Nishioji no Tsuneomi." He wanted to spit out the name in disgust. "Being a Kirishitan is bad enough, but this one is a samurai. An embarrassment. He interfered with our master's plans in Himeji. We should have killed him there. His presence here taunts our work. How did your brother meet him?"

"He arrested my brother."

Wakizashi nodded, his heart beating louder in his head. "It's him. He works at the Justice Building."

"Why is he here?" Riku's voice sounded reserved, as if he worried it might be a problem.

"He served at the castle in Himeji. Now he chases criminals. It allows him to wear his swords. It's too good for him. He belongs with society's other outcasts."

Riku looked away.

"You have a question?" Wakizashi asked. "Say it."

The merchant rubbed his hand across his mouth. "Could this Nishioji have an interest in my niece beyond work?"

"Doubtful," he answered in a huff. "He is a man of his word." Wakizashi stared back at Riku. "The temporary delay may even benefit us."

"How?"

"Encourage your *daughter* to learn everything about Nishioji. His habits. His preferences. His cares. Once she is yours, duty will command she reveal all to you. It will be easier to kill him"—he rubbed his chin and smiled—"and more enjoyable."

"You sound like you know him well."

"We stared at each other once on the battlefield. I remember him."

Riku grunted. A rude habit for an inferior in the presence of his lord. *When this is over, it may be time to eliminate him.* "Questions, Riku?"

The merchant paused. "Killing samurai is bad for business. It will create questions."

Always about money for this one. "I'll make it so that no one knows how he died. Kirishitan are foolish, and their passion is pathetic. I will show them meaning of faith."

"Then kill him now. I'll push the marriage. It will increase our profits."

Wakizashi drew his sword and sliced a strip from Riku's cheek.

Riku grasped his face. Blood seeped between his fingers.

"Don't give me orders," Wakizashi barked. "I could cut you in half in public, and no one could touch me. Do you understand?"

Riku shook. "Yes, sir." His voice trembled.

"On your knees."

Riku complied.

Wakizashi pressed his sword against Riku's neck. "Remember this, I will sever your head and strip your family of your assets if you ever address me like that again. Support of our cause is the only important thing. Do not forget that."

"Yes, sir," Riku said.

One cut would do what he wanted, but he needed the merchant. Once they were done, there would be nothing more to hide. All would fear and fall in line.

He withdrew his sword and sheathed it. The merchant sighed and relaxed. *Even this worthless pile got the message.* "That's all for now. Rise. Complete the adoption and push her to finish her service. Report to me with any updates."

"I will. He may yet use her for his own needs."

Wakizashi grabbed his sword hilt. "I didn't ask for your opinion. Nishioji is not one to use a young girl. Just report the facts as you learn them."

"Yes, sir."

"Lord Eijiro will come to Osaka soon. No delays, or you will pay with your life. Now remove yourself from my presence before I make your removal permanent myself."

Riku bowed lower than he had before. Wakizashi was impressed. The merchant needed to be taught manners, but maybe there was hope. Age was but a number. Class was the true differentiator. If the merchant proved useful, Wakizashi might allow him to live.

CHAPTER SEVEN

Tomi stared at Hisa in disbelief. "I have a message? From whom?"

Hisa glanced between Tomi and the padre. "That is hard to say."

"Who brings the message?" Alvares asked.

Hisa hesitated. "The traveling brothers."

"Traveling brothers?" Tomi faced Alvares. "Who are they?"

"Members of the Society and others who support us. They preach in places where we have no churches." He turned toward Hisa. "They traveled at night?"

"They did," Hisa said. "The group lodged at the house of a supporter. One of them rose early to bring the message. He planned to give the message to you, Padre-sama, but it is intended for Tomasu-sama. He was delighted to learn that he was here."

The hair stood on the back of Tomi's neck. His hand dropped to his katana. It must be a trick. Who knew to send him a message here?

"Show him in," Alvares said.

"He is behind me. Come in," Hisa called out.

A short, slender man wearing an orange robe like the

one worn by Hisa entered. His head was clean shaven, and a thin mustache decorated his face. He had a mole on his right cheek and pock marks on both sides. He resembled a Buddhist priest, except for the cross hanging from the sash around his waist.

Hisa stepped behind the visitor and left, shutting the door behind him.

Padre Alvares put his hands together to bow while Tomi tapped the hilt of his katana. "Welcome," Alvares said. "You must know Ozaka well to make it here in the dark."

"I lived here before. I worked on the boats bringing stone from the Inland Sea to the castle. Part of the Regent's push for 7000 new homes in forty days."

Tomi eyed him. "How did you join?"

"Padre Frois used to watch the ships with stones every day. He preached from the shore often. I became a believer and volunteered to help. Some things have changed here, but much remains the same." He bowed. "My name is Ruka."

Tomi returned Ruka's bow, still eyeing the man out of curiosity. "What is the message?"

"Yes, I regret not coming last night, but we reached the house late, so our leader insisted I get some rest. I bring news from Himeji and your friend Tokoda Ujihiro-sama."

Uji? Could he be sending a message? "How do you know Tokoda? Why would he use you as a courier?"

"We met in Himeji at the baptism of Tokoda-sama's brother Nobuhiro. I understand from Tokoda-sama that you and Nobuhiro are…old friends?"

Tomi nodded. The mixture of wordplay was as close as Uji would get to making a joke. It's also how he identified the courier as trustworthy. "You must have impressed him."

"I did my duty. Meeting Tokoda-sama surprised me, since he is not a believer."

"I'm not surprised," Tomi said, rubbing the scar on his cheek and remembering how he acquired it. "The Tokoda brothers are close."

"I saw that." Ruka's gaze swept the ground. "After the ceremony, Tokoda-sama asked about my travels. He pulled me aside and requested my help."

Alvares's face tightened. "You trusted him? You just met him."

"He has a reassuring face and a confident tone. He asked if I could pass along a message."

The padre's eyes grew wide with concern. "For a non-believer?"

Ruka's gaze grew resolute. "I believed his request. He did not wish to use a messenger service but said he needed help. I received approval to help."

"From whom?" Alvares asked.

"Padre *Oregan*," Ruka said.

"Who's that?" Tomi asked.

"Padre Organtino," Alvares said. "He lives in the capital and has so embraced your culture he acts more Japanese than any of us."

Ruka's lips thinned. "Tokoda-sama first requested we pass a message to his brother, Toshihiro, in Kyoto, which I did."

The winds blew hard again. Noises sounded within the mission. Kazu must not be resting. "Your friend Tokoda-sama must be trustworthy," Alvares said. "Discretion is important."

"I delivered a second message to the brother in Kyoto. Tokoda-sama then asked me to reach Nishioji-sama."

"Anything besides the message?" Tomi asked.

Ruka's face grew sheepish and turned red. "It is unimportant."

"What is it?" Alvares asked.

"Tokoda-sama expressed that all padres should bathe more than the once a month that is required in winter."

The padre laughed. "I see. What was the recommendation?"

"Weekly at least," Ruka said.

"Agreed." Tomi fought to maintain his composure. If only Matsu could see his reaction. "Where is the message?"

Ruka reached under his orange robe and pulled out a folded piece of paper. He handed it to Tomi. "Tokoda-sama was most urgent with this."

Tomi accepted the letter with both hands, noting the wax seal: an incomplete rendition of the kanji for happiness. The reference to the anti-Christian group they'd defeated in Himeji was a signal to Tomi that the message was authentic.

Tomi placed the letter beneath his outer garment, brushing his fingers on it, and then nodded his thanks. "I must leave."

Alvares eyed him. "You are not going to pray? Coming here, that was your purpose."

"I'll say a brief one," he replied. He didn't wish to appear rude, but the news was urgent. He needed to find Matsu now.

Aki stepped outside the shop to get a breath of fresh air and check the morning weather. Two nights ago the young samurai, Yori-sama, had stopped by for her answer. That same night, her uncle informed them he would start the adoption process.

"Are you nervous, Aki?" her father asked.

Her father's reserved tone suggested *he* was. Anxiety swirled in her chest like a typhoon. *Yes, Father, I am.*

"Too nervous to speak?" her father asked.

"I apologize, Father. Did I not say anything?"

"Your lips moved, but no sound came out." He flashed a doting smile, a sign that he was about to pass along some fatherly advice. "You've always been that way. When you're nervous, you believe you are talking when you're saying nothing out loud."

Aki brought her left hand to her mouth, rubbing her fingers against her dry lips. "I am a rude daughter then. My apologies. I am nervous."

"Why?"

She held back. When she agreed to serve Nishioji-sama, she thought of how handsome he was and the chance to get away from her uncle. Now she recalled her father's treatment and how lowly her family was. "He is a samurai. I should not be in the company of a samurai."

"Would you rather your uncle plan your wedding?"

"He is planning already. Contact the fish dealer you mentioned. Maybe he has other sons. Ever since I agreed to this, I have had time to think. The samurai is a decent man, but he still arrested you. What should I expect?"

Her father nodded. "What happened was a misunderstanding. Most people believe merchants are hiding something. There is a reason for the proverb 'Screens and merchants are crooked.' Truth in those words. Some are not reputable."

"You are an honest man," Aki said, her voice rising with her indignation. "You should not be put with criminals."

"Daughter, learn this now. People who do not earn a living from trade are often suspicious of those that do. Not just officials but farmers, as well. We serve as best we can."

"Your father speaks the truth." Her uncle's voice rang out, sending a shiver along her skin. He had entered the house without announcing his presence. "Officials always cite merchants for imagined crimes and make us explain ourselves. It's how they justify their oppression to their superiors, by scaring more tax money from those who have it."

Aki bowed her head to avert her gaze. How long had her uncle been listening outside the door? Had he heard her comment about her willingness to marry anyone else rather than become his daughter?

"Fewer merchants cheat than the officials believe," her father said, interrupting her thoughts. "Are you suggesting there are—"

Her father's voice cut off mid-sentence, and he stared hard. She turned to look at her uncle.

His face bore a slash across the cheek. Aki shuddered. She had never seen a cut so deep. What could do such damage?

Her uncle crossed his arms and eyed them both with a feigned owl-like gaze. "I am saying there are many merchants who use unscrupulous methods."

"Uncle, what happened?" Aki asked in earnest.

"I…am touched by your concern," he replied with a slight grin. "An accident at my home. I fell and cut myself on a display rack. I tried to dress it myself, but this was the best I could do."

"Aki, fetch a wet cloth," her father said.

Aki hurried to the back room, grabbed a fabric scrap, and wet it with hot water from the hearth. She stretched out her arm and patted the cut. Uncle gritted his teeth. *The pain must be intense.* Aki cleaned her uncle's wound, seeing him stiffen with each press of her hand. She allowed herself a brief touch of sympathy while suppressing her revulsion at being close enough to smell his sweat.

Aki poured more water on the cloth and pressed with a lighter touch. The hot water drew fresh blood. Aki shivered. She feared causing more pain, but she pushed herself to clean the wound. When the blood ceased, she stared at the gash. It was a straight cut, almost neat. That clothing rack of Uncle's must be sharp.

Did a similar cut cause Nishioji's scar?

She rubbed honey on a cloth fragment and then applied it to the wound. "Done."

"This is why I need a daughter at home," her uncle said, "to care for me. Would you not like that, Aki? Once the adoption is recorded, it will be official."

A vile flavor rose in her mouth, erasing the scant bit of pity that had arisen. *The idea of caring for her uncle and being at his call. The nerve of him.* She hoped her father did pair her with a family that sold fertilizer.

"We can discuss that later," her father said. "What were you saying, Riku, about what merchants believe?"

"Only that there are merchants who put their thumbs on the scale. It's a way to get more coin."

Especially people like you, Uncle, who have big thumbs.

"What did you say, Aki?" her uncle asked.

Did I speak aloud? "Nothing. I thought of something Father said before you arrived. Is not the penalty for cheating severe?"

Her uncle traced a line with his thumb across his own neck. "Severe, indeed, but most would pay additional taxes or sell their children before having their heads chopped off or being skewered on a wooden cross. Officials will make a few examples of offenders. Others will fall in line."

"Why only a few?"

Her uncle glanced at her father with disapproval. Obviously, there was something he thought she should know.

Her father turned toward her. "Because, Aki, if there are as many cheaters as your uncle implies, then there would be insufficient workers to pay taxes."

"Exactly," her uncle said.

Aki bowed. Anything to avoid her uncle's smug expression.

"Come, Mori," her uncle said. "Get your records. We have much to plan for when Aki returns from her duties to the samurai."

"I will fetch the information," Aki said, as she headed toward the back room. "Please wait here."

"I'm hungry, too," her uncle said.

"I will get you something."

"Just get the records. I'll take care of it myself."

Her uncle sauntered away, acting as if he owned the place. Her father looked at her sternly and then approached and broke into a smile. "Your uncle does have a big thumb," he whispered.

"I said it aloud? Is that why he asked?"

"I could hear you, because you're *my* daughter. Your uncle likely heard noise."

"Like you mentioned before, when I am nervous?"

"Also when you're angry. When you're angry, your thoughts are clear."

Her cheeks warmed in embarrassment. "I will work to keep them more silent."

"See that you do. In the meantime, fetch the records and then prepare tea for us. I will need you to join. There is much to do."

Yes. Much to do while waiting for the approval of an adoption and the end of my life.

CHAPTER EIGHT

It was the start of the hour of the monkey when Tomi and Matsu settled at Tomi's house. He never expected it to take until midafternoon, but at least they had daylight left.

"Open the message from Uji or not?" Matsu asked, his feet crossed under him. He sipped water in the main room, relaxing near the back door.

Tomi shook his head. "I'm wondering if we should wait for Yori."

"After depriving me of a restful few hours, you're going to make me wait?" he asked, a light glow on his face. "You spent nearly all day looking for me."

"Not *all* day. I went to the jail and questioned the man who attacked me."

"Any success?" Matsu asked.

"None."

"Could have rested more," Matsu said, "if you were going to make me wait."

"Were you planning another tea ceremony?"

"Planned to watch the boats on the canal and listen to the sanshin. In some places, there are patches of plum blossoms already blooming."

"Plum blossoms?" Tomi stared at his friend. "I hadn't

noticed."

"You deprive yourself. Ujihiro's father, when he was alive, was an accomplished poet. One day, he challenged Uji and me to a poetry contest. A joy to listen to him. Our portions of the poems never matched his.

Renga. Another pastime I didn't know about my friend. "I sent a messenger to find Yori."

"Tell him later. Doesn't know Uji like we do."

Tomi nodded, both in agreement and curiosity. He broke the seal and scanned the note. "Uji says another group has been located. A pocket of traitors following an unnamed person in the capital who is close to the regent."

"Unnamed? Or unknown?"

Matsu was right. "Unknown," Tomi said. "Some of the ones that have spoken refer to him as 'Master'. Others as Eijiro. No other information."

"Isn't 'Eijiro' a name?"

"It is, but there's no one near the regent named Eijiro."

"Where were the traitors?"

"Kamakura." Tomi drank a deep draught. The barley flavor proved filling. He listened for the approach of Yori and then read the note again. Uji's detailed missive showed no corrections. Either he mulled his first words carefully, or he drafted a letter and then destroyed it. "There is no church in Kamakura. Uji says the criminals were discovered watching a Buddhist nunnery there, a special place controlled by the empress. A local constable arrested them."

"The divorce nunnery?"

Tomi stared at his friend. "You've heard of it?"

"Only rumors and the image of women throwing shoes onto the grounds to get someone's attention. Go there to rid themselves of bad husbands. A personal patronage of the empress."

"You sound like you know it well."

"Only in passing," Matsu said. "Toshi chides Uji about his marriage, saying one day Uji's wife may seek her own separation when he gets older and fatter."

Tomi laughed hard. "One day, Uji is going to drop Toshi off a bridge. A joke, of course."

"Anything else from the group in Kamakura?"

"They were looking for a woman."

"Name?"

"Iri," Tomi said. "That's all we know. Some followers took their own lives to avoid arrest. The ones that lived were hired help who knew little else."

"Why a Buddhist nunnery? It's the wrong target," Matsu said.

"Uji thinks this mysterious Iri is seeking a divorce."

"From whom?"

"Maybe this Eijiro or Master, whoever he is. One option is the place in Kamakura."

Matsu grunted. "Makes sense. What else does he say?"

"They continue to find eye patches, like we did in Himeji, but Uji has no idea what it means."

"Probably a ruse of some kind to make us curious. Anything about Toshi?"

Tomi reached to the side and grabbed a tray, offering Matsu a confection. "His results match ours. Nothing." He extended the message. "You can read, if—"

A snap of twigs sounded from beyond the thin paper of the shoji door. Tomi held up his hand to silence Matsu and pointed at the entrance to the back.

Yori? Matsu mouthed.

Tomi swiped his hand across to say no. He gestured toward the front door and repeated Yori, then pointed again to the back and shook his head.

They both stood and drew their swords at a measured pace to tamp down on the surprise, then both nodded *ready*.

Tomi flashed three fingers and then signaled the cadence. *One. Two.* He slid the door open, sword drawn, and stepped into the entrance. "Show yourself," he barked.

"It is me," Yori said, his hands extended in open palms

of supplication.

Tomi exhaled slowly, trying to calm the fire in his body. "That was foolish, Yori. What do you mean by approaching the house this way?"

The color disappeared from Yori's face and embarrassment turned to shame. "My apologies. I should have announced my presence first, but I heard your voices and decided to come around."

"Voices," Matsu said, more an inquiry than a statement. "How much did you hear?"

"Murmurs, except for the comment about someone named Toshi. Who is he?"

Tomi thought of Uji's brother working alone in Kyoto. "A person you should meet one day, if you have the chance."

"Gomen kudasai," someone called from beyond the front door. Whoever it was had more sense than Yori.

Tomi opened the door to reveal a man with a grizzled but familiar face. He wore a coat that stretched to his knees, leaving exposed shins. The man bowed low as Tomi tried to recall his name.

The husband of his mother's caregiver.

"Junichiro, what brings you here? I'm surprised to see you."

"I beg your forgiveness, Nishioji-sama. My daughter has the pains. The *koshikakae* who assists with all births in my area is at my house. The old woman examined my daughter and said it is time."

Tomi motioned the man to wait. He reached the room where his mother napped and conveyed to the caregiver her husband's arrival. Tomi requested she keep him updated and then watched as the couple departed.

He would need to reach Aki tonight and tell her to start tomorrow.

It had been a long day, but it felt like it was only the beginning.

###

Aki had hoped for a pleasant dinner with her family, but her uncle had returned early in the evening to discuss more wedding plans with her father. Had she not shown him enough kindness this morning when she had cleaned and bandaged the wound on his face? Could he not have left her alone? At least he had not made any more *daughter* comments.

Aki helped her mother put away the dishes from dinner. Genta's wife, Sadayo, directed the flow, failing to assist but making sure everything was done "as Genta would want." She shrugged off Sadayo's criticism, knowing that her brother had a good heart. She wished Shuji's wife, Ogin, was here, but she and Shuji were visiting Ogin's family tonight.

Uncle had ordered her mother around earlier in the evening. Aki did not appreciate it. Could her brother divorce his wife and Uncle adopt her? It would make several people happy.

"When does your service begin, Aki?" her uncle asked.

"Two mornings from now."

"Then you will be done," He accented the last word as if implying a debt, "in about three weeks, and we can move forward from there?"

"Riku," her father said, "Aki knows no more now than she did when the samurai first asked. It's our understanding the caregiver's daughter is some time away from giving birth."

Aki uttered a silent thanks. Father was trying for time. She could not prevent the caregiver's return, but her father's vagueness would delay her uncle's plan.

"I will do my service as the samurai sees fit. It is temporary, but I do not know how long or when it will begin."

Her uncle contained his temper under a controlled stare. "I await the day I adopt you. I hope your samurai will provide you time to meet my future son."

"Your future son?" Her voice carried an edge. "I am not even your daughter yet, and you discard me."

"How dare you raise your voice to me!" he yelled.

"Aki," her father said in a commanding tone and stepped between the two of them. "We will discuss everything later. Riku, she has no sway with the samurai. You must understand that."

Aki looked at the others. Shock radiated on the faces of her mother and Sadayo. Aki had never raised her voice to an elder. If only her sister, Hoshi, were here. She would at least get a reassuring glance.

"My apologies, Uncle," she said, knowing she must express regret because of her low status. "It is not my place to speak to you in such a manner. It is also not my place to ask such questions to the samurai. Please be patient. I am certain my service will be short."

She grabbed another tray and headed out of the room.

"Aki," her uncle called her name as a command to appear.

She approached and trembled in his presence. "Yes."

"You will be my daughter. Think of yourself as my daughter." He stretched taller, and the bandage on his cheek opened. "You do this for *our* family. When you work for the samurai, you must learn everything you can."

"That sounds like spying."

"It is not spying. It is business. You will do what I say and report to me everything you learn about him."

Aki sighed. "I understand." She reached out and pressed a cloth on his cheek. Could kindness change her uncle?

"What are you doing?"

"It was open."

"Oh. See. We can do this."

Uncle's reaction was what she needed. Everyone understood her outburst, but her actions remained improper.

Reconciling with her uncle would give her father more opportunity to find an alternative with less pressure.

Uncle said his goodbyes and saw himself out the door. She stared at it and imagined him walking away. The revulsion at being Uncle's daughter left her in sorrow. The bandage did not heal her situation.

A light touch on her shoulder brought her back. She turned and saw Father, who had given her a reassuring pat. The rest of the family had left the room. "Father, there must be something we can do. I will do anything you ask."

"I will do my best. Have faith in me."

She nodded. Her father was a man who kept his word. Even he, though, might not have hope to hold Uncle back.

The door slid open. Had her uncle come back? She looked toward the entrance.

Nishioji-sama stood there, his face somber.

Aki's heart sped up as she could not hide her eyes. *Will he tell me he no longer needs me? That would make this bad day worse.* "Nishioji-sama, what brings you here?" She paused for a second. "Is there something wrong?"

"My servant had to leave today. It was time for her daughter. Earlier than expected." He appeared tired, as if embarrassed or under strain. "You must start tomorrow."

Aki sighed in relief. He still needed her. "I understand."

"Good. Be ready to depart at the hour of the rabbit."

Nishioji-sama turned and headed down the street in the darkness. People side-stepped to move out of his way. Tomorrow, she would see his face every day.

But it would not last long. If the daughter had given birth, then her father's time was shorter. Aki had little more than three weeks left before the caregiver's return. Uncle would demand that she marry his choice for her.

The candle was burning.

CHAPTER NINE

Aki opened the door for the third time in the last few minutes. A massive chilling wind blew raindrops onto her face. It was the hour of the rabbit and still no Nishioji-sama. She glanced at the family room, which was poorly lit and cold. *So odd to see it empty, given all the work done here.*

She smoothed her dark green kosode, as if her hand could take out the wrinkles there. She wore another garment underneath and kept a *mino*, a straw cloak for protection against the rain, in her hands.

"Daughter, what are you doing?" her mother asked.

Aki grimaced inside, sorry to have awakened her. "Preparing for my first day with the samurai."

"With the samurai?" The scant light cast a glow on Mother's plump face. She yawned. "I thought you were caring for his mother."

Aki's cheeks grew warm. "Yes, I am, but I want to appear presentable."

Smiling, her mother shook her head. "You look fine." Her tone was sharp. "A simple garment will suffice, and add another one, given how cold it is. You will prove your worth to them."

"I know," Aki said, smoothing the kosode again, "but

I want to make a good impression."

"You did that already," she muttered. "You're not his wife, and you're not part of the willow world entertaining men for money, unless you're hiding something from your father and me."

Aki shook her head. "It is—"

"Look at me," she whispered in a tone that brooked no discussion.

"Yes?" she asked.

"What's troubling you, daughter?"

Aki stopped primping and put her hands by her side, staring into her mother's intense gaze. Her hair, usually held with a blue clip, was down. *Odd to see her this way, almost relaxed and refreshed and still so young.* Her sisters inherited her mother's looks. She did not.

"What is it?" her mother asked.

Aki sighed and paced the tatami floor. "Nothing."

Her mother sidled next to her. "When are you going to admit it to yourself?"

"Admit what?"

"You're infatuated with this samurai."

"Infatuated?"

"Yes, you mew like a cat trying to decide whether to eat or sleep. Infatuation."

Aki pressed her palms together in front of her chest. "This man arrested Father."

"Yes, and he protected your life. Your feelings are confused. I understand."

Aki felt her chest swell. The samurai prevented a man at the jail from hurting her and Father. He had also stopped the young samurai from striking her.

The memory of his protection lingered in her mind.

"At least admit he's handsome," her mother said.

"Handsome?"

"Yes, and that scar on his face is a samurai's dimple." She crossed her hands over her chest. "That one can even make old ladies like me swoon."

Aki tried not to laugh. "He is handsome. I admit that. I have never met anyone like him."

Her mother inched closer. "This explains why you are smoothing your clothes. You want to look your best. For him. I welcome it."

She considered asking how she looked but decided she would check a mirror later. "Welcome it?"

Her mother whispered in her ear. "Anything to keep your uncle away from you is welcome. He will be here any moment." Her mother smoothed Aki's shoulders. "There. You are beautiful."

"Gomen kudasai," a voice called out. Aki's heart leapt into her throat. *He is here.*

Her mother shooed her toward the door where a cloaked figure stood at the entrance. She walked to the front and the figure lowered his hood.

Her heart sank to the floor. Standing there was Yori-sama.

"Was it a good idea to send Yori to bring your new *servant* here?" Matsu asked.

Tomi ignored Matsu's sarcasm. "I couldn't do it myself. I wanted to make sure everything was ready."

"Should have told her the location last night. Could have come herself."

"The street captain wouldn't allow her entry at this hour."

"Leave instructions with the street captain."

"The sun won't have risen. It'd be dangerous. There are bandits."

"Stood up to Yori. Can take care of herself."

Tomi glanced at his friend and returned to preparations. "That's what Yori said when I sent him to fetch her."

"Getting smarter. My respect is increasing. You said?"

"That there are bandits and I forgot to tell her the way."

When Matsu quieted, Tomi enjoyed knowing he had his friend. "Also, Yori can talk to the street captain. That way Aki will have no issues."

Matsu stared at him, wide-eyed and grinning. "*Aki* is it now?" He reached for the kettle. "Interesting."

Tomi considered throwing the wooden tray in his hand at Matsu but knew he would only spill his tea. That would create a mess he needed to clean. "Change the subject."

"Fine. Weren't you going to enlarge your hearth?"

"Yes. Why?"

"You keep saying so. Every time I come here, it's the same."

"Found a carpenter I like. Then he got ordered onto another job."

"Ordered?"

"Someone closer to the castle than I am."

"Oh. Outranked. Not in the neighborhood with us lower-class warriors."

Tomi held up his hand and hastened to the window. Cold air blasted his face.

"What is it?" Matsu asked.

"I thought I saw Yori and Aki coming. Hard to tell at this distance. It was only a quick glance."

"Nervous?" Matsu asked.

He rubbed his clammy palms on the sleeves of his outer garment. This was just a merchant girl, and he was preparing the house. "Why would I be nervous?"

"Because it's *Aki.*"

Tomi drilled his gaze into Matsu, who slipped his shoes on and headed out, disappearing into a shaded darkness punctuated by the early morning sounds of nature. Matsu no doubt enjoyed the noise. Tomi less so. Once Aki arrived, he would have to leave.

When a clap of thunder sounded, a heaviness weighed on his gut. He hoped she didn't get drenched coming here.

Did she have an umbrella? Would it hold off?

Light drops of rain struck the porch, going from faint to strong though not heavy. Hopefully, she was close.

Hopefully sending Yori had been a good idea.

"Time to move," Yori said. "I'm here to take you to Nishioji's house. The rain will only get worse."

Aki's arms tensed by her side. Disappointment at the sight of the young samurai drizzled like raindrops that slid down the door awning and puddled at his feet. She had hoped for Nishioji-sama. Nothing to do but obey. "Good morning. I am honored that you are here."

"You're wasting time." The young man's gruff voice cut through the wind. "We move now before it gets worse."

She grabbed an umbrella and offered it to Yori. "*Kasa?*"

"Unnh." His stare froze her more than the wind, but he nodded and took it. At least he had not yelled at her.

She bowed low, glancing at his feet, which were turned to the right. He was ready to leave. Her mother brought her another umbrella. She opened it and stepped outside.

"Where is Nishioji-sama?"

He frowned at her and clenched his teeth. She had said too much. "It's not your concern. He requested I bring you to his home. Remember the way, I won't do it again." He pointed to the street. "We leave. Now."

"I am ready."

"It wouldn't matter if you weren't."

"I—"

"Silence," the young man growled. "Three steps behind. Maintain your distance and keep up. Don't make me look back for you."

Aki nodded, afraid to speak. Her neck tensed as the wind blew mist on her cheeks.

"This should take thirty minutes. Don't slow us down."

The young man sped forward, and she hurried to

follow. When the door closed behind her, she uttered a silent thanks and goodbye to her mother.

She followed Yori to the street and looked for signs of slipperiness. Grayish clouds provided scant light. Periodic stone lanterns provided a little more. The samurai turned left, toward the city's edge, and then a right on a main road and quickened his pace.

With another quick right, they passed through a section of houses belonging to cloth weavers. Aki tightened her kosode to protect herself from the stiff breeze, struggling to stay close but three steps behind. She hurried, noting stores and other landmarks. A left turn at another street took them by a row of oil pressers. Her sister, Kiku, lived nearby. She should talk with her if the chance arose.

The rain increased in intensity. Drops splashed her face and trickled down her neck and arms. Yori moved like someone who could navigate streets in pitch darkness. Water from puddles drenched her feet, chilling her toes like an icy dip.

He glanced back at her. "Keep up," he said. "I don't have time to wait for you."

She hurried behind him, her arms crossed and her hands inside her sleeves to keep them warm. They passed more rows of thatched-roof homes and businesses, not an area she knew well. She tried to rouse her burning muscles. It would not be good to show up exhausted on her first day of work. Hopefully, they were close.

Rain fell harder, but at least it was not a downpour. Aki rubbed her hands under her clothes and against her skin. They were not far from the Administrative Building, though she could not see it or the Justice Building. Many samurai houses were northeast of most city merchants and closer to the castle. High-ranking samurai of visiting daimyo also lived in the area, supporting their lords when the regent required their presence here or in the capital.

The wind blew hard again and more rain fell,

drenching her hair and running down her cheeks. All her worries this morning about how she looked fled. By now, she must look horrible. Wherever they were going, she hoped it would be quick.

Yori doubled back south and led her toward two rows of homes, buffered in the rear by bushes. He pointed his finger. "Wait here."

Aki stared as he moved toward the guard. Why were they waiting here? Did the samurai not live much closer to the castle than this?

Yori spoke with the man on duty, pointing towards her and one of the houses. The man appeared to write something down, but it was difficult to tell from this distance. The young samurai hustled back to her. "I've given your name to the street captain. He has noted you in the records."

"Thank you. Nishioji-sama lives here?"

He pointed to a house at that end. "There," he said.

"There?" Aki asked, making certain.

"Are you a simpleton?" The young man huffed. "Why Nishioji—" He stopped as if reconsidering his words. "Don't expect me to do this again."

She bowed low and rain pelted the back of her clothes. "Thank you again for your kindness." She stared at him, seeing in his eyes the part of him that was her age.

"What is it?" he said.

"Nothing, Osamurai-sama."

The young man handed her back her umbrella, then turned and walked away. For a few moments, she watched him depart. The wind blew harder, echoing in her ears as it froze them. She glanced at the house and then back toward Yori, who was already far away.

If only she had a mirror to tell her how horrible she looked. *Maybe it is better not to know*. Time to start. It made no sense to arrive early, only to be late from fear of announcing herself.

Aki introduced herself to the street captain, a man

about the age of her father but with more gray hair. He was kinder than the young samurai but still gruff. He waved her in, and she headed for the house.

More rain flowed over her eyes. What else could go wrong this morning? A small eave stretched out over the front door. She stepped on the stoop, wiped her face and hair with her hands, and flung the excess water away. The umbrella shielded her some, but she was still drenched.

Aki paused and reached for the bell that hung in front of the door. It opened, and Nishioji-sama stood before her.

Her heart fluttered and her hands shook as she bowed. "Good morning, Nishioji-sama."

She raised her gaze and looked into his eyes.

His mouth dropped open, but he said nothing.

The man who'd protected her from Yori and in the prison was now speechless.

Tomi caught himself staring at his drenched young girl but regained his composure. "Enter. Enter." He waved her in, his hand flapping twice to urge her out of the rain. "You're on time. Good morning."

"Yes, sir. Good morning."

Aki stepped into the *genkan*. Tomi grabbed a nearby cloth and handed it over, then closed the door behind her. She wiped the rain from her face and proceeded into the main room.

Water dripped onto the floor from her cloak and from her soaked kosode.

He looked at her neck and saw two collars. She could change here. "I'll get you something to dry yourself." Tomi walked across the room, stepping to a closet on the other side. He grabbed one of his mother's older garments, a light blue one, and a larger cloth.

"Here. Use this, and put this on," he said. "I'll tend to the hearth."

He walked to the fire and added charcoal, keeping his

eyes down to allow her privacy. Heat wafted over him as he spread the coals across the pit.

He glanced over at Aki, who was ready, her green raiment draped over her arm.

"Hang it on the hook in the genkan. It will dry."

She obeyed and bowed again. "I am sorry, Nishioji-sama." She looked at the water on the floor and used the smaller towel to clean it. "I am making a mess."

"Don't concern yourself. How was the walk with Yori?"

She grabbed at the collar of the blue kosode. "It was fine. I hope I did not inconvenience him."

"He met you this morning—as a favor to me."

Tomi's stomach fluttered like a small bird in a strong wind. He did not know what to say. Why was he nervous? *She's only a merchant girl.* If Matsu knew, he would never let Tomi forget it. "Was the walk good? Other than the rain? And Yori?"

She paused. "He kept a quick pace, which I needed to stay warm. I did not wear enough to be outside long. I will change that tomorrow."

"I should've told you how long it would take."

He motioned for her to follow. "Come with me. It's time you met my mother."

She kept her hands in front and moved to step behind him but then stopped and raised her head. "You are burning sandalwood?"

He turned and faced her. "Yes, it provides my mother comfort. How did you recognize it?"

She angled her body away. "My mother and my sister Kiku teach at temples. I recognize it from where Kiku does lessons. I like that scent." The pitch of her voice rose in another show of respect. "It always makes me stop when I smell it at a temple, and I try to breathe in the air. Can your mother move around much?"

"Yes." Tomi mulled over what he should say. Her

caregiver, Matsu, and the padre knew his mother's secret, but no one else outside the family. "My mother can move about, but she spends a lot of time resting."

"If the weather warms, can I walk with her?"

The answer dug into his gut like a dull, heavy sword. "She has pain in her hands and feet. Sometimes, she feels nothing. She complains that her knees and elbows hurt. Make sure she is bundled well, so she doesn't get cold. Keep her in the neighborhood only. Don't go far."

"That must be tough for her. Is it getting any better?"

Tomi debated what to tell Aki. She would be here about three weeks. Could he hide it from her? If not, he could order her to stay silent. "Not much change, but some days are better than others."

"How about—"

He waved his hand to stop her from asking more. Part of him was grateful for her questions. It showed she cared. It was why he hired her. However, he had no answers for his mother's condition, a reality that stung like the cut to his face once did. He saw the red pin in her hair, a pin that had stayed put through the rain. Like Aki. "Do whatever my mother requests of you. She enjoys practicing calligraphy and was good many years ago." He pointed toward a desk in the room with paper and brushes. "The two of you can discuss that."

Aki bit her lip and looked away. Something he said had bothered her. "What is it?" he asked.

"I will do my best."

"I am sure you will suffice." *Suffice?* Tomi cursed himself. That's not what he wanted to say. He wanted to tell her she impressed him with her diligence. Her presence distracted him, like that pin in her hair.

"I do not feel worthy, but I will make your mother comfortable. My sisters, though, are better calligraphers."

He focused his eyes on her. "You challenged us when we arrived at your house that morning. Your brothers should have done that, but they didn't. That is the type of caregiver my mother wants."

She opened her mouth as if to respond but instead nodded and averted her gaze. "Is there anything else I should know?"

It was Tomi's turn to glance away. Could he tell her everything? "Nothing for now. You'll learn soon. My mother will explain."

When Tomi motioned for her to follow, she fell in step behind him. When they reached the room where Mother rested, he extended his hand, palm outward to Aki. "Are you ready?"

"Yes."

Nishioji-sama cleared his throat and then slid the door open. The scent of sandalwood grew stronger.

"Mother, the girl is here."

Aki followed him inside, bowing to the figure on the stack of tatami mats. "I am honored to meet you."

The woman pushed herself into a sitting position and moved her wooden pillow to the side. Her black hair contained numerous gray streaks with part of it mashed in, showing how she had slept. Wrinkles creased her face. Her eyelids fluttered and then opened for good, accompanied by a wince and a smile.

She ran her fingers through her hair to freshen it then placed her hands, palms down, on the tatami floor to make a bow herself. "I'm honored to meet you, as well."

"I'm certain things will be acceptable," Tomi said, a slight hesitation in his voice. *Why? Was he nervous?* Her hire had been sudden.

"Yes, we'll be fine," his mother responded. She gestured toward a nearby small ornate table. "Hand me that pin. I want to go out front and do what everyone does when they wake."

Aki stifled a chuckle. Early morning humor, just like

her own mother. She scanned the table, seeing a pin, a cloth, and some kind of ointment. She grabbed the pin and extended it out. "Would you like my help?"

She waved her back. "I can do this myself. I have joint pain. I'm not an invalid. My son worries too much." She placed the pin by her side then brought both hands to fix her hair into a bun.

The woman's sleeves slid down her arms, revealing red splotches and a few bumps. Aki averted her gaze. "Are you sure I cannot help you?"

"No, I'm fine." The woman grabbed the pin and jabbed it through her hair. Her smile grew wide. "What do you think?"

"Healthy, Mother."

"You always say that." She turned to Aki and met her gaze. "What do you think?"

"I agree with Nishioji-sama."

"Not a good start," she said while shaking her head. "If you're going to assist me for a few weeks, you need to be honest. We'll work on this." She held out her hands. "Now help me up."

Aki gasped. A drop of blood pooled on one of the woman's hands. "You cut yourself."

"Oh, dear. There's a cloth over there." She gestured to the table. "Hand it to me."

Aki grabbed the cloth and glanced at it, seeing dark spots of dried blood. She handed it to Nishioji-sama's mother, who pressed it against her fingers. "It'll be a second. I'm so clumsy." She moved the blanket and inched her feet under her, getting into a sitting position on her knees. The woman had not flinched when she poked herself. Had she not felt it? Why would a hair pin have a sharp point like that?

The woman held out her hands again. "Help me up."

Aki knelt in front of her, grasping both wrists and rising. The woman pressed against her to steady herself and then stood. She swayed and pressed again. Pain streaked across her face. Aki added support. The woman gained her balance and lowered her hands. "That's fine."

"How do you want to do this?" Aki asked.

"Hold out your arm."

Aki held out her forearm, and the woman placed her hand on it, maintaining her balance as she took a step. Aki glanced at Nishioji-sama, who nodded as if to say she was doing well. She guided the woman out of the room and toward the front door.

The samurai's heavy footsteps sounded behind Aki on the wooden floor. *Is he making sure I can do this?* His mother walked without leaning on her for support. Instead, she was using Aki's arm for balance.

Nishioji-sama stepped forward and opened the door. Fresh air wiped away the sandalwood fragrance. The three of them slipped their shoes on and stepped outside. The rain had stopped, and the sun was rising, though a bitter cold enveloped the street.

Movement to the left caught Aki's eye as a familiar figure with hair swinging behind him headed toward them at a run.

The samurai's voice broke through the wind. "Yori, what brings you back here?

"Nishioji-sama," Yori said, his voice on edge. "Emergency. Constable Oeda sent me to get you. We need to go now."

Nishioji's posture turned rigid. "I must leave," he said. "When my father returns this evening, allow him to assist you. It'll be dark. Wait for me to return."

Aki nodded, seeing both samurai break into a hurried pace. Hopes for Nishioji-sama to say goodbye floated away as he talked with Yori-sama. What could have happened that forced him to cut the morning short?

Whatever it was, the day would be long.

CHAPTER TEN

"What happened?" Tomi asked, keeping pace with his young charge. "What's the emergency?"

"An incident at a vacated temple. Three men heard something strange and went inside. Two of them are dead and one is injured badly. A carpenter looking for wood found them."

Tomi nodded and allowed Yori to lead. Some temples left from when Nobunaga defeated the Jōdo Shinshū, the militant Buddhist sect that controlled Osaka, remained in outer areas of the city. When the regent started expansion in the city, he forced some northwest across the river and others south along the route to Shitennōji, the sixth century temple built by Prince Shotoku.

That was the limit of Tomi's insight, but Yori had lived here for over ten years. He knew the area well. It made him valuable.

They hastened through the Administration District and turned on one of the main roads toward the river. "Do you know who was killed?"

"I do not. Only that Goto was one of them."

Goto.

Tomi increased his stride. He'd last seen Goto when

that prisoner had escaped his bonds and tried to kill him. Tomi wanted to make sure he was okay.

A few merchants were open at this hour, but the lack of carts meant it wasn't a market day. He dodged two deliverymen coming his way, hearing apologies for impeding him in his wake. They passed through a carpentry and jobbers district and reached the temple a few minutes later. Several men dressed in a mix of blues and browns milled about in front.

He slowed to a brisk walk.

"Constable Oeda should be around somewhere," Yori said.

"How about Matsu?"

"Matsu, too."

As if hearing his name, Matsu signaled from the right. They walked toward the two men guarding the front. The officers flinched at their approach and then relaxed. A nervous reaction. Tomi would be on edge, too. Yori talked to one man who ran inside and then returned. "They will find Oeda."

"What happened?" Tomi asked Matsu.

'Don't know. Oeda ordered Ishii and me to survey the outside. Haven't been in yet."

"Find anything?"

"Nothing. Just odd holes."

"Why odd?"

"The carpenter district is near here. When carpenters take materials, they do it to reuse them. The holes here are destruction." Matsu pointed over to the right. "See that?"

Tomi studied the hole. The wood underneath suggested it wasn't for carpentry. He stepped back, bumping into a guard who moved, and took the entire building into view. The temple occupied a sizable plot. Rows of stones overgrown with large weeds made a straight path to the entrance. Moss-covered statues marked each side. Empty stone pedestals where statues had once stood also extended out on each side. Open patches of thatch dotted the roof.

Constable Oeda strode toward them a few moments later. Perspiration trickled down his red face. "It's good to see you. We need all ideas."

"Your face is—"

"We have three men dead in there." He sighed and glanced back at the entrance. "I am stunned."

"Three? Yori said two dead and one alive."

"Goto died a few minutes ago."

Goto dead. The words struck Tomi like the kick of a horse. He nodded. "Show us what happened."

The constable motioned them to follow, leading them through the entrance onto the inner grounds. A rock garden marked one side overrun with weeds that marred its once tranquil beauty. The inner grounds were thin, barely enough to separate the building from the outer wall.

"I remember this place when it was beautiful and restful," Oeda said, regret coating his words. "Sad to see it this way."

Something within Tomi concurred. Temples brought stability to a neighborhood and a sense of belonging. He hoped Christian churches might be seen the same way one day.

"Follow me," Oeda said, waving them to hurry.

The constable led them toward the front entrance, which, like the gate, was missing a door. A scrawled message marked the left wall. *So many wives. Still no children.* Tomi puzzled over the meaning as he ascended the squeaky wooden steps so close he could hear Oeda's labored breaths.

The smell of blood struck him before he reached the top, overriding the incense that permeated the walls. They followed Oeda across the threshold and to the right.

Two bodies lay motionless on the floor, their weapons next to them.

On the left sat a third figure, unmoving, his back to the temple wall.

Goto.

Tomi's stomach churned liked the sulfurous pools near the volcanoes in Kyushu. He'd seen death in battle before and sent enemies into their own next lives, but this fight had been over before it started.

Streaks and slashes of blood draped Goto's garments. Stab wounds and visible skin revealed which strikes killed him.

Matsu knelt on the other side. "His face. Impassive in life and death."

"Mmm. He accepted his fate before the end came." Tomi's chest tightened. He'd seen too many friends die for nothing. Sometimes he had to draw a sword but only when he had no choice.

Two men worked nearby, searching the bodies for a hint about who could have done this. Yori joined them, stepping back to observe. They bowed to Tomi and then resumed their duties, their gazes askance toward Goto. At some point, they would have to disturb him.

Who would disturb the repose of someone who had met death with such grace?

Oeda approached Tomi and Matsu. "What happened here?" Tomi asked. "Goto's expression is serene, like he knew what was happening and couldn't fight."

"I know very little." Oeda stared at the floor, one of the few times Tomi had ever seen him stunned. "The men over there"—he gestured to the bodies—"were recruits from the city defense group. Goto was training them. When we found them, Goto was alive but barely. He told us they saw two men skulking about. They tried to surprise them. A floor squeak gave away their approach. Goto said the men were as quick as you and Matsu. They were no match for them."

"Were they samurai?"

"No, the men who did this only carried only a single

sword and dispatched the new officers."

"Did he say anything else?" Tomi asked.

"He said one man looked familiar, but he couldn't recall where he'd seen him. He didn't know the other one."

"Familiar?" Matsu asked.

The hair rose on the nape of Tomi's neck. His thought had been the same as Matsu's. "Goto thought he'd met the attacker before?"

Oeda covered his mouth with his hand. "I don't think so. More like he should've known him. He faded at that point."

Tomi looked at the walls, a mixture of dust and destruction. They exhibited holes, like the ones outside, with remnants strewn everywhere.

"Constable, this destruction, is it like this everywhere?"

"Yes," Oeda replied, his voice carrying sadness. "Everywhere. Some new and some old. There are places where carpenters took materials. That's expected. Damaging the building serves no purpose. Like the scrawled writing."

Tomi walked toward one of the holes, comparing it to the places where carpenters had collected wood for other projects. Dust covered the worked over sections, but they were neat. These holes were fresh and carried subdued levels of incense.

Matsu walked over to him. "Intrigued by these holes, too?"

"Nothing makes sense," Tomi said, his eyes drawn toward Yori, who worked elsewhere in the room.

"If some are old," Matsu said, "that means others likely caused the destruction."

Tomi scratched. "Or the same attackers were here before and making holes."

"Why would they do that?"

"Could they be looking for something?" Tomi asked.

The constable arrived from behind. "What makes you say that?"

Tomi bit his lip. "Not sure. Just a feeling. Let's take a walk. Yori," he called out, "come with us."

Matsu and Yori got behind him. Oeda followed at his side. They headed toward the corridor on the left, an area lit by open shutters and scarred outer walls. He stopped at the wall's edge and pointed to one hole.

"Look at this wall. It separates us from the outside. What the carpenters left remains untouched, but these holes have specific places, places with possible space behind the wall. The only reason to do this is if you're searching for something."

Tomi peered inside the hole, taking an angle to allow light. Debris littered the space.

Matsu followed and checked. "Nothing."

"Exactly," Tomi responded, "anything there would have been taken. Did Goto say anything else before he died?"

Oeda sighed. "Not about this. We hoped he might revive, but he didn't."

Tomi glanced at the rest of the corridor, which showed similar damage. "More holes. They were searching for something." He looked at Oeda. "What could it be?"

The constable bit his lower lip, his face taut with hesitation. "Jade."

"Jade?" Matsu asked. "Why would that be here?"

"Harima," Oeda answered.

Oeda glanced in Tomi's direction, as if Tomi should know the answer, but he remained puzzled. "I do not understand."

"You're the Kirishitan. Are you not familiar with Harima and its former daimyo, Takayama Ukon?"

"Ukon-*dono* lost Harima when the regent issued his edict three years ago," Tomi said. "He lost it as he refused to renounce his faith."

"Yes," Oeda said, "when Ukon-dono was appointed to oversee Harima five years ago, he eliminated many Buddhist temples and statues. He burned the wooden statues but shipped the jade ones here to Osaka. Shitennōji, the other temples near there, and the ones in Nakajima, claimed some of them. The rest were stored elsewhere."

"Where?" Yori asked.

"No one knows," Oeda said.

"So they are searching for missing jade from Harima?" Matsu asked.

"Not just there," Oeda responded. "Some of it is from Nobunaga's takeover of Osaka. It may have been forgotten, but it's still out there. Someone's trying to find it."

"We should search this place ourselves," Tomi said. "Look around the building."

"Good idea," Oeda said. "Matsu and Yori," he pointed to a nearby hall, "you take that corridor. Tomi and I will go this way. Stay alert."

"*Hai*," they responded in unison.

Oeda joined Tomi down the hall lit by openings from the ceiling and a lantern on a hook, likely set there to help the search. Tomi tightened his long-sleeve outer garment as wind whipped through his frame like roof snow falling on his neck. Two stone pedestals where a brazier would have been stood empty, and one of crumbled stone sat idle.

"You know a lot," Tomi said.

Oeda motioned Tomi closer. "My family is from Osaka. When I was young, one of my grandfathers called this city Naniwa, the prior name, though my grandmother chided him for it, calling him old-fashioned. Prince Shōtoku built Shitennōji centuries ago. My late brother was a priest. I considered taking the tonsure and becoming a priest, too."

"Things are changing here," Tomi said. "Your family is well?"

"Yes, both my old and new family are well. Grab the lantern. We'll check this first room."

Tomi complied and entered. The place appeared to be for storage. Empty damaged shelves lay on the floor. Two ragged tatami mats lay in one corner, a spot for a homeless person, someone to help if only the church could find them.

Three holes marred the walls. "Your new family?" Tomi asked.

"I was not born with the name Oeda. I was a younger brother. There was no need for me to be a Buddhist priest like my father, so I married into a police family with no sons. I took my wife's name to continue their line. Once my wife birthed a son, her parents no longer concerned themselves with me."

"That explains much," Tomi said. "but your brother is dead, and your wife's family has an heir. You could help your old family now."

He shook his head. "Too many disagreements with them. I had to find something else. Wisdom comes from knowing one's limits."

Tomi studied Oeda's face. "Kenkō again?"

"Of course. Let's check the next one."

Light shone into the second room from a hole in the roof and water pooled on the rotting floor. One section was lighter than the rest, likely once covered but now laid bare. Maybe a place for meetings or meditation.

Tomi pointed toward two holes in the wall. "You really think someone was searching for excess jade?"

"Certain temples would have it. We should look for signs."

"What signs?"

"I don't know."

They returned to the waiting area. Matsu and Yori soon walked toward them in rigid steps.

"Nothing," Yori said, his voice harsh.

"Any ideas?" Oeda asked.

"None," Matsu answered.

"If any jade was here," Yori added, "it has been taken"

"How old is this building?" Tomi asked.

Oeda looked around. "Ever since I've been here. Why?"

"Why is the temple here?"

"Not following you, Tomi," Matsu said. "What do you mean?"

"Many temples were burned when the Buddhists here surrendered to Nobunaga."

"Yes," Yori said, still agitated. "Others moved north and south."

"So why was this left?" Matsu asked.

Oeda coughed hard. "Somebody might want to keep the land. Or they want to sell and can't get approval."

Tomi stared at Oeda. "Approval?"

Oeda nodded. "All land transfers require magistrate approval. Remember?"

Tomi seldom thought about such things. Mundane details appealed to his father. It was the reason the sake company employed him.

"What is it, Tomi?" Matsu asked.

Could the jade answer be in the main Administration Building? "We need to know which buildings remain. If the people who killed Goto are looking for jade, then they won't stop. How many abandoned temples remain?"

Oeda glanced toward the ceiling as if counting in his head. "Most would have been transferred and put to other uses by now. The Administration Building would have that information."

"Yori," Tomi said, "go there this morning. Get us a list."

"Understood. I will start now."

"Wait," Oeda said. "I have another task for Yori first. We have three dead men. We must tell their families. Matsu, you take him."

"Can do it alone," Matsu said. "Yori can do the research."

Oeda shook his head. "Goto has a son named Gyu. A few years younger than Yori."

"Understood."

Matsu and Yori left together, taking Tomi's prayers with them

"Nice of you to remember Goto's son," Tomi said.

"Yes, but I wanted to talk to you alone."

Oeda's tone suggested something was wrong. "What is it?"

"The old temples in new use must be careful."

Logic punched him in the gut. How had he not realized it?

Oeda was talking about Tomi's church.

Aki put away the trays from dinner and then breathed a sigh of relief. Everything was ready for tomorrow. Her first day had been tiring. The morning had been slow, but Nishioji-sama's mother had helped her clean the house in the afternoon. Not once had Aki looked at the door in fear of her uncle walking in and making a new demand.

"You're a hardworking girl," the woman said.

"Thank you," Aki said, trying to hide a smile.

"And helpful, too," the samurai's father added. "We are done."

Aki acknowledged his praise. Her initial impression of him had surprised her. She had expected someone the samurai's height only aged. Instead, he was the same height as her own father. He had returned home about an hour ago and set to work on a dinner of rice and vegetables but had said little.

Questions continued to amass in her mind, things she wanted to ask about Nishioji-sama, but any question would be intrusive. It was not her place.

The day had gone well. The woman had allowed Aki to clean herself more from the rain, and she was not as ill as Aki had expected, though she did tire. During the day, she walked around the house, going out for brief moments in the neighborhood. The ground had dried a bit, but Aki feared the woman would hurt herself if she fell. There was not much that Aki could do except to keep her company. She insisted on cleaning, so Aki learned where everything was. Did every samurai have a five-room house? The houses in this neighborhood all appeared the same.

Memories of the blood from the morning made Aki tense all day. She asked about calligraphy, as the samurai had suggested, but the woman put it off and said she would prepare things for tomorrow.

One tray remained in the room, set aside for when Nishioji-sama returned home.

As if in response to her thoughts, the door slid open, and he entered. "I'm home."

He glanced at Aki with a nod then headed to his parents. The soft murmurs reached her ears. She caught half the words but did her best not to listen. He walked over to her, his face somber and serious. "My mother says you had a good day."

"I did what she asked."

"Which is acceptable. It's time to leave."

"Yes, Nishioji-sama."

Aki visualized the walk home. It was cold. Her kosode had dried during the day and it was not raining now. If she walked fast, she would stay warm. "I will be here tomorrow."

"I'll see you make it home."

Make it home? Had she heard him right? He must be busy, and his eyes cast a tired gaze. When her brothers looked like this, the day had been rough. "I know the way. You have not eaten yet."

"I'll eat later. It has been a long first day for you, and it isn't safe for a young woman to travel alone at night. We depart now."

Aki quashed any concern in her mind and bowed.

"Yes, Nishioji-sama."

He strode out of the door of his house. She followed, closing the door behind them and then doing her best to maintain a proper distance. Other samurai dotted the area, most chatting with each other. Two monks introduced themselves at neighborhood doors, likely the ones who bless houses and ask for donations.

Twenty minutes passed. Nishioji-sama set a slower pace than the younger samurai had this morning, but it felt as if they made more progress now. As the wind whipped through her, she pulled her garment tighter. Soon she would be home to the warm hearth and fire.

After a few minutes, he turned to her but said nothing.

"Is something wrong?" she asked.

"It's colder than I thought it would be. I don't want you to be ill."

More wind shot through her, and she crossed her arms in front to press her clothes against her body. "It is no bother. I will be home soon."

He grunted. "Walk closer to me. I will block the wind as best I can."

Block the wind? The samurai's broad shoulders could block avalanche of winds. Was he asking her to stand closer? Her mind blanked for a few seconds before she could answer. "I must stay back. I would appear to be insulting you."

"You must keep your health." His face grew taut. "Don't disagree with me."

She'd seen that face the morning at her home when he'd admonished Yori. Was he always stern? "I do not deserve your kindness."

"It's not a question of deserve. The woman you are replacing is away for a few weeks. I cannot afford to have you fall ill."

She nodded. "I. Understand."

A brief smile tilted his lips, warming Aki's heart. He

waved her closer. "Think of it this way. Servants maintain proximity to their lords to protect them from attack."

Aki pressed her stomach to keep from laughing. Her protect him? He was twice her size and a trained warrior. "I will follow your orders."

Aki's body warmed as she drew nearer to him, as if her heart were closer, as well. Evening deliverymen carrying boxes on shoulder rods swerved around them but maintained a brisk pace. Laughter rang from noodle restaurants on both sides of the street. She seldom ventured out at night. There was work to be done.

She remained a respectful distance away, but it was difficult. Nishioji-sama continued to glance back to make sure she was close. Half the time he tilted his head as if listening to her footsteps and other times as if surveying the streets. People still milled about the open businesses. She could not remember when Osaka was not busy, though her father said it was calmer here before the regent built the castle.

They passed through the weaving district, a place that was always busy. Father said weavers worked late in the evening. It was the one place where Father said he would not marry his daughters off. One of his sisters had married into such a family. Father said she overworked herself and looked older than her years when she died.

A few minutes later they reached her district. A lone figure approached the front of her house.

Nishioji-sama's hands flew to his waist and grabbed the hilt of his sword. "Who is that?" he asked.

"My uncle," Aki said. Her heart dropped into her stomach.

His sword hand relaxed. Nishioji-sama turned to her. "Does he come often in the evening?"

"Yes, he and my father work on things together. He always wants to discuss his"— thoughts of the wedding and adoption soured her stomach—"business plans."

"Does he live nearby?"

"He lives closer to the castle. He handles fine goods for rich officials, so his wares are in demand."

Nishioji bit his lip in thought. "I know merchants like that." He continued forward.

Aki stopped. "Nishioji-sama, I am certain I am safe from here. You have been most kind and have not eaten. I do not want to keep you any longer. Or"—she thought how to ask appropriately—"you could come inside for a minute. My parents could provide you with something to eat."

It was hard to read the samurai's face. The light from the nearby stone lamps on the street provided little more than shadow. "Your concern is noted. I cannot stay."

"I understand."

"My mother mentioned you will practice writing characters tomorrow. I'll leave things out for you to do so. Get someone to escort you before dawn else come at first light.

Aki bowed and then turned to approach her house. The closer she got, the more she could see Uncle's face by the bright lamp near the front door.

The only reason Uncle would be here at this time was to discuss the arranged marriage.

It was good that Nishioji-sama did not stay. The longer she could hide her misery from him, the better.

CHAPTER ELEVEN

"Make it home?" Matsu laughed. "You really said that to *Aki* last night?"

The morning sun peeked from behind the clouds. It warmed Tomi's face and illuminated the Justice Building ahead. Tomi focused on the entrance as he increased his stride. He'd thought walking to work with Matsu would distract him from the weather, but he hadn't expected having to answer questions about his new servant.

"Yes," Tomi said, rubbing his rosary beads through his clothes, a silent request for forgiveness. When he'd told Aki the reason he'd wanted to walk her home, he'd hidden the truth. When he lied about anything, he rubbed his beads. Tomi hated to lie. Something within him had demanded he ensure her safety. "It had to be done."

"Why? Can walk home on her own. Nights colder but no problem."

"It's a long walk. I feel responsible."

"Knows Osaka."

"The city has changed. Walking with her sends a message. She is under a samurai's protection."

"Then why are you with me right now instead of her?"

"My mother was well this morning. Also, I told Yori to follow her from a distance."

"That sends a message, too." Matsu stared at Tomi with a dubious gaze, not hiding his usual wellspring of criticism that often flowed in Tomi's direction. "Escort her home tonight?"

A Buddhist monk in black stood on the right, his gnat-like humming droning for donations. "I'll decide later."

"Make her wait for you?"

Tomi glared at Matsu to silence his friend or at least make him change the topic. It would only be temporary. Matsu was a hard man to cow.

They finally reached the building. People in the streets pivoted away, offering a clear line to the front. Arai stood on the top step, moving back-and-forth between the two guards. He looked in their direction and then closed the distance at a full sprint. "Matsubara-sama. Nishioji-sama," Arai said, "I've been looking for you. Constable Oeda is at the prison. He demands your presence."

"What happened?"

Arai inhaled sharply. "I've been instructed to find and bring you…and to say nothing more."

"We know where the jail is," Tomi said.

"I have my orders."

Tomi motioned for Arai to lead. Usually, Arai wouldn't refuse to answer Tomi's question. *Oeda must have ordered his silence.*

The walk to the jail took only ten minutes. A waste seller passed ahead of them as they approached, walking away from them and toward the river. The acrid smell of his cargo lay on the air, leaving a foul trail.

Oeda waited in front of the facility, which was set at the edge of a canal under construction. Prisoners spent their days providing labor. The swampy area proved treacherous. If something befell a prisoner, then it demonstrated his guilt.

Oeda flashed a few hand signals, then Arai pivoted, leaving Tomi and Matsu to talk with the constable alone. Oeda's narrowed, determined eyes conveyed the grim news.

"What happened?" Tomi asked.

"I called you here about your *friend*."

"My friend?"

"The man from a few days ago whose life you spared. He's dead."

###

Aki glanced at the neighborhood captain and watched as he processed others arriving. Were these also servants for nearby residents? She had waited until morning to leave, as Nishioji-sama had requested. The walk had been cold enough to see her breath. Thankfully, there'd been no rain.

She announced her presence.

The samurai's mother was up and moving around.

"Welcome, Aki. Happy you're here."

"Hello." Aki paused for a second, her voice having risen in pitch.

"You sound surprised to see me."

Aki nodded. "I am. After yesterday, I did not expect to find you up."

"Some days are better than others. Today is one of those days. I'm excited about my first calligraphy lesson."

Aki walked to the desk and found the brushes and paper laid out on top. "This is perfect."

"Open the back door," the woman said.

"Are you certain? It's cold."

"Trust me."

Aki opened the doors and saw single walls to shield the winds. "This is…nice," Aki said.

"Tomi saw the design at the house of a high-ranking samurai," the woman explained. "He made the change here himself."

"Made the change?" Aki asked.

"He's gifted at building things." She smiled with a mother's pride. "He has worked hard to make my life here easier."

"Will we not be cold?"

"There is more. In the chest to the left is a large cloth. We hang it in front of the opening. It keeps in the heat."

Aki opened the chest and found cloth that reminded her of those businesses used at entrances to indicate being open while keeping it warm for customers. She hung it as if she was at home. "This works."

"He's a wonderful son."

Aki matched her enthusiasm. "What else he has done?"

"I'll show you later. If it warms up, we will take a walk this afternoon. For now, I'm excited to do this."

The woman's smile calmed Aki's nerves. She had long practiced her calligraphy, hoping to give lessons, but today was her first opportunity.

Aki watched her do a few basic characters to judge her skill. Her strokes wavered as she struggled to steady her hand. Was she tired? Had she pushed herself too much already this morning? Did her illness leave her too weak?

After thirty minutes of practice, Aki looked at the woman. Her eyes appeared heavy. "Should we rest?"

"A little more," she responded. "It's been so long. Could you show me how you do it again?"

Aki recalled her own mother teaching her strokes when Aki was younger. Steadiness and repetition brought speed, but speed was not the most important thing.

"My mother always taught me to keep my movements slow." She demonstrated. "Breathe and express yourself with the beat of your heart."

They worked for another fifteen minutes. "That will do it," the woman said. "We should sit and enjoy the weather. The morning feels warm."

"Let me clean the brushes. I will help you outside."

As she handed Aki the brush, Aki noted her fingertips, misshapen and rough as if cut with a jagged blade. Her fingers also curled in, and she struggled to extend them. Were these symptoms of the illness Nishioji-sama mentioned? What caused such a condition? The tips of her fingers resembled frayed yarn. No wonder the brush wavered in her hands. She couldn't hold it steady. It was slipping as she wrote.

Yesterday, she had stabbed her own finger with a pin and had not noticed that blood flowed from it. *What kind of disease rots one's hands and silences pain? Why can the woman not get help for this?*

"Dead?"

Tomi shook his head, repeating the word to himself. He stared at the wall that surrounded the jail, seeing the open wooden structure beyond the entrance. He'd never gone past the outer structure before; instead, he'd required prisoners be brought out during previous visits. "How did it happen?"

"Another prisoner," Oeda said. "There was a fight. Both men are dead, as well as the prisoner captured with the man who insulted you."

"Leaves one, then," Matsu said. "Where is he?"

"With a doctor. Secluded. We're fortunate. He was scheduled for execution."

"We need to see him," Tomi said. "Who was the new one?"

Oeda went silent then found his voice. "Someone who works on the river. A samurai from Awa Province caught him, and his servants brought him to us."

Awa. One of the provinces now storing rice in Osaka. "Did the prisoner say anything when he arrived?"

"Nothing." He wiped his hand down his face, knitting his eyebrows into one line. "It might have been planned."

The word piqued Tomi's curiosity. "Planned? Why?"

"The man that brought him said he was foolish. Could have escaped and didn't."

"Wanted to be captured?" Matsu asked.

"An assassin," Tomi said.

Oeda grunted his concurrence. "It's reasonable. A man easily captured kills two prisoners on his own and then takes his own life."

Tomi pressed his fingers to his forehead, but it failed to help him make sense. It was like looking at shadows through a *shoji* screen, moving images undefined. "Why would someone do that? Why were they important?"

Oeda wiped his face, clearing away small beads of sweat. The events troubled him. "It's like a map with no landmarks."

"More like it has holes."

Oeda smiled. "The writings of philosophers have missing chapters."

A proverb. I should have known. "Nice thought. Kenkō?"

"Yes. Kenkō."

"Fill in the holes?" Matsu asked.

"I don't know where to begin," Oeda said.

"We use the one landmark on our map." Tomi turned north and listened for the water. "The river area where rice is stored. I recommend we check it as soon as possible."

Oeda nodded. "We have work here first. You can start tomorrow. Early."

Early morning. That would have to do. Aki would need to be early. That would be fine. She understood duty.

So did Yori.

Nishioji-sama stepped into the house and announced his return home. His return elated her, but his arrival coincided with a conversation she was having. She'd hoped to learn more about the handsome samurai. His mother had chatted a little, but learning more would have to wait. Now he was escorting her home again, but for much of the walk he'd said nothing.

It was a warmer night than the previous one, but he insisted she stay close. He slowed his pace, maybe to avoid tiring her. Evening food cart vendors yelled out their offerings of noodles and cooked vegetables. The aromas made her mouth water. She'd eat soon.

"Your mother enjoyed working on her calligraphy," Aki said.

"That's good," he responded, half in speech and half in grunt. "It's important to her. How did she do?"

Could she describe how her hand slipped or the chewed appearance of her fingers? His mother was ill. A rash that ate the skin, but nothing she'd ever seen. "She had trouble holding the brush steady. Has she had this problem long?"

Nishioji-sama tilted his head in her direction, his gaze soft and sad. "No, it's the illness, but I feel she's getting stronger." He smiled. "I expect her to improve."

"I will do my best."

Small groups filtered through the streets, stopping at the vendors. Some bowed toward him. Others turned and gave him space. The lanterns on the road and the smaller ones that hung on the sides of buildings provided openness. The walk to and from her house was safe. She should tell him she didn't need an escort.

"Why does your family know calligraphy so well?" he asked.

His question broke into her thoughts. "What do you mean?"

"It's not common."

"I know many who can. How would we keep records if we did not write?"

He smiled. "Writing, yes, but not trained in calligraphy. One can write, but this is an art."

"Oh…it is, but Osaka used to be a temple city. Buddhist priests and nuns offered classes for years. My mother's family learned well, exchanging lessons for silk. They passed down the skill.

He stared at her for a second. Whether her answer

made sense she was not certain. It was something her family just did and she had never thought to question.

They approached the weaving district. Activity hummed from behind the doors with occasional soft thuds. The area was well lit, and home was near. Another sign that she should be fine by herself.

A few more minutes later her house came into view. The samurai slowed. "About tomorrow," he said. "I need you to come before light. Expect Yori. If he does not show, make sure you have an escort.

Come early? It was a common request, and she must honor it as his employee. "I will be there. Nishioji-sama, may I ask a question?"

A tender look crossed his face. Did many people see this side of him? "Yes, what is it?"

"I do not need an escort. Yori-sama…." Heat rushed to her cheeks. "My apologies for my use of his first name. He would be insulted."

He laughed. "What option did you have? You don't know his last name. There is a reason for that." He drew his handsome face closer and whispered. "I will say nothing. One day you may learn it or at least understand why you can't use it now."

Aki looked into his eyes, and her skin tingled. Any more of this and she would faint. "I wanted to say I do not need an escort. I watched all the way home. The streets are fine. I will stay on the main roads. I should have no problems."

His lips thinned like a teacher preparing to impart advice. "I watched the streets, too. Yes, they are lit, and the stone lanterns would be the same in the morning. However, some districts have lights only because they are busy at this hour."

She bowed her head, seeing dual shadows of the samurai on the ground, one that danced and one that remained still. She noted the swaying flickers of a nearby lantern then raised her head skyward. The moon, not quite round but looking large, loomed low in the distance. "The moon is out. It will light my way before the sun rises. I beg you do not ask," she hesitated, still afraid to say the name, "him."

Nishioji-sama looked pensive, as if mulling it over. He glanced at the moon and then back at her. "I won't ask Yori," he answered with hesitation in his voice, "but I ask that one of your brothers escort you due to thieves. Make sure the walk to my home is not too dark. I will accept your word."

Aki nodded. *Accept her word* he had said. She would need to maintain that trust. Shuji would do it. Genta would complain, and so would his wife. "Yes, sir."

They started walking again and soon reached her home, saying their goodbyes. Aki watched him leave and then realized the results of her request.

She had just talked Nishioji-sama out of walking with her each night.

CHAPTER TWELVE

Tomi and Matsu nodded to each other then turned to scan the river. Another waste of time. It was the third straight morning since the death of the man at the jail, and they had hoped watching the river would help them learn more about the assassin. Unfortunately, little had happened this morning or any of the prior two that they had come. A few ships had passed, likely headed upriver after paying duties at the river entrance. There were also other docks, larger ones downstream, where they might disembark. This dock was closest to the rice storage warehouses and remained the best option.

Nothing suspicious had come near the buildings or any of the docks within eyesight. Not that they could distinguish much. The low fog on the water made it difficult to see anything. Small fishing boats had passed, the swashing of water providing a beacon of sound in the mist, but those boats had moved further upriver. So had the fertilizer boats.

Tomi blew on his hands, trying to warm them, then rubbed them against his sleeves. The first two mornings had been comfortable, but a winter freeze had arrived overnight, leaving Tomi craving a return to a fire.

"Could be better used elsewhere?" Matsu said, his

voice matching the hope within Tomi. "No sign of anything."

"Oeda's request was that we be here for a few days." Tomi stared at the horizon. If only the sunlight would peek through the dark. If only a clock were nearby. Waiting 'til dawn was vague, at best.

"After this early morning duty ends," Matsu said, "I will find my inspiration. A few sips of tea. Relaxing strands of sanshin. The scent of plum blossoms. The chirps of birds. After that, I will persuade Oeda to try another option."

"The sanshin will scare the birds away," Tomi shot back. "Poor plan."

A few coos from the air sounded their agreement. Matsu emitted a chuckle. "A joke? You made a joke. Spending time with me has done you some—"

Tomi extended his hand, palm outward, and motioned Matsu to silence, pointing toward the water with his other hand. Murmurs from the river rose over the fog. The words? Unintelligible. The tone? Menacing.

Matsu signaled Tomi to allow him to lead, and Tomi nodded. They walked at a slow pace for several minutes, listening for the boat as it neared.

A crack in the distance brought them to a halt. A large, portly figure appeared in the moonlight, someone ill fitted to silent work. Something about the man looked familiar, but Tomi put it aside for now. He reminded Tomi of a merchant. His walk created an appearance of both age and money. Two other men followed behind, like rats serving a leader.

The figure headed to the water and then whistled twice. One whistle came in response. A few minutes later, a boat approached the shore out of the fog, one like those that brought goods upriver for ships too large to enter. It resembled a cargo craft Tomi had seen on Biwa, the large lake northeast of the capital.

The wind whipped through as if blowing clear patches

through the fog. The boat sat low in the water, likely loaded down, though as a cargo boat it was wide compared to other craft.

A man alighted from the front, splashing water as he reached shore holding a rope. Other men jumped to the side and helped bring the boat closer.

Tomi's teeth chattered. *Water this cold strips the skin.* The fog reasserted itself and shrouded the two men. The one from shore gave another whistle behind him, and six more men appeared bringing ornate palanquins. These men were dressed well for cargo carriers. They set the carriers aside, opening them when they did, and then joined on the rope. The men then boarded and unloaded what looked like large spools.

Silk thread?

"What do you think?" Tomi asked in a whisper.

"That cargo boat could not have come all the way from the inland sea. Not big enough."

"Agreed. There must be a ship nearby?"

"Yes," Matsu said, "maybe guards from one of the daimyo on the river saw them."

"Not likely." Tomi's heavy breaths created wisps from his mouth. "The fog is thick, and ships are common. Even if they noticed, they might not have paid attention. Maybe one of the diving families along the water's edge."

"They would be asleep."

"Probably asleep. Hard to follow with the two of us."

"Unnh." Tomi wished Yori were here. He'd requested the young man watch Aki each morning to ensure her safety, a task to which he'd grudgingly agreed. Matsu had been correct. Aki could make it to his home without concern. He and Matsu needed Yori's help now.

Each of the men brought cargo ashore and loaded the thread in the palanquins. Tomi now understood the logic. No one would stop the carriers for fear of detaining a prominent official. Additional men arrayed more finely than others wore swords to complete the ruse.

"What do you think?" Matsu asked.

Tomi stared at the men from the craft. *Rough and unkempt, like common thieves.* "*Kaizoku.*" *Pirates.* The men on the boat worked for money. The men on the shore, though, worked with a purpose. Devoted followers.

"I agree," Matsu answered. "Though something is odd." He scratched the back of his head as he stared. They finished loading the silk, and then the leaders of each group distanced themselves as if repulsed. The men in the boat pushed away from shore while the remaining ones chatted.

Tomi's eyes grow wide. "They didn't pay," he whispered.

"What?" Matsu asked tone sounded irritated.

"The men on shore didn't pay the men on the boat." Tomi stared at them. "They're together."

"Lot of work to avoid taxes."

Tomi grunted. "But where do they go from here?"

Light peaked from the east. The men on shore worked faster. The ones on the river started moving west.

"What next?" Matsu asked.

"We follow." Tomi's chest swelled. Whatever was happening here involved a coordinated effort. "You follow the boat as best you can."

"Going downriver. Cannot keep up on foot."

"The fog will slow them, and the growing light will help you. A boat that size will hug the coastline for safety and meet up with a larger ship. Do your best. Maybe we'll be lucky."

"And you?"

"I'll follow the smugglers. The large man looks familiar. Need to see where they're headed. Meet later at the office. I'll locate Yori. We'll discuss what we find."

"Understood," Matsu said and nodded. "Are you good alone? If my quarry sees me, I'm too far away to do anything."

"I will be." Tomi motioned for Matsu to hurry as he rubbed his rosary under the fabric of his clothes. "May the Lord—"

Matsu silenced him with a wave. "Tell him to care for you. You need him more. Talk soon."

Aki bid her brother, Shuji, goodbye, watching him leave in the early morning light. She uttered a silent thanks for his presence, knowing he had felt coerced. He commented he did it in fear of the samurai, though Aki believed he wanted to avoid his own wife's disapproval. Shuji's wife, Ogin, often complimented Aki for her business skills. Ogin was also the best choice to replace Aki, if Uncle pushed hard and did not allow Aki to help Genta.

On the first day he escorted her, the street captain had denied Shuji's entrance. There was no advance approval. However, the captain looked away and then changed his mind, as if he had received a message to allow Shuji to pass. Aki wanted to look around but knew it would anger the man if she and Shuji dallied.

The door slid open. Nishioji-sama's father stood before her. Something about his jawline reminded her of his son. It was the one physical feature they had in common. "Nishioji-sama?"

He nodded. "Aki, you are early." He turned to Shuji. "Thank you for bringing her."

Shuji bowed and left, his footsteps sounding as he sped off.

Aki surveyed the man's humble attire. He was dressed warmly. "Are you home today, sir?"

"No, just waiting until you arrived. I must work and need to leave."

"I am sorry I delayed you."

He shook his head. "Don't worry. My wife is up this morning. She wants to get outside today if the weather warms. She's waiting for you."

The man nodded as he passed her, his glance also a reminder of the samurai. When a sharp wind blew, she headed in, closing the door behind her. "I am here," she announced.

The samurai's mother looked up from the table where she sat enjoying a meal. She smiled in Aki's direction. "It's good to see you. Come here."

Aki hurried over, drawn by the excitement in the woman's voice. "Your husband said you wanted to go outside later this morning."

"I do," she responded and held out her hands. "Help me up."

Aki grabbed the woman's right hand to steady her and then glanced at her fingertips. They were dry and disheveled. Aki swallowed a gasp. Was this an injury of some kind? The woman pushed against Aki's hand and rose to her feet. "You are well this morning?" Aki asked.

"I am. After we go outside, I want to practice my writing again. I have something to show you."

The woman's enthusiasm piqued Aki's curiosity. She studied her but saw nothing. "What is it?"

The woman pointed toward the wall. Aki saw a bigger desk. Brushes and paper were laid out and ready. "What happened to the old one?"

"Tomi added more space and replaced the top. He surprised me last night."

Aki walked over and studied it, kneeling and running her hand over the smooth wooden finish. When did he find time to do this? "I am excited about helping you."

Nishioji-sama was as talented as he was handsome.

She looked forward to his return that day and hoped he would walk her home.

Tomi nodded and watched as Matsu circled out of sight of the men nearby. When he approached the shore many yards down, Tomi lost him in the dim light.

He turned toward the remaining men and stared. They modified the boxes, changing the appearance. They then shed their outer garments, shifting to plain brown ones low enough to cover their *fundoshi*, the basic undergarment. They slid their swords into pockets at the sides of the palanquins. They now resembled workmen and were not important enough to stop. They could add items on the top that no one would notice. If something happened, they could reach the swords. Deadly workmen indeed.

Tomi backed away, leaving himself space to move about. He recognized none of them, meaning they were not local criminals. The one in charge intrigued him. Where had he seen him before? If Tomi knew him, the man might know Tomi.

The men reached the road and continued south, staying outside the city and the area of the new canal. There were a few businesses there, but it was more an expanse of farmland. Given Osaka's growth, Tomi expected more of everything. Instead, it was a blend of openness and darkness, which provided him cover to hide.

The men turned away from the city, taking one of the few roads that went west. Tomi stayed back. Someone might notice him. People were few. No others to distract his quarry. An open field gave less room for Tomi to hide. The men turned left, toward shops, and Tomi ducked between two buildings, catching the men as they emerged and headed into open area.

Tomi darted behind a tree line as the men reached a small, decaying shrine with a gap-filled surrounding gate. If the numbers were true, Nobunaga had destroyed over 2000 temples after the militant Jōdo Shinshū monks surrendered ten years ago. Shrines were affected, too.

The men set the palanquins down, so Tomi narrowed his eyes. A single monk in dull robes rushed out, opening the gate and allowing them in. His wild hand gyrations showed irritation and anger.

Tomi approached from the tree line on the side. It meant swinging out, but he was still in the open. The shrine resembled a place established as a neighborhood memorial set aside for visitors to drop money. Having someone monitor it was odd for so small a location, though it appeared large enough for storage rooms in the front and back. *Could one or two people be living there or access quarters to spend occasional nights there? Was it a residence or a hideaway?*

The monk's voice erupted in shrill tones. He appeared upset about the time. The shrine resembled a mix of maintained and decrepit ones, well enough to be in use but poor enough so people would ignore it. Devout followers might drop a coin in support.

It was the perfect location for smuggling. Tomi watched as the men worked a few minutes with the priest then headed out. The silk thread was stored away.

Tomi could return or get assistance to have this place observed. It would be difficult. He did not know whom to trust. A subject to discuss later with Matsu and Oeda. For now, he needed to follow and learn more.

The familiar man gave directions to those remaining. They dispersed, and Tomi followed the leader. He gave thanks for the man's beard. Not an uncommon trait, but one that would make following him through the streets easier.

Tomi again stayed back to ensure he wasn't noticed then swung around, using the same route he'd used to get close. The man made his way back to the business area, which meant more people, more places to hide. Tomi could also lose him in the growing crowd. Tomi confirmed he himself hadn't been followed and that the other men were nowhere near. He quickened his pace on the bearded man, who walked side-to-side, occasionally stopping as if attempting to guard his steps. Was he a trained criminal or a trained samurai? Both would give him the knowledge to detect Tomi.

The bearded man headed south, where street vendors were setting up for the day. Tomi closed the distance to avoid losing him, shifting behind passersby to avoid being seen.

More people entered the streets as the growing light made an impact. Merchants congregated, talking to neighbors, and good spirits filled the area. A dog barked, catching Tomi's attention as the white ball of fur crossed in front of him. Tomi took the dog's appearance as an omen and hid behind a crowd.

The bearded man headed toward the center. Tomi rushed to get a better view, stepping left to allow him to make his turn. He passed through the street to hide himself, in case the man himself turned.

A glance right showed fewer people than on the main street, but the bearded man remained on course. Tomi allowed the distance to widen. If he'd noticed Tomi earlier, he might suspect something. He studied the shop signs. A dry goods area. Tomi crossed the street and tried to lose himself behind a group on right. They would notice a samurai and create a commotion, but Tomi could defuse that with a glare. His height gave him a few inches to see over people. He needed to use that advantage.

The man turned right and then headed straight toward an area of houses and temples refurbished as businesses. This was the southern edge of the city, with newer temples, a growing, dynamic area, and a straight path toward Shitennōji, the oldest temple in Japan. The path might provide cover, but he would be more difficult to follow. He went left toward a side street and then moved between two groups of men. *Should I cut early or still follow?* He hastened and stayed. He had to know where the man was going.

His quarry darted left and quickened his pace. There were fewer people, though it was busy with those bringing shipments or headed to work. The man hit the next street and appeared to go right. Tomi hugged the left side and then stopped at the edge, taking a knee. The man might be waiting. Tomi paused his search.

A sharp action on his left drew Tomi's attention. The bearded one, now a block down and on the right side, glanced toward Tomi. Tomi gripped his sword and withdrew it an inch. Another delivery man, this one in a hurry, sped into the street with poles on his shoulders that he swung over people's heads. Nothing of concern. Tomi released his sword.

The bearded man stopped and then turned in Tomi's direction. Had he been seen? He looked away to hide his face. If the man was doubling back, Tomi would hear his approach. Noises bustled to the right of another delivery, this one to a tatami mat dealer across the street. Cries of children cut through the air. Women with children entered from another alley. Would the man challenge Tomi with children nearby?

The man shifted right and maintained this path for several minutes, the longest in one direction. He turned right, and then a quick left, heading down a side street. Tomi hurried to the position but didn't see him. The next street over Tomi knew well. It had housed several temples. The area had been rebuilt and the land reused but was still dead in ways. Tomi went back. He could not chance an ambush at the end of the cross street, but he would be away from children if forced to fight.

Tomi moved again and scanned the next street. A man in gray clothes, like the bearded one but with a sash over one shoulder bowed towards a building that appeared under remodel. The man clapped then gave a half-glance toward Tomi's direction.

That man was clean-shaven and had a scar under his eye. Unfortunately, Tomi didn't get a good look at his face.

Tomi again searched the area. His quarry had fled. He crossed streets and checked north. Had the man turned south, Tomi would have seen him before he emerged.

Nothing.

Tomi continued to search, but there was no sign of the bearded one.

He punched the side of the temple with the base of his fist.

His quarry was gone.

CHAPTER THIRTEEN

"You're late." Wakizashi stared at Riku, the cloth merchant. "Lateness is not tolerable. What is the reason?"

"My apologies," Riku said, unable to stand still, "but I felt like I was being followed. When we picked up the silk thread this morning, I saw no one, but a presence was there."

Wakizashi approached the merchant. "Are you certain?"

"No." The merchant paced a few steps in each direction. "But this morning's delivery was uneventful. Nothing stood out."

"No one saw the shipment?"

"No one. Of that I am sure."

"When did you notice you were being followed?"

The man sighed and rubbed his chin. "In town."

"Could it have been at the shrine? What reason is there to follow you there?"

The merchant moved side-to-side. Was he thinking of a lie? "None. I've smuggled goods past checkpoints many times and never been caught. My instincts are good. They keep me safe."

Wakizashi rubbed his forefinger across his lips as he read his underling's face. He followed his own instincts, as well, and his said this man was foolish. Unfortunately, he was still the best option. For now. "Is that why you removed the beard?"

"A precaution. It allowed me to disappear."

Wakizashi huffed. "No one saw you remove it?"

The man didn't budge. "I made sure of it."

"See that your movements remain secret. We have few places as beneficial as that shrine. We must protect it."

"I understand. What do you suggest?"

"Improve it. Make it look better."

"Will that not draw attention?"

"Maybe, but it will also keep it away. No one develops a place that they want to keep hidden."

"How do we stop the curious?"

"They will not come at night, and it gives us reason to have people there. Adding to it may even inspire people to donate." He smiled. "We can serve people spiritually."

"It will be done."

"Good. One more thing, Riku. If you feel like you're being followed, then scatter. You risk our entire operation."

"Yes, Master."

The underling departed, drawing Wakizashi's gaze with him.

If you chance bringing a person following you here, I will kill them and you.

Tomi watched the door of the room, waiting for Matsu to arrive. He had asked Oeda for privacy. Oeda had placed him and Yori in the file room, one of the few in the building with no window. Shelves lined two of the walls, with a table included for study. The room was a mix of dust, accented with the aroma of burning lamp oil set on the front wall and away from shelves.

Oeda had brought him files of pending cases and asked for Tomi's review and input of interrogations. The cases appeared mundane, likely already decided. Tomi understood the assignment. Train Yori. It would be his job one day. He'd thought about filling Yori in on the morning's activities but decided to wait until Matsu arrived.

The door slid open, revealing Matsu. His face appeared downcast.

"You look like you found nothing," Tomi said. "Did you have any success?"

"Went as far as I could. The smaller ship reached a larger one and sailed away."

Tomi pointed to an empty chair at the table, suggesting Matsu should sit. "Did it have any flags? Any idea of who might be behind this?"

"The flag furled away from me. In the distance, it looked like lines and leaves."

Tomi stared at the wall, trying to place such a design. "Lines and leaves? Can you explain?"

Matsu chewed his cheek, a sign of deep thought for him or to ensure he explained it right the first time. This was the serious side of Matsu, the side Tomi knew from Himeji. "Looked like the regent's crest."

Tomi's gut tightened. "The regent? You think him involved in this?"

"No. Couldn't see it all. Just looked like the crest of Hideyoshi, but it was odd."

"Odd? It was displayed wrong?" Yori asked.

"No one would dare," Matsu said. "Would bring a painful death."

Tomi coughed and cleared his throat, tapping the top of his chest with his fist. "What if it's someone else's crest?"

"Another daimyo?" Matsu asked.

"We're assuming pirates. Pirates could be involved, but many now work for daimyo. Especially now, as the Hideyoshi has tried to put pirates out of business."

"Becoming personal navies," Matsu said, though his tone sounded unsure.

"It makes sense. The regent wouldn't need pirates to

smuggle silk. It's likely another daimyo."

"Why not?" Yori asked.

"The regent has first choice of silk shipped from Macau," Tomi said. "He also controls Osaka and wouldn't concern himself with taxes."

"We should discuss it with Oeda later," Matsu said and then paused. "What happened to you after I left?"

Tomi replayed the morning's surveillance, showing the bruise on his hand where he'd slammed his fist against a temple wall.

"How do you think it happened?" Yori asked, his tone more polite than usual, as if he had somehow increased his respect.

Tomi reflected on the smaller points. There had been occasional crowds to hide in, and the man had disappeared after he'd come toward him.

Matsu grunted in response. "Let's retrace your steps, starting from where you last saw the man. See what options he had. You may have lost him. This does not mean he went far after you did."

"Then we should go now," Tomi suggested.

Tomi led Matsu and Yori to that section on the west side of town where business was growing, expanding into farmland. Two places he'd assumed abandoned appeared active, one appearing to be a warehouse and the other being remodeled. Crowds milled about, making it difficult to talk privately, though people always provided them with space.

Tomi showed them each of the streets he had taken and the ones the bearded man had used. Frustration welled inside as his steps from the early morning blended in his head. *How did he avoid my notice? Where did he hide himself?*

"Any ideas?" Matsu asked.

An image of gray flashed in his head. The man with similar clothes. That must be it. "The beard. It must have been fake," Tomi said. "It's the only thing that makes sense."

"What does it mean?" Yori asked.

Tomi smelled the air, catching a light scent of muck. "If I head north along the main road, what do I get?"

"The river," Matsu answered

"Yes, I do. What happens if I go west?"

"Farmland," Yori said.

"Correct. Yori, you're from here. Do you know this area well?

"I used to walk here often with my grandfather when I was younger. He tried to teach me about it. He died three years ago when I was thirteen."

"Your point?" Matsu asked.

"There are businesses here. He wouldn't go there. But there are also some standing ruins he could have used to hide. He couldn't have gone far.

"They must be using an abandoned building for their activities," Tomi said. "It's the only option."

"Like the ones with hidden jade," Yori said.

"Exactly."

"What do we do next?" Matsu asked.

Tomi bit his lower lip, a habit his mother always said meant he was thinking. "Yori, did you go to the Administration Building and ask for that list of buildings transferred?"

"I did. They say it will take time to make a list."

"Tell them to hurry," Tomi said.

Yori looked down and inhaled before looking again. The request was a challenge. "I will follow with them. One more thing."

Tomi eyed him. "What?"

"We may need help."

"Who do you trust?"

"Yaesu. My older brother."

Tomi had met Yaesu once. He resembled Yori except he was calmer—that, and he didn't shave his forehead into a bald pate. "Is he trained how to fight?"

People continued to stream around the three of them. Yori glanced both ways, afraid to talk until it was clear. A light wind blew, carrying hints of moisture. Rain would come later. Aki would need an escort home. He doubted she had an umbrella.

"Yes, he is trained, but he cares not for it. He works with the castle planners, improving the grounds and defenses."

"We'll discuss it later," Tomi said, "after the shrine."

"How close is it?" Yori asked.

Tomi pointed north. "If we go that way, it's not far, but let's go toward the castle."

"Why?" Yori asked.

"I want to retrace my steps."

"Think he might have doubled back?"

"Possibly, but I don't want to come at it straight, either."

"I don't understand."

"Yori, I have no idea what I'm searching for. Just follow. Try to remember your grandfather's wisdom. It could help."

They headed east, toward the direction of the castle, then turned left after a long stretch.

"You sure?" Matsu asked.

"Yes. The tatami mat stores were here. A lot of children, too."

"That early?" Matsu chewed his lip. "Likely headed toward the temples south."

"Let's keep going," Tomi said.

They turned left and then right again, reaching the dry goods district. Tomi looked around.

"What is it?" Matsu asked.

"Aki lives that way. Most of the fabric district is there."

"Is that important?"

"I don't know."

They continued cutting between each side, seeing the street vendors. They had changed since the morning, singing different chants and selling different wares. Women shifted side-to-side as they walked toward the main road, likely headed for the vegetable stands nearby. Daikon was still available, along with the late kabocha and winter greens that his mother loved.

He looked east again. Beyond were weavers. Further up were warehouses.

"You keep staring toward the castle," Yori said. "It's not Aki."

"No, but there's something else.

They turned left. The shrine appeared in the distance. Occasional drops fell as they neared it. While Tomi didn't welcome more rain, he thought it might distract notice from their arrival.

They reached a closer vantage point. In the daylight, the shrine's decay showed like blackened weather marks on rotten wood.

"Yori, circle it and come back."

"Yes, sir." The young man sauntered out, darting between each side of the street, checking the businesses as he neared the shrine. Ten minutes later, he returned.

"What did you see?" Tomi asked.

"The wall in the back was repaired."

Someone was now using this place. Repairing a wall indicated such. No one would risk the ire of the gods by raiding a shrine amid a restoration.

"Anyone there?" Matsu asked.

"Appears unattended."

A wooden object in front drew Tomi's gaze. "I'm going to look. Matsu, come with me. Yori, keep watch."

He and Matsu headed toward the shrine, stopping at a nearby table of hats that merchants appeared to be clearing before the downpour. Tomi's eyes remained ahead. "Do you see it?" he asked.

"There's a new donation box."

"Are you certain?"

Rain fell a little harder. "It wasn't there this morning."

"You remember that? It was dark," Matsu said.

"I do."

"It looks ordinary."

"I'm certain it's new, or it has been placed since this morning."

Two passersby arrived at the shrine and said a prayer then held their hands over the box. A clunk followed.

"Yes, it's new," Tomi said. "They're asking for donations."

A man appeared from the side of the building and waved at the couple. Tomi glanced at him, but a hat hid part of his face, making him indistinguishable.

They returned to Yori. "Did you see the man come out?"

"Yes," Yori said. "It looks active. I don't remember this place ever being in use. We should have the place searched."

"No," Tomi responded, eyeing the box. "We watch it for now. Get an idea of who uses it."

"Will need help," Matsu said.

"Agreed," Tomi said, his thoughts focused on what to do next. "You stay for now, Yori. Matsu or I will relieve you before nightfall. Did you bring anything to sustain you?"

"I will last," he said in an annoyance he tried to hide. "Do not concern yourself."

"I know you will," Tomi said. "Keep sharp. If someone leaves, follow them."

"As you command," Yori said.

Tomi motioned to Matsu, and the two of them departed.

When they were out of vocal range of Yori, Matsu

spoke. "Good to leave him there for so long?"

"He'll do fine. One of us will spell him early."

"Won't be easy. Need more than the three of us to watch a place."

"I understand," Tomi responded, "but I wish to keep this from Justice Building. Can we trust his brother?"

"No one else. Both raised here. Their presence less noticed."

Tomi shook his head. "I know, but I remain suspicious. We have dead officers and prisoners."

"Don't like adding more people?" Matsu responded.

"We have no choice. For now, I need to go home. Please meet me there in two hours. I have a greater challenge."

Aki turned at the sound of the sliding door, glancing at the sun, which was lofty in the early afternoon sky. Tension raced across her skin as she put her brush down on the table. He was early.

Nishioji-sama entered and put his shoes to the side.

"Nishioji-sama," Aki called out as she rushed to meet him. "May I bring you some tea?"

"I'll have some," he responded gruffly.

Aki hurried to the hearth and prepared his tea while Nishioji chatted with his mother. Something about his posture conveyed his concern. The morning had passed well. She and his mother had even taken walks, though the woman had remained bundled, covering the bruises on her hands and arms. She also carried something in a pocket under her kosode. The item resembled the kanji for the number ten. What importance did that character have for her? She wished she knew the woman well enough to ask.

She brought the tea over, served it to them, then left and tidied up the room. The conversation continued, and Aki pushed herself as far away as she could. Best not to appear to be listening.

The door slid open. "*Gomen kudasai,*" a voice said.

Aki hurried to the entrance. The other older samurai, the one called Matsu-sama, stood there. Worry etched his face. Wisps came from his mouth in heavy breaths. His swords appeared askew, instead of tight inside his belt.

Had he run here from a great distance?

"Osamurai-sama, please enter. I will fetch him."

He shook his head. "No time. Tomi," he called out.

Tomi. So that is what his friends call him.

Nishioji-sama strode toward him and grunted. "You're early."

"Plans have changed. Need to leave now. I'll explain on the way."

"Understood."

Nishioji-sama turned to Aki. "My mother is tired. Help her rest. Wait for my father to return and then go home."

Aki nodded. The two samurai hustled toward the street captain and then headed right. She watched them as long as she could. When Nishioji-sama had returned early, she hoped for a chance he might walk her home.

That chance faded with the day.

CHAPTER FOURTEEN

"What happened?" Tomi asked, glancing back toward his house. "Why the urgency?"

"Another rumor," Matsu said. "Oeda wants surveillance."

Tomi breathed deeply. The timing was convenient for the smugglers. Had they been noticed? Were the smugglers trying to draw them away? "Does Yori know?"

"Ordered to find him and bring him. Thought I should find you first. Gives him more time."

Tomi nodded. "I agree."

The two hurried to Yori's position. Leaving him there had been acceptable, but they'd been ordered to return. Workmen paraded in both directions, offering them visual protection as they approached the shrine. Yori was likely to have shifted his position. Five minutes passed before they located him.

Yori's eyebrows rose at their approach. "Both of you?" He glanced at the shrine while turning half a gaze toward them. "I thought only one of you would relieve me."

"Another rumor," Tomi said, "like when we surveyed Aki's family. We've been ordered back to discuss it."

"*Aki's* family again, is it?" Matsu asked. "Not the cloth

dealer."

"You know what I mean." Tomi stopped and looked at Yori, catching the earnestness on his face. "You saw something?"

"I will explain while we walk," Yori said. "We need privacy."

They backed out of the area. Yori maintained his attention on the shrine while Tomi and Matsu pretended to converse. They didn't know if they'd been seen, but caution was warranted.

Heading back to the Administrative Building, Tomi suggested taking a side street that led toward the canal under construction. This would allow them privacy for a few minutes. Osaka teemed with expansion, so it was difficult to find any street during the day without activity.

Clouds covered the sun, keeping the air cold. In the back streets, the width between shops was tight and the roads were less maintained. They reached an empty area, as good a place as any. "What happened?" Tomi asked.

Yori licked his lips. "Two men visited the shrine. Priests. One stayed outside while one entered."

"Stayed outside? Why?"

"He appeared to test the outer wall and looked around as he did. He also glanced in my direction twice but did not look for long. I doubt he saw me."

"Did you get a good look at him?"

"Enough. I would recognize him if I saw him again."

"How about the man who entered?"

Yori sighed. "Him, too. He hid his face, but his hood slid down, and I caught a glimpse."

"Why the sigh?" Matsu asked.

The wind whipped through the narrow corridor between the buildings. "Because he looked in my direction, and it was more than brief."

"You think he saw you?" Tomi asked.

"I do not know."

They took a right into a busier street, ending the conversation. Yori's voice had held embarrassment. Would Oeda allow for a quick search of the shrine, or would they focus on the emergency?

With another left turn, the Administrative Building came into view. They hurried to reach the front. Constable Oeda was already outside with a small group, motioning them to move faster.

There would be no chance to search the shrine.

Aki entered her home from the back, hoping not to interrupt business out front. The samurai's father had returned home earlier than usual and had sent her home. She'd hoped to see Nishioji-sama before leaving, but he had told her to leave when his father got home. Tomorrow would be a new day.

She entered from the rear and removed her shoes, glimpsing herself in a nearby mirror as she announced her return. Had she looked like that all day? It was bad enough that her sisters had inherited their mother's looks while she had not, but this was too much. Her hair resembled a mixture of stubble and splits. No wonder Tomi had sent her home upon his father's return.

Heat rushed to her face. Had she thought of Nishioji-sama by the name Matsu-sama had called him? She would have to be careful not to say it.

"Yon-ban, you are home," Genta said.

Yon-ban. Not a good sign. Aki cringed at her eldest brother's use of that nickname. *Number four.* Yes, she was the fourth out of four sisters. Yes, she was the youngest and least important. Genta had called her that when she was younger, switching to Aki as she had gotten older.

Then Sadayo, his wife, had learned about the nickname.

"Yes, I am home." She crossed her arms in front of her and tilted her head up. "I take it Sadayo has a request for me."

"Please do not sound that way. I only call you 'number four' to assure you that you are part of the family. Last children often feel left out. You are important."

Genta was treating her with kindness instead of using his position as older brother to demand her help. He was definitely in boiling oil. "So Sadayo does *not* have a request for me?"

Her brother opened his eyes wide and gave her that look, the one that always melted her resolve. Then he shrugged his shoulders and said nothing.

That said everything. "She has a request for me."

"There's no reason to be cynical."

"I would never do that, Genta." If her sister Hoshi were here, she would laugh at that statement. "What is the problem?"

"I was helping my in-laws with the work today at the trading house. There is some confusion on the accounts."

Sadayo was again trying to pull him away, like always. "Why were you there instead of here?"

"Learning the business."

"Why are you not learning this business? You are in charge when father retires."

"It's good to learn how trading works. My wife's company acquires things we need for our business."

"What error did you make?"

"Let us not talk about that. Will you help me?"

The pleading in his eyes suggested the trouble was big, but he was hiding it. "Let me wish father and mother well. Then we will go."

"They know I'm waiting back here for you."

"I need to eat something."

Genta reached into his kosode and withdrew a small pouch. "I have something already."

"How about a bigger snack?"

"Sadayo has prepared some things for us."

His wife cooked? Another reason to get a bigger snack.
"Just a little more."

"Please, my little number four—"

She silenced him with her hand palm outward. "I will come, if you promise never to call me that again."

He shrugged. "I cannot stop my wife from using the term."

"And her family."

He scrunched his face and nodded. "I will speak to them. I will tell them you're apprising me of something new. Perhaps after that they will view you differently."

"Last time, your father-in-law remarked that the best way to see me was in darkness."

He avoided her gaze. "His comment was unacceptable."

"You said nothing then."

He inhaled through his teeth. "He is my father-in-law. It's difficult."

"He has money."

"This is not about money."

"With your wife, it is always about money."

"Aki, we go now." His tone no longer pleaded for sympathy. Now he was the eldest brother and giving her an order. She nodded and tightened her garment. *Something must have gone wrong. Something big and he needs my help. Using his position. Just like Uncle.*

Aki's stomach tightened. What would happen if Nishioji-sama discovered her uncle had asked her to spy?

He would grant her permanent relief.

Tomi marveled at the clear night sky. His mother would appreciate an evening like this. The moon was full and lit the area along with the stone lanterns on nearby roads. A light wind whistled through the streets, mixed with the voices of nearby revelers out for an evening.

"How long will we be watching?" Yori asked.

"Hour of the rat," Tomi responded. "Matsu and others will take over then."

"Hour of the rat? That is a long time."

"At least it won't be half the night, though it'll still be late." Tomi blew on his hands. "We avoid the dark cold. Continue your rounds. It will keep you warm."

Yori nodded. He headed left and circled around the row of properties, stopping at other places and conveying messages. The goal was to catch someone. It was late. When they had watched Aki's house, nothing had happened in the time before they entered.

But then nothing had happened in the morning, either. That day had been a ruse. Was today the same?

A half-hour passed with nothing of interest before a casual movement along the street drew Tomi's gaze.

Aki.

The young woman trailed the man in front of her. Recognition dawned. Aki's eldest brother. The one who'd been left in charge the morning of the arrest of Aki's father. The man's name escaped him.

The two of them stopped in front of the target residence. The brother moved to a side door and opened it, announcing his presence after he entered. This meant he lived there or had some relation. Aki followed him in and shut the door.

"It cannot be," Yori said, hurrying to meet him. "Her again? This family?"

Tomi rubbed his chin. No one had mentioned it, but how would they know the connection? Aki's presence changed things. "It's---" Tomi paused "a coincidence."

"This is not a coincidence," Yori said. "This family *is* involved in the smuggling."

"Perhaps." Had either of the two men holding their positions noticed? Did they recognize Aki? Were they thinking the same as Yori?

"You should question her tomorrow morning when she

comes to your house."

More revelers broke the stillness. "I'll consider it. I'm often gone before she arrives."

"Should you not wait for her?" Yori asked. "Is that the best option?"

Tomi tightened his lips at his charge. "I will decide the best option."

"Is it not good to question her?"

Tomi frowned. "I will decide when it is good."

"But?"

"You will say no more."

Yori nodded and began his next rounds. Tomi stared at the door through which Aki had entered. Would she leave before Matsu and his group arrived? He trusted this woman in his own home. Could her family be involved with the smuggling operation?

Yori was correct. He needed to question Aki without making her suspicious. His gut told him she was not involved, but she might know something.

He'd wished to see her. Now they had to meet.

CHAPTER FIFTEEN

Aki pressed ahead into the crowded market. The samurai's mother was in good spirits and wanted to make a special dish. Aki wanted to learn. She could not cook. Another way she was not like her sisters—and the only thing she had in common with Genta's wife.

Aki rubbed her stomach, remembering the queasiness from two nights ago when she had eaten Sadayo's cooking. She should serve Sadayo's food to her uncle and then tell him it was her own. That would get him to change his mind.

People jostled her as she moved through the street. The cries of merchants rang through the crowd. The food sellers did not come out every day, but she knew what she needed.

"You are here?" Nishioji-sama said.

Aki froze. What would the samurai think of her not being at his house? She looked at him. Nishioji-sama, so imposing when they met, had softened in her eyes, though she had not seen him since the day of the emergency when Matsu had fetched him. The one her age, Yori-sama, stood next to him and maintained the same stare he always did—angry at her. He folded his arms and pressed them against his chest. Samurai intimidated her. The swords they carried were sufficient to do that. However, Yori-sama's face resembled someone seeking retribution.

"Yes, sir." Her stomach churned. Was she showing enough respect? She had longed to see Nishioji to ask about the emergency but had not yet had the chance.

"How is my mother?" Nishioji-sama asked. "Why are you out here?"

Aki smiled inside. This she could answer. "She is fine, the best she has been in the last few days. Calligraphy practice went well, and she wanted to give me a cooking lesson."

A puzzled look crossed his face. "I understand, but is my mother alone?"

That explained his concern. "She is not alone. The woman who normally shops for her food is ill. Her young daughter came by to tell us."

"She is a child." His voice carried an edge. "She is unsuited to care for my mother."

Aki rubbed her hands together but kept them low. His love for his mother ruled his thoughts. "Her grandfather is there, too. He is smoothing the rock garden in the back."

"Is the hearth stoked?"

"Your mother did not want it too hot. A corvee is digging on the canal near the house. The child's father is assigned to it."

Nishioji-sama appeared relieved. She had not met the girl's father, but the samurai's mother trusted the family. She was not the first neighbor to visit. Many came by to cheer the woman. On a night Aki had worked late, a fire watcher visited, as if he knew Nishioji was working.

"Hurry with your errand and get back," the young man said. "That is your duty."

Nishioji shot arrows with his eyes, and Yori fell silent. He could chastise with a glance as easily as anyone else could with words.

"I understand. I will return to the house as soon as I buy what Nishioji-sama's mother requested."

A sudden yet slow movement drew Aki's attention. The undesirable from her neighborhood, the one who had smiled at her the morning she had freed her father about tax evasion. Dressed in faded clothes, he appeared to approach but then turned to move elsewhere. The crowd allowed him to pass as he took a route to avoid all.

"What is that eta doing here?" Yori asked, a harsh weight on the word. "He should be where he belongs."

Nishioji-sama stared as if insulted, but he appeared to agree with the abrasive young samurai. Aki considered the man. She had spoken with him a few times when he worked in her neighborhood. Aki found herself repulsed by him, but the man still smiled at her. Father always pressed her to have a kinder heart for this one.

"I'll order him to return to his own district. Whatever business he has," Yori-sama said, his voice rising, "he can find more appropriate hours for it. He should not foul the air with his presence."

Yori took a step, but Nishioji grabbed his arm. "Stay, my young friend. We've more important tasks than to roust undesirables. Come."

Yori's eyes flashed, his face both enraged and calm at the same time.

"Acquire what you need and return to my mother," Nishioji-sama said. "I should make it home early for once. I expect a full report when I arrive. Tell her I will return at a reasonable time."

"Yes, sir." Aki bowed again, knowing he would not reciprocate.

The two men left, leaving Aki by herself, his command in her head. She turned to leave but glanced again at the eta, who headed out of the district, this time with a small white dog trailing in his wake.

The dog saw him as friendly. *Dogs know.*

###

"Did you ever talk with her," Yori asked as they

glanced toward Aki, "about why she was at that house?"

Tomi chewed his lower lip. He didn't like being questioned by Yori, but it was a valid question. "I've not had the chance."

The sun came out from behind the clouds, warming the air, but it still felt like the night. The growing crowd provided some heat. Aki was not the only one shopping. Delivery men carried boxes on their shoulders, creating obstacles to get around.

"Is that why you told her you would be home tonight and wait?" Yori asked

Tomi nodded. Yori followed his logic. He was smart, and, for once, not pretentious. "Yes, I thought it—"

"There you are." Matsu's normally jovial voice carried tension, as if something nagged at him.

"Have you been looking long?" Tomi asked. "How did the search go?"

"Fruitless. The shrine is just a shrine now. There are people there rebuilding it and trying to make it work."

"Priests?"

Matsu shook his head. "No. Carpenters. I saw someone in the robes of a Shinto priest, but another officer said he knew him. Said they had just received approval on the location."

"How about the house?" Tomi asked. "The one we've been watching."

"Oeda says it's now more of a patrol. Nothing happening."

Now a patrol? That made no sense. "What next?"

"Oeda wants to see you," Matsu said, his gaze flitting back and forth. "Alone. I don't know why. He told me to find you."

Tomi sighed, wondering if there was a different project or another discussion. He still needed to talk with Aki. Hopefully, he wouldn't get home too late. Would she be there?

His chest grew heavy. He'd given Aki an order. She wouldn't disobey.

"How are you feeling?" Aki asked, looking at the samurai's mother as she cursed herself. The woman had been walking outside with the young girl, watching the corvee work. She noticed Aki's return and walked ahead to meet her.

An icy patch on the ground marked the foolhardiness of doing that without assistance.

A few of the nearby workers helped her get back into the house. One female neighbor visited and wrapped her ankle, helping Aki with tea and seeing to the woman's comforts.

"I'm doing…better now."

Aki knelt and then bowed. "Again, I am sorry. It is my responsibility. I should have known."

"Nonsense." She pinched her lips shut and her nose wrinkled. "I felt good and was happy to see you return."

Aki's heart pounded. What would Nishioji think when he returned home? "Nishioji-sama will be unhappy with me."

"*I* was the one who ordered you to pick up the food. Do not worry. You were following my orders, and I will tell him that."

"Your son is a samurai."

"He was my son first, and I know him well. You're a good person and take excellent care of me. I will tell him the same."

Aki's belly knotted. How could she be good? Her uncle demanded she share information about the samurai, information she couldn't hide once she was his daughter. Maybe she would be fortunate, and Nishioji-sama would get angry, angry enough to release her.

"What troubles you, my child?" She smiled, clutching her odd juzu beads with the character for ten at the end. She was never without them, not that Aki had ever seen.

"I am still concerned," Aki said, as she helped her charge take weight off her ankle.

"I'm in good spirits. I felt a lift today that I haven't known in a while. I just need some rest."

Aki set a bell next to her. "If there is anything else, please let me know."

The woman closed her eyes, and Aki watched as she drifted away, her body relaxing with each breath. Sleep would be good. The hand that clutched the beads relaxed, and her talisman slid onto the floor. Aki picked it up, intending to place it next to her.

What was this?

Aki rubbed the wooden figure attached to the end of the string. It was unlike any charm she had ever seen before.

Two pieces of wood shaped like the character for the number ten but with the carved image of a man added. It resembled an execution.

She recalled her childhood. A prisoner had been convicted of robbery, and the officials wanted to make an example of him. They required everyone to watch while the man was tied to the wood, his legs and arms splayed out. Men with spears stood on each side and ran him through from waist to opposite shoulder, leaving him alive as he screamed in pain, then withdrew their spears and did it again. The second time they brought the man death.

For that man, his legs were spread and lashed to a second piece of wood. On the talisman, the legs in the image appeared together. It was still a crucifixion. *A strange symbol this woman holds close.*

Aki fought the nausea that always rose in her throat when she recalled that day. *Why would anyone carry this image?*

But it was important to her.

She placed it back in the old woman's hands, careful to avoid the reddish blisters and scarring on her palms. Aki closed her fingers around it and watched as a smile broke on her lips.

It was a religious image. It must be. That religion she had heard about.

Kirishitan.

Was this religion not forbidden? She had heard yes and no.

Her chest tightened so much that she could not breathe.

She now had information she knew her uncle would want.

CHAPTER SIXTEEN

Tomi watched as Oeda closed the door and then invited him to sit across from him at the desk. Like the few times Tomi had been in this office before, he first noticed the incense burning in front of the shrine of the constable's brother. The desk remained organized but stacked with reports. Tomi pointed to one. "Do those to go to the magistrate for final approval?"

Oeda chuckled. "Officially. Everything goes to the castle where someone approves it. You're forgetting this is Osaka. No one's ever sure who has the authorization."

That explained it. He was being forced to keep them for now. That meant both men who oversaw Osaka were busy. Just like the policeman, the regent was demanding assistance with preparations for battle, forcing Oeda and other constables to depend on the city militia for support. "Will they let you decide any of it yourself?"

"I was thinking of putting white sand behind the building and making prisoners to kneel on it while I pass sentence, but that is for serious offenses and most magistrates hold such court at their homes. My wife would demand my retirement if I did that."

Tomi suppressed a smile. He'd never met Oeda's wife

but guessed Oeda was making a joke. "I understand."

"On to other matters. We searched the shrine. Nothing."

Tomi nodded. "I expected that. Waiting two days to search may have given whomever time to clear it. Is that why you wanted to see me?"

"That's one reason."

Tension rose in Tomi's neck. Was Oeda doubting him? "You think it was empty the entire time?"

Murmurs from behind the door caught Tomi's attention. The office was always active. Oeda rubbed his chin as he glanced at the door. "No. I think the goods were there. We did not have enough people to do everything. The three of you did good work. My fault. I am thinking something else."

"Other things distracted us. Is that what you mean?"

Oeda signaled yes with his gaze. "To waste time in useless work makes one a fool or complicit."

"Is that Kenkō?"

"Yes. You're getting better."

Tomi puzzled the comment in his head. "What do you mean?"

"My dead philosopher is more illuminating than yours."

This time Tomi knew Oeda was joking. "Are you saying we're wasting time?"

"We need to be better. You remember the cloth merchant?"

Heat flushed Tomi's cheeks. How much should he tell Oeda? The man was his superior.

"Very well," Tomi said. "The woman who cares for my mother is away helping her daughter with childbirth. I hired the merchant's daughter as replacement while the woman is away."

Oeda eyed him curiously. "Interesting choice."

"Maybe."

"Has something happened since then?" Oeda asked.

A sliding door interrupted the conversation. A young officer entered to ask Oeda's concurrence on an issue from Constable Tanaka. The young man then left the office and Tomi stared at Oeda. "There may be a connection we didn't know about."

Oeda tilted his head. "What?"

"The young girl. She visited the new house we were watching."

Oeda froze. "Why haven't you mentioned this to me before?"

Tomi paused, hoping to hide the growing embarrassment for having kept this information. "I thought it a coincidence."

"Have you questioned her?"

"I haven't had an opportunity. My father returns from work early and sends her home, but Yori and I saw her today buying food. I told her to wait for me tonight."

"Then you must go home now. Ask without telling her. She needs to explain herself."

"I will," Tomi said, "Anything else."

"There may be some early mornings and long days ahead of us. I'll discuss it with Matsu and have him relay the information to you. Send him to me if you see him on your way out."

Tomi bowed and headed out to find Matsu helping with another prisoner. He conveyed the message and left the building.

It would be twenty minutes before he reached home. He rubbed the beads under his clothes. *Time enough to create convincing questions and regret lying in advance.*

###

The door slid open, catching Aki by surprise as the samurai announced his return.

He is early. Aki had known this moment would come, but she had hoped that his mother would be awake and willing to try her ankle.

She ran to him. "Welcome home." She tried to get the words out, but they caught in her throat.

"What's wrong?" Worry streaked across his face as his gaze flitted around the room. "Where's my mother?"

"She is resting." Aki had hoped to practice what she would say, but his early arrival had left her no opportunity. "She slipped and fell outside."

"How did you allow this to happen?"

"She hurried to greet me when I returned from my errand."

The samurai hurried to his mother's side, anger etched on his brow. "You were supposed to look after her."

"Hush, Tsuneomi." The woman's voice carried a tired reprimand. "She did nothing wrong. I sent her to get the food."

Nishioji-sama's face tightened, and Aki stepped back in surprise. *A samurai rebuked by his mother*. To see that status did not affect family actions warmed her. So did the concern on his face.

He glanced between the two of them and then focused on Aki. "My mother speaks wisely. I..." His voice trailed off. Did he mean to say more? Aki would not get an apology from a man, especially one of higher status, but his face suggested he seldom let status interfere.

"Aki," the mother added, "you should return home, since my son is here."

Nishioji-sama straightened, and Aki's tension grew. The woman may be saying yes, but did he want her to stay? "I thank you. I should prepare something for you first. Before I left to get food, you were excited about making dinner. I will do it before I leave."

Aki headed to the side area where food was stored. She liked the samurai's house. The living area wasn't a business. Leaving early, though, did not bode well. Uncle could drop by and ask for information. The later she stayed, the less chance of having to talk with him or her older brother. No conflict of duty.

Nishioji followed her, stopping at the entrance. Aki bowed her head, afraid to catch his gaze. His mother may have supported her, but he could discipline her away from his mother's presence.

"My deepest apologies for what happened, Nishioji-sama." She bowed, placing her hands near her knees, her upper body parallel to the ground.

"Unnh," he grunted as she raised herself up. "My mother is correct. You followed her instructions. It was not your fault."

The tension in Aki's stomach eased. Nishioji was as kind as anyone she had ever met. Her uncle said only moneylenders could make a samurai bow. She did not wish to see it. "People stop by often to visit. Your mother has many friends."

He nodded, as if considering it. "I know. We've not been in Osaka long, but people have made us welcome."

His voice trembled. Odd for a samurai. Her oldest brother acted the same way when his wife was making demands, preoccupied in his thoughts. "Can I assist you, sir?"

"You don't wish to return home?"

Aki bit her lip. He had noticed. She loved home, but she needed to tell him the truth. At least what she could. "My family is unimportant."

He tilted his head, appearing surprised. "Your actions toward your family are the reason I hired you."

She took a deep breath. The conflict remained. "It is my eldest brother. The last time I was home early, he insisted I go to his wife's family's home to fix a mistake he made. He asked that my help be in secret so that her parents would not know."

"Your brother's wife, I assume." Nishioji smiled. "What does her family do?"

"They run a trading business. They ship goods to the capital and buy them from there."

Nishioji continued with his questions. Each answer seemed to make him relax. Why would he be so interested in her life? Did it matter? The longer it ran, the longer she stayed. *Less chance of seeing Uncle.*

The rest of the afternoon passed quickly. Nishioji-sama informed her he would be busy for the next few days and requested she come as early as she could. Granted, no request from a samurai was merely a request.

The walk home was uneventful. Unfortunately, it was also short. She took a detour, going first through an area of coopers and then crossing through a block of blacksmiths. The blacksmiths took her back toward the samurai. It also took her toward her uncle's house, but he would never be in this section of town. Too dirty. It would ruin his clothes.

Part of Aki had hoped he would escort her home, but he had seemed preoccupied, likely worried about his mother's fall. And his father had not returned.

At least his mother had convinced him the fall was not Aki's fault.

Her father was outside when she arrived home. "How did it go today, my child?"

She related how the woman hurt herself. Her father's face turned ashen. "What did the samurai say?"

"He started to speak, but his mother said it was her fault."

Her father's expression remained concerned. "It is good she spoke for you."

Aki forced a smile. "If that changes, he will spare me from Uncle." She looked around, then leaned in and lowered her voice. "Is he around?"

Father's sigh equaled hers. "He's out with Genta. He continues to ask about your work with the samurai."

Fear crawled up Aki's back and raised the hair on her neck. "What did you tell him?"

"The same as before. I told him you could be there a while."

Aki nodded. "Thank you."

"Realize, Aki, that I don't want you to be his daughter, either. I have dreams of you helping Genta and Shuji. The longer you work for the samurai, the better the chance that the other family will grow impatient."

Low shouts sounded through the walls, the last vestiges of the workday. Aki's tension ebbed. Father was a wise man. She turned to leave and help the business close then held her place.

"What is it, Aki?"

"I saw something at the samurai's house that surprised me."

"What was it?"

"While his mother was resting, something fell from her hand. I think it was a Kirishitan symbol, Father."

"Kirishitan?" Her father scratched his chin. "She's a Kirishitan?"

Aki licked her lips. "I think so."

"That's dangerous, I've heard."

"I thought it was a crime," Aki said.

"It's not against the law," her father said, "but it is concerning."

"What is concerning?" Uncle said, sliding open the door and stepping inside. Father maintained special slippers here for Uncle, as if he belonged. How much had he overheard?

"It is nothing, Uncle. I find my work is different. It is a change from selling cloth to serving a samurai."

"I see." Uncle ambled toward her. "It sounded like something was dangerous. Maybe I heard it wrong."

So you were listening outside the door, you frayed fabric scrap. "No, Uncle, it is a grand opportunity to learn new things. Once I am working here again, I will be better prepared to serve high-ranking customers."

"I see," her uncle said. "Working here? Once I adopt you"—his pause hung like a poorly-shelved box—"your responsibility will be to your new family."

Father stepped between them. "That was not our discussion. Aki was to be allowed to work here, as well."

Uncle tipped his head back like a zealous official. "Yes, but the samurai's delay has created concern with the other family. I had to allay them."

Just what she and Father were talking about earlier. He was listening to them. Aki longed to spit into her uncle's face the sour taste that flooded her mouth. "I serve at the samurai's need."

"Yes." Her uncle smiled as if counting his silver. "And while you work for him, as I have mentioned, learn everything you can. It will benefit us."

The tone in his voice let Aki know he wasn't finished, but it was not her place to question him.

"Unnh," her father grunted. "It sounds like you have more to say."

Thank you, Father.

Background noises in the shop subsided, as if the others had grown aware of the discussion and were listening from a distance.

"I do. It is how I can address the concerns of your future family. I need you to make a request of the samurai."

"What is it, Uncle? I do not see him every day."

"Interesting." His voice had increased its pitch. For once, she had surprised him.

"He works long hours, so it may be days before I can make a request."

"We have a few days, but you must press. I need to choose an evening in a week where you would be available to be home."

Aki's stomach roiled, but her father again stepped between them and waved her to silence. "For what purpose? As she said, she serves at the samurai's request."

"To assuage the family's concern," her uncle responded as he crossed his arms and eyed her. "The parents wish to meet my daughter and begin the process."

That was it. Aki's heart sank.

"She is not your daughter yet," her father said.

"That's the best news. I received word from my contacts in the city. The paperwork is complete. Aki, you're now officially my daughter."

It could not be. "Uncle, I am not ready."

"We are not ready," her father said.

"It had to be done," her uncle said. "Make the request to the samurai."

Officially his daughter. Aki held her tears inside.

If only Nishioji-sama had gotten angry enough today and killed me.

CHAPTER SEVENTEEN

Tomi looked again at the inlet, glancing back at the sun as it descended behind the mountains. It would be dark soon, but there'd been a full moon only three days ago, and ships were using the moonlight to their advantage.

Would that he could walk with Aki in the moonlight, but it had been three days since he had seen her.

At least the house she had visited was no longer of interest. He'd presented his information. Oeda had seen no more need to even patrol. Now they were here instead.

They'd been ordered to search every ship that came to the docks. All the ships had complied. Searches were a common security measure, and no one argued with men who had swords.

Three other ships lay anchored nearby. One of them, a fertilizer boat, fouled the air while it waited to fill its hold. Officials maintained a minimal watch on them, but they'd been searched. Nothing to do but wait for the next one.

"Yori, did you ask your brother?" Tomi asked.

"I did. He is already working."

"What's he doing?"

"Spending his evenings looking at temples he knows."

"He sounds eager."

"It is a change from his normal duties."

The thought of Yaesu at work without instructions bothered and amused Tomi. From what he knew of Yori's brother, the man was more an artist than a fighter.

"Will the smugglers use a typical vessel?" Yori asked, interrupting Tomi's thoughts.

"You expect a pirate ship to resemble one?" Tomi asked. "Until we know otherwise, we search everything. Did you check on Matsu?"

Yori nodded. Matsu had been here as much as possible for three days straight, checking every vessel. Clearing out the shrine meant the smugglers were searching for another storage place, but the ship might not know it was seen. Matsu needed to check.

The young man's brow furrowed. "What is it?" Tomi asked.

Yori took a deep breath. "A question. A personal one."

Strange he would ask. He'd never done so. "What do you want to know?"

"Why are you kind to that girl?"

"What girl?" Tomi knew what he meant, but he wanted to keep his feelings to himself. Since the afternoon when he'd questioned her about why she had been at that house, he had felt duplicitous. "Who?"

"The one in your employ. She talks to you as if she is of higher status than she is."

Tomi shook his head. "Is one's station the only measure of judgement?"

"Commoners are commoners," Yori countered.

"Yes, just like the regent, who was once a commoner."

Yori gave a sideways glance as Tomi's words had their effect. Yori was young, but the regent's meager upbringing was still a known quantity. "You should not speak so."

Tomi kept the rest to himself. Yori believed in status. He would not understand equality. A belief in equality was a Christian one. "I speak of how I was raised, Yori. My father came from nothing and rose to make my life possible. Because of him, I have my position today."

"The gods have blessed you. Is that why you treat the woman so?"

Back to her again. Tomi ignored him and turned toward the harbor. Another ship appeared in the distance, but it was hard to see anything in the diminished light. The wind whipped across the shore as if speeding the boat forward. "All can be blessed with bounty."

"Even the eta? Your revulsion to him was the same as mine. Do you deny it?"

Yori had him there. Undesirables were part of society, yet no one, including Tomi, wanted them. They should just do their job and leave people alone.

What would Iesu think? He'd never visited Japan, at least that Tomi knew. Iesu would greet the undesirable. It was not a step Tomi could take. "Yes, I shared your feelings toward the man."

Darkness descended further. Tomi directed Yori to scan the horizon. "Make sure the lanterns are lit," he said, hearing the murmur of voices from other ships still active.

"Then what?"

"We wait until it gets closer. If there's a strange flag, we wake Matsu."

Yori left to check the ships in the harbor, a way to waste time until the far one got closer. Matsu had described the flag flown by the smuggling ship, but he'd been unsure of the design. It could even fly a different flag or none now.

The ship approached the shore. "Rouse Matsu," Tomi called out to Yori.

Yori hurried away to follow Tomi's orders, returning a few minutes later with Matsu at his side.

"Another ship?" Matsu's look was one of amusement. "Was hoping to finish the dream I was having."

Matsu's joviality brought a smile to Tomi's face. "I think it will be worth it." He gestured to the harbor. "What do you think? Is it them?"

"Yes," Matsu said. "Looks like it. Don't see the flag it was flying, but this is the ship."

"Think it will stop here?"

"Has to. Too big to put ashore at the docks upriver. It must stop here."

The ship positioned itself next to a smaller vessel designed to carry cargo around Osaka and toward the capital. Men from the larger ship dropped from the bridge and tied the boat off.

"This is the time. Give the signal," Tomi said.

Yori turned and pointed toward a guy at a warehouse. He and three other men strode toward them.

Tomi and Yori headed toward the vessel, with Matsu and the other men behind them. Three men appeared at the boat's edge, glaring and daring them to approach before one of the two men who tied off the boat waved them back to their duties. Their minimal clothes were wet and spotted. Both men had small beards, though one man was bald and maintained his, while the other had unkempt hair and didn't shave.

"What's your business, Osamurai-sama?" one man asked, his tone an abrasive form of respect.

"Are you the captain?"

"He's on board. I'm Soru. I'm the second."

"Nishioji. We have orders to search the ship. We have reports of goods being smuggled by *kaizoku*."

The man expelled a frustrated breath. "We're not pirates. The only ones are in the south or on the other side of the country."

"Then a search will reveal nothing."

The man's lips thinned. Was he considering what to do? After a long pause, he stepped aside, allowing them to proceed.

Tomi boarded the ship, followed by the other men. "Those on board will stay in the center. We will search."

"What is this?" a thin man about Tomi's height shouted as he approached. "What are you doing?"

"You the captain?"

"Yes."

"We have orders from the constable to search all arriving ships."

The captain fumed but remained silent. Tomi directed his men to search the top deck. Likely nothing was stored here unless for ease of disposal. The men made quick work of it but found nothing.

Tomi looked at the captain. "You and your men stay here. Some of us are going below."

The captain gritted his teeth, more defiance than any other captain he'd seen in the previous three days, all of whom had acquiesced, hoping to move along. They were hiding something.

Yori reached for a door to go below. It opened hard, knocking him to the deck.

Three men rushed out, swords brandished, their feet slamming down as they took positions. The captain and his men spread out. Each carried a weapon hidden beneath his clothes.

Tomi drew his katana. The captain and one other man charged him. He pushed up and punched one in the gut, then shoved him backwards against the rail. He turned to face the captain, deflected a parry, then sliced his sword against the man's arm.

The captain fell back and jumped over the side. The cold splash of water stung Tomi's face. He longed to stop the man, but there was no time. He turned toward the others. Steel clanged and clanged again. Three men lay on the deck, two pirates and one officer.

We need men to surrender. We need to question them.

The first man charged again. Tomi deflected and struck the man in the face. He fell backwards over the rail. A splash followed a loud thud. Tomi checked the side. The man floated, unmoving. He would regret the man's death later.

Matsu and another officer each dispatched a pirate. The remaining men lost the will to fight. One jumped overboard and disappeared under the water. The rest sank to their knees, their swords clamoring on the wood. The pirates had outnumbered them, but the officers outclassed them.

Tomi ordered two of his men to search below for others. The men returned a few minutes later but had found no one. A movement caught Tomi's eye. He signaled the officers to keep the prisoners silent, then circled, and saw the captain with packages in hand. He had gotten back on board. Tomi crept toward him, watching his step as he did.

A cry erupted, followed by a gurgling sound. The captain whirled about, glared at Tomi, and turned to flee. Tomi knocked him to the deck, scattering packages, and wrapped the man's arm behind his back.

"Unnh," the man groaned.

"Silence," Tomi thundered.

Tomi unwrapped a package with his free hand.

Jade.

Tomi forced the man to his feet then took him to join the rest of the prisoners. He shoved him to his knees. His wet clothes clung to his body.

A prisoner lay unmoving on the deck, blood pooling from his neck.

"Did you do that?" he asked Matsu.

"Yori, but I agreed."

Tomi sighed. Another unavoidable death.

"Talk," Tomi barked, bringing his sword under the captain's chin. "Who do you work for?"

The man coughed and breathed heavily as a slow smile emerged from his lips.

A smile?

He brought his hands up under his chin, snapped his

wrist, then drew a small dagger.

Tomi lunged to knock it away.

Too late. The captain plunged the dagger into his own throat.

"No!" Tomi screamed.

The captain's eyes rolled back in his head. Tomi gulped hard. The captain collapsed and thudded onto the deck. The man who could tell them everything would now yield nothing. They were getting nowhere.

No, they had gotten somewhere. They had the jade. They had the ship. They would search it until they found something.

They questioned those remaining but learned nothing. The prisoners were hired men working for money. All they knew was that they were transporting cargo.

Tomi ordered them taken to jail, leaving one remaining officer, Arai, who guarded the jade. He surveyed the dead. His belly knotted in regret.

"It's a shame we could not get answers," Yori said. "It would have helped."

"Would have been hard for anyone," Matsu added as he pointed to captain's body. "A failed shinobi, the way he produced a knife."

Tomi scanned the men lying on the deck. The officer who died would need to be honored. Oeda would see to it. "The three of us will go below again to check."

They signaled Arai to wait for them and then headed below and split up. Sleeping quarters appeared sparse with nothing of note: small weapons and a few extra clothes. Tomi tapped the walls. Empty.

Tomi exited the room and found Matsu waiting for him. "Anything?"

Matsu nodded. "Sizable amount of silk thread in cargo, along with food. Oeda will be pleased. Where's Yori?"

The young samurai emerged. "Much to see in the captain's room. Come—"

A scuffle and muffled screams sounded from above.

The sound slapped Tomi with the truth. He hadn't seen Soru, the second, among the dead.

The three of them rushed to the top. Soru stood behind Arai, a garrote twisted around the officer's neck. Tomi leapt forward and shoved the men apart, knocking Soru to the deck. The man reached for a weapon.

Tomi drew his sword.

Soru threw away his dagger.

"Nice work," Matsu said. "I thought he was dead."

"I did, too," Tomi said, his breaths coming out in a relieved tone. "How is Arai?"

Yori ripped shards from Arai's clothes and used it to bandage his wounds. "He is injured, but he will recover."

"Who are you working for?" Tomi demanded. "Tell us. Now."

The man spat at him and then laughed, coughing as he did so. "Myself."

Yori slapped him. "Who are you working for? Answer him!"

The man lurched forward. Tomi covered the hilts of his swords.

Instead, the man grabbed the beads tucked into Tomi's belt. His rosary.

The man held it up, his face defiant. "Kirishitan." He spat on it and then threw it on the deck.

Matsu stepped forward and pointed his sword at Soru.

Tomi reached down and picked up his rosary, rubbing it against his clothes. He sighed, relieved the man hadn't destroyed it.

"Everything fine?" Matsu asked.

Arai groaned. Tomi glanced at the officer. He was now sitting up but showed pain. Yori supported him and helped him slide toward a wall.

A shuffle on the wood grabbed Tomi's attention.

Soru slipped under Matsu's blade and grabbed his

knife. He broke toward the side then paused at the rail. "See you in hell."

He stuck the blade in his mouth and then dived over the side.

The crash against the dock told the story.

"Sorry," Matsu said, "was concerned about Arai. Distracted me."

Tomi looked over the rail, though he realized what he would find. Soru's body lay still.

"Two took their own lives rather than talk."

Water lapped at the side of the boat, the only sound breaking the now silent dock. This Soru knew the difference between rosary and juzu beads. Few would. The strands were similar, yet he recognized which beads Tomi carried. Or the man noticed the sun symbol on the sword guard and recognized its association with the padres. Either one meant something. Tomi wished he knew what.

Another group who hated Christians. It was Himeji all over again. They now had proof of such a group in Osaka, and that the group was involved with silk smugglers. Unfortunately, no one was left to answer questions.

No. The one with a beard and his men knew the answers. Tomi had to find them.

"These men were good," Tomi said. "We must be careful. If only we had more information about them."

"We may," Yori said. Yori looked at Arai, who waved him off to say he was fine. He strode toward Tomi and Matsu. "I found some letters below."

A jolt of energy surged in Tomi's frame. "We'll take them to Oeda today."

Maybe they had a chance.

"Lord Eijiro," Riku called out, seeing the man who had just entered. "I heard you were coming. Welcome to Osaka."

"Spare me your obsequiousness. What happened to the

jade shipment and the silk threads with it?"

Riku swallowed hard. Lord Eijiro oversaw operations throughout the country and would one day rule. If Riku didn't complete his duties, he wouldn't be around to profit from it. A queasy feeling washed through his stomach. Wakizashi stood nearby and would have given him a second scar on his cheek, but the look on his face suggested he was bubbling like a sulfur pool at a hot spring. "The ship was boarded. After issues with our last shipment, we tried an upriver port where I had associates who could deliver our goods. The police learned of it."

"You didn't assist?" Eijiro directed toward Riku.

"I arrived too late. I'm a merchant and would not have been much help."

"That shipment was important. Who was there?"

Riku tilted his head toward the man on his right, a sailor on the ship who had escaped by jumping overboard. Riku didn't know his name but had seen him swim away. The man related the details to Lord Eijiro, who maintained a calm demeanor.

"Is there anything else?" Lord Eijiro asked.

"Yes, my lord. Someone called Nishioji was in charge. The captain and the second are dead."

"Nishioji?" Wakizashi said, more an expectoration than a question. "That foul Kirishitan again?"

"They haunt like demons," Lord Eijiro commented.

Riku stared at the man. "You know him, as well, Lord Eijiro?"

"I know of him from his actions in Himeji. Wakizashi knows him from battle. We owe him for his insolence. Why do you know him?"

Riku eyed the sailor and Wakizashi ordered the man to wait for him outside. From there, Lord Eijiro ordered Riku to continue.

"My adopted daughter works for him while his mother's caregiver is away."

"Your adopted daughter?"

Riku lowered his gaze under Lord Eijiro's stare. "Wakizashi's plan to expand our money. I adopted my niece and will marry her to another family with opportunities in the capital. They are connected to the guild in Gion. It will be beneficial for operations. The wedding will take place as soon as the caregiver returns."

Lord Eijiro nodded an approving smile. "I see. Does she know about Nishioji's foreign faith?"

"She does not know I know. I heard her tell my brother that his mother dropped a cross."

"Discuss it with her," Lord Eijiro said. "None of my associates here are women. She could be valuable."

"The caregiver looks after her own daughter, who just gave birth. Once she returns, it will be done."

Lord Eijiro stiffened. Riku froze. He had angered him. Lord Eijiro was quick. Riku had seen it before. He could dispatch a man before the man could move. So could Wakizashi. Lord Eijiro's smile made him resemble a smug teacher imparting knowledge. "How little you understand them. Every opportunity to add another believer is worth their time. If your daughter expressed an interest, this Nishioji would face ten men on his own if it meant adding another believer to their group. You must start now."

"Yes, my lord," Riku said, relieved to still be standing. "I will do what you command."

"Good, your daughter must become an asset. It is her duty."

"Yes, sir."

Lord Eijiro did not acknowledge the response. "Wakizashi," he barked.

"Yes, Lord Eijiro."

"You have orders, as well. Silence any pirates in jail. Have *Tantō* take care of it before they can tell what they know about our operation. He will not be recognized."

"All of them?"

"The Captain and Soru were trained warriors and understood the need to die. Their loss is deeply felt. The rest are unimportant."

"Yes, my lord," Wakizashi said. "It will be done."

"One more thing, Wakizashi," Lord Eijiro said as Wakizashi and Riku waited for the pronouncement. "Find other work for the sailor outside. Keep him away from the dock."

"Yes, Lord Eijiro."

"Riku." The man uttered his name with the sharpness of a blade. "You have questions."

Riku remembered the one time he'd met Tantō. The thin, coarse man maintained an odd grin throughout, his eyes flashing death. He hoped never to look into his eyes again. "None."

"Good," Lord Eijiro said. "Do not fail me, else Wakizashi will hide your body next. To both of you, the future of this nation is at stake."

Riku kept his gaze down. He had heard that tone before. To look at him would be perceived as a challenge.

His life depended on his obedience.

CHAPTER EIGHTEEN

"Nishioji-sama?" Aki said as she opened the door, breathing in the wintry air before realizing her mouth gaped open.

"Aki, you are awake. Good." His steady tone was softer than she had ever him speak.

She bowed, her nerves racing like a waterfall down her spine. *Why is he here? Has something happened? Is the caretaker already back*? "I am surprised to see you. Your work has kept you occupied."

"We have been busy at one dock. However, we found the people we were looking for yesterday. I came as I need to see you."

He needs to see me? Something must be wrong. "Would you come in for tea?"

He pressed his lips together. "We'll have tea at my house. My father must leave early today. He will not be waiting. Can you leave now?"

"I am at your service."

She bade her parents goodbye, grateful that Uncle was not around to remind her of her promise to request a night to meet the man he had arranged for her to marry. She would address it today.

The morning walk was warmer than it had been the last

few days, and the city was awake in response. Street cleaners were out early, taking advantage of the weather but also cleaning up after last night's rain. She maintained her respectful distance but stayed close to hear him.

"It has been a few days," the samurai said, looking back as they neared his district. "How have you been?"

How had she been? Was he really asking about her? "Your mother is stronger since her injury. Yesterday, she mentioned wanting to walk around today. Did she tell you?"

A puzzled look crossed his face. "She said the two of you worked on writing to allow her to rest her ankle. If the weather warms, she wants to sit outside. She enjoys listening to birds."

"She has told me, Nishioji-sama, but I did not think I would be in your service long enough to get that warm. Your mother is a kind woman. I enjoy my time with her."

"She says the same," Nishioji said, "but I was asking about you."

"I am well. There is much going on with my family. It would not interest you."

The samurai's neighborhood came into view, and Nishioji-sama waved her closer. She followed his order but did her best to show deference.

The samurai's father appeared at the door. She saw him break a small smile before returning to a serious expression.

"*Chichiue*," Nishioji-sama called out. She could not recall hearing the samurai address his own father before. He used the same term she did for her father. Nothing formal. "You're still here," he continued. "Why haven't you left?"

His father's mouth opened, and he rubbed the back of his neck. "Today only I'm late. It's the new place. We've been delayed again. Would have told you before, but you've been busy. The rice harvest may be months away, but we need to move soon."

"A new place for sake?" Aki asked.

"Yes, an abandoned temple. Local officials used it for meetings after Nobunaga defeated the monks. It's close to the new rice storage areas."

Aki thought about it. "I know that place. Not well."

The father nodded in an assuring way that reminded her of her own father. "Yes, it's perfect. Nobunaga ordered the monks moved both across the river and near Shitennōji, and the place avoided being razed by carpenters. However, we still cannot get ownership. The magistrate has yet to approve it. There must be some money involved." He nodded to Nishioji. "Can you not assist? The owner would give you a barrel of sake."

"I would be no help."

"I can still hope. Your mother is sleeping. She asked that you wake her."

Nishioji-sama grunted. He would not disappoint his mother. His father drew the belt around his outer garment taut and then headed toward the main road.

"Your father sounds happy," Aki said as she watched him.

"The family who runs the sake business treats him well. We were fortunate when he found the job."

The wind whipped through the street. Nishioji-sama pointed at the door. Aki stepped aside to allow him to go first. She then entered and shut the door behind them. Aki enjoyed the warmth of the fire crackling on the hearth.

He removed his shoes and stepped from the genkan to the main room then turned and held her gaze. Her pulse raced. Something was on his mind. "I will be busy for the next few days. I need you to be here as early as light allows. The same at the end of the day."

"I will," she said, bowing as she did, her uncle's words, her promise coming to mind. "I must, for my family's sake, beg one request."

He stiffened. "What is it?" he asked in a flat tone.

She took a deep breath. "My family requests I be

allowed one day next week to not work late."

His cheeks flushed red. "What is the reason?"

Her gut sank. She often imagined more time with Nishioji-sama. Telling him would end those thoughts. "My uncle has adopted me as he has no children. He plans to marry me off to have a son to inherit the business. He wishes me to meet the family he has arranged."

His shoulders slumped, and his smile disappeared into a tight-lipped blank stare. "That'll be fine. Inform my mother. Don't tell her why."

"I will say nothing. May I ask why?"

"She enjoys your company. After her regular caregiver returns, she hoped you would come by." He emitted a garbled chuckle. Was he nervous? "For calligraphy lessons. She fears you won't have time."

Her first official student. For so long she had wanted to teach like her sisters. Her family would be proud. "I will arrange it when the time comes."

"Good," he said. The color returned to his cheeks.

A door slid open, and his mother stepped out, her walk buoyant. There was no limp.

"Father said you were sleeping."

"I pretended so he would leave." She sighed. "He worries too much. I am much better. The best I've been in days. Would you pour some water for me?"

"Yes," Aki said. She grabbed a nearby tray and brought it to the hearth then filled a teacup and presented it to the woman. She reached out her hand.

The cross Aki had seen before fell to the floor.

"Oh my," his mother said. She reached for the cross and brought it to her lap, hiding it under the folds of a blanket.

Aki tried to hide her gaze as if she had seen nothing.

Nishioji-sama's approach said that wouldn't work.

"Mother, I must leave. Aki, outside," he uttered, knowing she would obey without looking back.

"Close the door," he said.

A breeze lighter than before blew through the street, but it did not match the look in the samurai's eyes. His face grew stern, like the day she first met him. He paced as if giving a lecture. "I know you saw it."

She let out a breath. "Is it Kirishitan?"

"Yes, my family is Kirishitan. Mention it to no one. Do you understand?"

"Yes, sir." Aki quivered in place. She had already told her father. Her uncle had overheard. "What shall I say to your mother?"

"It will give her more things to chat about with you. She doesn't have to hide it."

"Is this religion not banned?"

"Yes and no. We will talk more. For now, say nothing to anyone."

"Yes." She watched him leave. Her heart pounded in her throat.

The samurai's mother wanted to chat. Aki had told him of her uncle's plans.

She was now keeping secrets from his family and her own.

Tomi walked the short distance to Matsu's house, the conversation with Aki still bouncing in his head.

Matsu's wide eyes told Tomi what he was thinking. "Unexpected."

"I didn't want to talk at work."

"Never seen you look more in need of my *deities,* as you call them."

Tomi pressed his lips tight. Matsu's jokes sometimes stirred frustration, but Tomi knew Matsu was trying to make him laugh. "You ready to leave?"

Matsu barked at his lone servant and then closed the door behind him. "Always. What happened?"

"Once we get on the way."

They passed the street captain and headed into the business district. Tomi pointed to the less traveled alleys between principal streets and used for some deliveries and personal home entrances. *Fewer people to overhear.*

"What happened?" Matsu asked.

"Aki knows about my faith."

A half-dressed man stepped outside. His eyes widened when he noticed Tomi and Matsu and hurried back in. Just as Tomi expected. Privacy.

"How?" Matsu asked.

"My mother dropped her cross in front of her."

"Wash it in water and perform a prayer ritual."

"What?"

"Heard some rumors about your practices."

Tomi shook his head. "We do nothing like that."

"What did you say to her?"

"I told her to say nothing and that we would talk later.

Matsu patted him on the shoulder. "She won't say a word."

They turned left and headed back toward the Justice Building, which was now in the distance. The main street was congested with construction workers carrying supplies through the streets. Tomi pointed toward another alley.

"Your morning was busy," Matsu said, almost laughing at Tomi as he did. "What else happened?"

They turned right down another street. "Aki is getting married."

The smile on Matsu's face disappeared. "Sorry. Why?"

Tomi explained about the adoption and Aki's scheduled meeting with her future family. Matsu's dry wit remained silent until the end.

Then he rolled his eyes. "The woman you love is promised to someone else, and now knows about your faith. Hardly worrisome."

"I never said I loved her."

"Not in words."

Tomi paused. "You're right."

They reached the Justice Building. Tomi surveyed the nearby crowd at the Administration Building, their indistinct murmurs reaching his ears.

"What now?" Matsu asked.

"A favor my father asked. The sake company has been trying to expand and take over a larger building, but the transfer is not yet approved. He asked if I could do something. Offered a barrel of sake for my efforts."

"Sounds worthwhile," Matsu said. "Get Yori started."

"This is not for your amusement."

Matsu laughed. "Trying to cheer your mood. Where is it?"

Tomi explained the location.

"Know it well. I have seen *kawasemi*, kingfishers, over there."

"You should have been my mother's son. Enough with the birds." He shook his head. "Kingfishers. Really?"

"It—"

"Can we talk about something else?"

Matsu smiled. "No problem. Should ask Yori. If it's a former temple, it should be searched for jade.

As if in response, the young samurai rushed toward them. "Oeda wants to see us."

The three of them entered the building. The smell of smoke from the hearth produced a pungent aroma, as if someone had used too much charcoal and then tried to dampen it. They pivoted and sped toward Oeda's office.

They found him pacing as if they had made him wait. Papers covered his normally organized desk. Something had gone wrong.

"What is it, Oeda-sama?" Tomi asked.

"They are dead. The prisoners are dead."

Tomi's mouth dropped open. "The men from the boat yesterday? What happened?"

"We don't know." Oeda glanced at the ceiling as if searching for an answer. "They died during the night."

"How were they murdered?" Tomi asked.

"Likely poison." Oeda shook his head. "There was no sign of struggle."

"These men were pirates," Yori said. "They fought well but knew nothing. Who would kill them?"

"I don't think they all were pirates." Tomi paused. "Only a few fought well. We defeated most of them without effort.

"I agree," Matsu said. "Some of them were awkward. Great numbers can sometimes hide great incompetence."

"There's one more thing." Tomi recalled the man who spat on his rosary and grabbed it, gripping the cross between his thumb and forefinger. "One of them knew these are not juzu beads without seeing the cross on the end. Only a devoted monk would know the difference without a cross."

"Those that were pirates may have spent time in Nagasaki," Matsu said. "Maybe they have seen them."

"Or maybe the one on board saw my sword guard," Tomi said. "The sun image would be known in Nagasaki."

"He likely did it to insult you," Oeda said.

General murmurs sounded from outside. Oeda nodded toward the open door, a small sliver of space. Yori closed it, sending quick footsteps away. Was someone listening? It would explain much.

"Another thing," Tomi said, lowering his voice. "What about the jade thrown off of the boat?"

Oeda hesitated. Was he holding back? Worry danced on Tomi's spine. "We found only a couple of items. Nothing we can identify, but it is jade. We'll search more today. We also still need Yori's list."

"I will inquire again today," Yori said.

"Has this building been searched?" Tomi asked.

Oeda inhaled sharply. "Not yet. I will set Arai to the task today. He is still recovering from his injuries, but he can do that."

"What about the letters Yori found yesterday?"

Oeda pointed to his desk. "They are there. Yesterday, other duties called. I glanced at them but could not see their importance. Then I got the news of the death of the prisoners. You can review them yourself later."

"I understand," Tomi said.

"What now?" Matsu asked.

"We ask more questions at the prison. Someone must know something." He stared at Tomi. "You and Matsubara go. Be quick."

"What about Yori?"

"I want him with me. We'll take the jade. We will show it to the monks across the river at Honganji. Maybe they will have a suggestion."

Tomi and Matsu left the office and headed toward the prison. He hoped the visit would be fruitful and quick.

He wanted to return home early and discuss the cross with Aki.

"Those are excellent," Aki said, examining the latest efforts of Nishioji-sama's mother. The woman's hands shook, despite her efforts to be steady. Earlier attempts had been one stroke at a time. Then she tried to do characters all at once.

When the woman yawned, Aki peeked at the clock, which burned into the next hour. "Are you tired?"

"Yes, I need some rest."

Aki helped her to the room where she slept and then went to get her some water. Was this the time to keep her promise to Nishioji-sama and tell his mother about leaving early next week?

When Aki set the tray next to the tired woman, she reached out for the cup.

The cross fell out of her sleeve and hit the floor.

The woman's face grew red.

Aki picked it up and placed it in the woman's hand. Chills danced in her fingertips. "Here you are."

The mother nodded, wrapping the chain around her right hand until she held the cross itself in her palm. She gazed at Aki. "Does this make you nervous? I cannot tell."

Aki's throat ran dry. She tried to speak, but nothing came out.

"It's fine, child," the woman said. "There is nothing to be afraid of."

Aki swallowed hard. "I am not afraid."

"Then what is it?"

"Nishioji-sama mentioned I should ask you about the cross."

"Nishioji-sama?" She smiled at Aki. "I know you feel you must use that, but it sounds too formal when I hear it."

"His status is much higher than mine. Even when I think about him, it is Nishioji-sama."

The woman laughed in a quiet tone. "That is too much. You should think 'Nishioji'. That is sufficient. For me, his name is Tsuneomi. His friends call him 'Tomi.' Much less formal."

She shook her head. "He is of higher status."

"As are his friends, but samurai still laugh, especially Matsu. I like him. He has a few vices, but Tsuneomi needs friends like him."

Aki nodded. She had never viewed Nishioji-sama—Nishioji—like this. "I will think as you say."

"Sit," the woman continued. "Do you have questions?"

Questions. Aki focused on the smoldering scent of sandalwood. "Did I miss something?"

The woman extended her open hand, showing where Aki should sit. "I meant questions on the cross."

"Nishioji-sa..., your son, said I should chat with you about it."

"He did? Do you wish to discuss it?"

"I—"

"Sit."

Her tone was now a polite command. Aki obeyed, wondering what she would say. She often looked haggard. Now, her eyes shone like the stars, as if she had reason to speak. "This is special to you. I see it in your face."

She flashed an open smile. "That's true. I've not been a follower long, but it means much to me."

"How did you learn about it?"

"Tsuneomi taught me about it three years ago. He went to Kyushu to fight for the regent and came back with the faith. So odd that it happened."

Aki wet her lips. "Why odd?"

"It was three years ago that the regent banned the missionaries. Wild accusations, but Tsuneomi listened to the words of a few prominent daimyo and became a believer."

"But the ban?"

"He could not deny how his heart felt. A high-ranking samurai's wife here in Osaka did the same. The faith changed Tomi. It changes all."

"And you, too?"

"I find comfort in it, especially with my sickness. My husband also believes."

Her family took great care of her. Nishioji had only mentioned his mother had been ill. Aki had seen the skin rashes. Was there more? "You have a difficult burden."

"Tsuneomi is my greatest joy. He was a bully as a boy but has grown into a good man. His father's prowess as a lowly *ashigaru,* a foot soldier in battle, made it possible for Tomi to achieve his status."

The woman pointed toward the sandalwood. Aki carefully added more. Nishioji a bully? She could not imagine it. "Why was he that way?" she asked.

"He thought he had to prove himself. He bullied a boy named Nobuhiro." She paused. "Nobuhiro's brothers took revenge."

Aki wondered what lesson that could be, but it was not her place. The more she learned, the more she was impressed.

"Do you have other questions?"

Aki glanced at the cross in the woman's hand. What to ask?

Was there a way to be faithful without lying?

CHAPTER NINETEEN

Tomi stared at the door of Aki's home. It was earlier than yesterday when he'd surprised her pre-dawn.

He'd hoped to get home in time and talk with her more. Work had prevented that. Oeda and Yori had returned from the monk village. They'd found nothing. Meeting Aki early in the morning was his only chance to talk.

The lasting bite of the night seeped into the gaped areas of his garments. It was not a raid, but he still trembled at the door. Why did he hesitate?

Something about Aki made him nervous.

The hair rose on the back of his neck. Was someone watching him? He scanned for signs of movement. There was little at this early hour. The moon, a little less than full, lit the area, leaving nowhere to hide. *Must be my own nervousness.*

Tomi took a deep breath and raised his hand to ring the bell.

The door opened, revealing the face of Aki's oldest brother. *Genta,* if he recalled correctly.

"Osamurai-sama?" The man's voice trembled as he bowed.

Tomi bit his lip. Aki working for him had done little to

change Genta's fear of Tomi's status. "Your sister. I need to speak with her."

"Yes, sir." He opened the door and indicated the genkan. "Please enter. Can I get you something?"

"Unnecessary. Fetch Aki. I'll wait here."

Tomi stepped through the door and closed it behind him while the older brother headed to the left. A light from the right cast a glow on the wood floor loaded with stacks of cloths and a mixture of lacquer dishes. Hurried footsteps soon made him smile.

"Nishioji-sama," Aki said, rushing forward. "My brother said you needed me."

Her hair was held by a clip that provided both a rough yet fresh look. *Not a hint of the facial covering that some women like. None needed.*

"I need you to come immediately. My mother had a fitful night."

Aki's head bobbed. "I will leave now."

"I'll escort you there. It's not safe to travel the streets alone at this hour."

"You are busy, Nishioji-sama." She bowed. "Genta can escort me. We will make haste."

"You will?"

"You have given me an order. I will follow it."

Tomi bit back a smile. One story the padres told arose in his head. The soldier with a servant. Iesu did not need to go, only give the order. Tomi always liked that story. That soldier could have been Japanese. He trusted the word of Iesu because he believed in it.

Did Aki follow his order because of his status? Or did she follow it because she cared for his mother? "I am grateful," Tomi said.

Tomi left, taking one last glance at Aki before he did. The young woman's presence calmed his mother. Him, too. It would have made her suspicious if he had stayed. He would find another time. Maybe return early tonight.

Matsu would chide him if he mentioned it. Nobuhiro would listen, but he was in Himeji.

How would Nobuhiro feel about his old bully asking for his advice?

He hoped to know soon.

Aki stepped outside to enjoy a morning break. The samurai's father had met her when she arrived. She had not known what to expect when Nishioji had expressed his concern but had only found her unable to relax. When exhaustion finally overcame her, she fell asleep. Aki left the door ajar in case the woman awakened and needed her.

"Are you Aki?" a young male voice called out.

Aki turned to see a boy of eight or nine stacking twigs and branches. He wore a headband and moved like a squirrel, darting around like a game but with purpose. "Yes, what's your name?"

The boy's face turned red. Was he embarrassed to talk with her? "Ruri."

Ruri. Unusual for a boy, but it suited him. "Why are you here?"

"My father visits once a week to clear the samurai's yard."

Aki nodded. The man had come by twice before, and Nishioji's mother had mentioned it. "Where's your father?"

"At the doctor. I am here in his place."

The boy bounced on his toes and looked around the yard. He must be eager to get started. "Your father is a hard-working gardener."

"He is not a gardener. He helps the samurai when he can."

Not a gardener? What commitment could the family have? Had Nishioji done them a service and this was how they repaid his kindness? "Come here, Ruri."

The boy hustled to her. "Yes."

"You are here to help your father. What does he do?"

"My family has a *ryokan*. Guests stay every night."

"Why does he come each week?"

"The samurai treats us well."

Good to the child's parents. "I see. Like you are good to your parents. You help your father when he needs you."

The boy blushed again. "I must finish. I have chores at home. My older brother and sister need me."

"I will leave you to it."

The boy smiled and resumed his activities. Aki craned her head to listen inside, but she heard nothing to suggest that the woman was awake. A strong wind whipped through the yard. For once, she did not feel it. Time to check on the woman, just in case. She stepped inside and closed the door.

Tomi cursed his misfortune.

He'd wasted the morning. They'd finally reviewed the letters Yori had found on board the ship and found nothing important. There was only a reference to a mysterious Iri, the same woman Uji had mentioned in his message.

A woman's first name. No last name. No hint of who she was, except that she was hiding.

Tomi would rest at home but then go back tonight. Fortunately, his father could watch his mother.

The early return home offered Tomi a chance to stop by the mission and say hello to the padre.

His mood cheered as he saw Alvares outside working on the grounds. The white dog lapped at his heels. Hisa worked on the side of the building. Kazu was nowhere in sight. Tomi approached Alvares with a lightness in his step,

The man's haggard expression said all was not well.

"Padre-sama, you're ill," Tomi said, trying to examine the holy man's eyes. "What is wrong?"

The man stopped and stood straight. Foreigners, in general, were taller than Tomi's countryman. Tomi was one of the few who could look them in the eye. "We lost Yamagawa last night. Very sudden. No one knew he was sick."

Thoughts raced through Tomi's mind, but he struggled about what to say. "When did you find out?"

"This morning. One of his children brought us the news."

"Did you see him?"

"I did, Tomasu-sama," Hisa's voice called out. "I saw him last night. Very sad."

"What happened?"

"I do not know. I went to bring him the blessed host and express my hope he would return to Mass soon."

"I will miss Yamagawa," Tomi said. "He had an easy manner."

"Was he ill when you were there?" Tomi asked, turning back to Hisa.

"No, his health was good. We prayed together before I left."

Tomi sighed. "I can't believe it."

"Neither can I," the padre said. "I visited the family this morning to offer my prayers for them and for Yamagawa's soul. At least he found God before he died."

"Tomasu-sama," Hisa said, "will you help me on this? My background is not yours. Your presence will soothe his parents."

"I'll do that, though I must leave. Tomorrow?"

"You're coming to services then?" Alvares asked.

Aki's image raced through his mind. He would like to bring her with him. She would be welcome. All were, but he didn't know how she would respond.

"I'll be here."

Wakizashi eyed his associate like a master training a young samurai.

"So, Tantō? Your idea worked?"

"Yes, the need these fools have for their *bread* makes them easy to find."

"Is this Yamagawa dead?"

"Yes, his refusal to obey the regent's edict is now his downfall. There are others to be found. I could use assistance."

Wakizashi shook his head. "We've lost several associates. The few we have left must search for the jade tossed overboard."

"Do the police still watch the water? I can dive for the jade."

Wakizashi crossed his arms and smiled. "Your persistence gives me hope."

CHAPTER TWENTY

"Nishioji-sama, you are home early," Aki said.

"It is brief. I must return." He paused. "Aki, come with me."

Nishioji's serious tone weighed on her like a load of heavy fabrics. Was he upset with her?

No. This must be about the cross.

They went out to the back area. A bluster filled the air, but extra walls and an extended roof protected them from the wind and sun. A garden of pebbles covered the patch, with smoothing tools set nearby. The garden often calmed Aki. Today, she tensed at its sight and longed to run.

The samurai pointed toward the side where two chairs lay next to the wall. "Sit," he said.

Aki grabbed the chairs, setting one for him and then one for herself. Nishioji seated himself, but Aki hesitated. She was not his equal.

"Sit," he repeated as a command.

A tingle ran up her spine. How could she relax around this man? She wiped her mouth, feeling tremors in her lower jaw. "Y-y-yes, sir."

The samurai chuckled. "Are you nervous? Have you done something wrong?"

She shook her head. Nothing. *Except twice seen the cross your mother carries and now know you are a Kirishitan.* "Has my service been adequate?"

"If your service was inadequate, I wouldn't be asking you to sit. I want to talk with you."

Aki took a deep breath. Her nerves prickled like an assault of needles. "I am ready, Nishioji-sama."

"The cross." He hesitated. "Did you discuss it with my mother?"

She glanced down to avoid looking at him. "Yes. Yesterday. She told me a few things. I asked about the ban."

He sighed. It must be a difficult question. "The regent told the missionaries to leave. He destroyed many places throughout the country, but others remain."

"What happened here?"

Again, he hesitated. This faith affected him. "We lost a church, a house, and a place for training padres."

"Was that everything here?"

"A mission survives, and there is a new place to live across the street from it. There are other places in Osaka, as well. These are supporters who welcome our faith."

"Does your mother visit the mission?"

"Her illness limits her, but the padre visits here."

Visit? Like the Buddhist priests? "They sound honorable, Nishioji-sama."

The samurai smiled, then his somber face returned. "They are, but you must not talk about what happens here. The law is the law. Faith is faith. We continue as we are, but we must keep everything private. That is your duty as a servant in this house."

Aki knelt and bowed. "I will follow your instructions."

"Do you have questions, Aki?"

Did she have a question? Ever since meeting the samurai, her first thought was how handsome a man he was, the most handsome she had ever seen. His gaze made her quiver. "Your family all follow this religion?"

The samurai paused.

Her hands shook again. She should not have said anything.

"Yes," he finally answered. "I am a Kirishitan. Does this trouble you?"

"No, sir. Do I look troubled?"

"You're trembling."

"I did not know I was." Of course she was. This was information her uncle wanted to hear. Why does it matter to him?

"Is there anything else?"

She should change the subject from this faith. "Your mother told me about you. Your childhood. She said you were a bully, but that you learned."

Nishioji's face turned red. She had never imagined a samurai could be embarrassed. He rubbed the scar on his cheek with his finger. What caused it? Her uncle had cut his face. Would that leave a scar?

"It is a long story," he replied.

"Is that how you got the scar?"

"Why do you ask?"

"My uncle cut his cheek recently. He said it was an accident, but it was deep. I asked him about it while I cleaned it, but he did not want to talk about it. I wondered if he would have a scar, too."

He paused. "If I meet your uncle, I'll look at it."

"How about yours?"

He sighed. "Another time."

A stiff breeze blew, and he motioned toward the door. "We should go inside. You need to stay late today. I have a lot of work. When my father returns, please assist him with whatever he needs."

"Yes, sir. I will." Changing the topic worked. If he said more, Uncle would want to know more. The challenge was to keep his words to herself.

From uncle.

"Her uncle has a deep scar?" Matsu asked Tomi. "Important? Why?"

"You know how I got this scar?"

Matsu nodded. "Told me. Several times. Tell Yori."

"He's with his brother."

"My luck," Matsu said. "Why again now?"

"I got this from a sword. It was deep and took a long time to heal.

"I remember. Nobuhiro's brother, Toshi, gave it to you. Your point."

"Aki said her uncle had a deep cut," Tomi replied

"*Aki?*" Matsubara's expression lightened. "You called her Aki again."

"That's her name."

"Yes, but your tone is tender."

Tomi grunted. "I'll ignore that. We need to discuss her uncle. Twice we've been led to this family but found nothing. We know Aki's family is innocent. Maybe her uncle isn't."

"Basing this all on a scar you haven't seen?"

"Just suspicious.

"Suspicious?" Matsu turned pensive. "Have Yori follow."

"He has much going on with the list and the jade."

"His brother."

"He's helping Yori. You trust Arai?"

"Yes."

"We'll get Arai to work with Yori."

Matsu nodded. "Agreed."

It had been a long day.

Aki wiped her hands across her eyes again. Darkness descended quickly, but the lanterns made it easy to see the way. Passersby made the evening busy. Nighttime sellers of warm food called out their tunes. Not much to fear in the darkness.

She stifled a yawn and then focused on the road. She typically was not this tired, but talking with Nishioji had left her drained.

This faith was important to him and his family. It touched them in a way she had not seen elsewhere. *What is its power? Am I interested in it, or am I just interested in Nishioji?*

The samurai was handsome. How many women likely wished they—

A shove from behind drove her forward. She tried to balance but hit the ground. Her face smashed into the dirt. *Who did it?*

Aki looked up. A group of drunks argued with two palanquin carriers. They must have bumped into her. The palanquin continued, and the drunks did not care. *People are consumed with themselves or their work.* She was nothing to them.

Aki pushed herself up but slipped and fell. Her skin tingled as she glanced around. She was tired. Had anyone even seen her fall?

Movement from the right entered her sight and approached her.

The undesirable?

The man moved slowly, nodding his head in a bow of respect with a smile. For as long as Aki could remember, he'd watched her life, as if he knew when she needed help. Yet what help could he offer without touching her?

"Remove yourself, scum."

A surge pulsed through Aki at the sound of that voice. It provided the strength to rise that her previous effort lacked. It brought her the energy to stand.

"I said remove yourself," Yori-sama said. "Your stench is not welcome nor wanted."

The man trembled, his fright obvious as he sank to his knees, his forehead touching the ground in abject servitude.

He then rose and slunk away. To watch Yori-sama was to believe the man had committed some kind of crime.

Other groups stepped aside as they acknowledged the young samurai's presence, but he did not acknowledge them. Instead, he strode toward her.

Aki bowed as her hands and knees trembled, not in fear of his actions but at his likely thoughts of her. "You were going to let him help you. What were you thinking?"

Aki quavered. "He approached only a little. I would not have let him nearer."

"You serve Nishioji-sama. You cannot allow yourself to be soiled by an eta."

"I understand." She glanced askew at the young man, afraid to look at him.

"Good. Don't let it happen again."

"Is there anything you need, Osamurai-sama?"

He eyed her with curiosity. "Why would you ask?"

"You were here when I fell."

"I…don't have to explain my actions to you. Is that clear?"

"Yes."

"Is that the same eta from before?"

Aki nodded. "Yes, he is the same. I have seen him, but he keeps to himself."

"Then he avoids good people," Yori said. "That is a relief to hear. Carry on."

"I will." Aki bowed again and then craned to look while the young samurai walked away. Her questions remained. Why had he been there? *Was he watching me? Did Nishioji send him to ensure I made it home?*

Stop those thoughts. Nishioji had better things to do than care for her. She was of little importance.

Her family then?

Were they still under investigation? Did they watch her because her family was a concern?

Home was close. Hopefully, Uncle was not there to

trouble her.

Ten minutes later, home came into sight, and Aki uttered a prayer to the gods.

Her Uncle's appearance at the front door let her know it had not been answered.

"My beloved daughter," Uncle said, "it is so good to see you."

Daughter? Aki desired to spit right into the cut that was healing, but she knew her father would not approve.

Her father appeared behind her uncle. "Aki, why is there dirt on your face?"

Leave it to Father to notice, something Uncle would never do. "I fell on the road." She brushed her nose and cheeks, feeling and then seeing the particles on her fingers. "Is my face clean?"

Her father touched her cheek with his thumb and brushed something away. "Now it is. Have you eaten?"

Nishioji's father had provided her a little, but her stomach growled at the prospect of more. "I should."

"Come in, and I will fetch you something." She followed them in as her father hurried to where Mother busily prepared a tray.

"It is good to see you, Aki," her uncle said again.

"You, as well." She tried to sound polite, but could she push him to leave? "It is late. Should you not head home?"

She regretted her choice of words. Uncle would use it against her. His smile lodged a pit in her stomach.

"We should go together then, since it's your home now, but there is much to discuss."

"Much?" The pit grew larger.

Her father brought rice, but it was not quick enough to silence the demon whispering in her ear.

"Yes, much. The family is ready to meet you. The dinner is three days from now."

Aki wished she was back at Nishioji's.

Uncle could never get her there.

CHAPTER TWENTY-ONE

Riku again searched the morning darkness to make sure he was alone. The air had been brisk, warmer than expected for this time of year. Clouds shaded the moonlight, making it hard for anyone to follow him.

He looked toward the sides of the building. A figure stepped out of the shadows long enough to signal silent approval. He was alone. Few would be out this early.

Once inside, he was greeted by a rough figure he recognized but did not recall his name. "Take me to Lord Eijiro," Riku said.

The man carried a lamp that cast a shadow over his face. "Is he expecting you?"

Impertinent. "This is urgent."

The squat figure nodded but said nothing else, motioning for Riku to follow. Small braziers on the floor provided heat, a welcome feel, but the building worried him. How had it remained empty? Would they still be able to hide here?

After two turns in the hallway, he reached Lord Eijiro's presence.

"The merchant Riku, master," his escort said.

Lord Eijiro gave a deadly stare, his piercing gaze

locked onto Riku. "This visit is unadvised." Wakizashi stood nearby, his face frozen with a wry, silent grin.

"An update before you depart, my lord. You are leaving today, correct?"

"Yes, I must return to Kyoto before my absence is noticed. What is it?"

"My daughter will meet her future husband in two days. After this meeting, I will push to complete the marriage."

"This is good news." His deadly stare remained. "Keep her in contact with the samurai. We may need to press that connection soon."

"Soon?" Riku puzzled over the word. "Is there a problem?"

"Yes, progress. We must find another place. We have one benefactor here, but he can no longer protect us. Has your daughter made progress at that church?"

"When I saw her last night, she claimed to have learned little."

"Speak to her again," Lord Eijiro said. "If my beloved Iri is in Osaka, she is hiding with a Kirishitan."

"Why is that?"

"That is not your concern. Demand your daughter attend the church and do her duty."

"What about the jade?"

"Continue that, too. More cloth sales equal more jade sent to China and more money received." He looked right. "Wakizashi."

"Yes, Lord Eijiro."

"Tell Tantō to press harder. Our associate in China expects as much jade as we can deliver."

Associate in China? Riku stored the information in his memory. No inquiries for now.

"I will tell him."

Lord Eijiro turned to Riku. "You have your orders."

Riku nodded. Time to force Aki toward her future.

###

Tomi rehearsed the words in his head as he approached the door of Aki's house. How much should he tell her? He had hoped to see her today, but work had kept him away.

Twice that he knew about, Aki had contact with an eta. He could barely tolerate their presence. What would Padre Alvares think of Tomi's feelings? He had meandered during his walk, allowing himself to stroll other parts of the city before making his way.

He glanced behind him to check who might be watching. People dotted the street, some in couples and some alone. Typical bustle for an evening. A Shinto priest approached in the distance, but the man took another road.

As a policeman, he would normally open the door without announcement. He listened intently. The smell of grilling food provided a last distraction, long enough for him to hear the laughter. A family enjoying time together. He was about to interrupt that.

It had to be done. He called out.

Voices stopped and then started again, followed by hurried footsteps. The door opened to reveal the face of one of Aki's brothers but not the oldest. He should know the name, as much time as she spent at his home. The man snapped straight and bowed. "Osamurai-sama," he said. "Are you here for Aki?"

"And your father. Bring them both."

The young man hurried away and returned a few seconds later, bringing Aki and her father. Aki's smile warmed him. He wished he could speak with her alone, after the conversation he dreaded, but she must be tired.

The father stepped forward. "We are here."

"I need to talk with both you and Aki."

"Will you honor us by entering?"

He hesitated and then nodded. "I will."

Tomi removed his shoes in the genkan and stepped inside. The last time in this house, he'd been here to arrest the father. Now he was a guest, an undeserved one. The darkened area of the storefront led to the main room. Aki's entire family rose and bowed at his presence.

His heart trembled. It would be easier to face an enemy in battle than to face his feelings for Aki. Would she see through him?

"Sit," he told the family and then turned to the father. "This is a matter of urgency. We must talk in private. Aki as well as you."

The family moved to leave. Tomi told them to remain where they were.

Aki's father stepped forward. "We should go to the outside storeroom then. It is a warm enough night."

They moved outside to the back, and Aki's father opened a small building which Tomi had noted before. Inside he saw a few chairs lining the wall and a light amount of stored fabric. "What building is this?" he asked.

"It is the neighborhood birthing room, but it has not been needed for two months. That will change in a few weeks as well as when our daughter Hoshi's time comes."

A birthing room. Tomi knew of such things but had never seen the inside of one. Few men had. He took a chair and bade Aki and her father seat themselves, as well. They hesitated. Aki clutched her hands. Her father moved side-to-side on his feet. When he said it again, both followed Tomi's orders out of respect or fear.

Aki's mother brought tea, which Aki served to him and her father. She had changed since she left work and the green kosode she wore suited her. A matching pin kept her hair from her face. He could lose himself in her eyes.

Tomi inhaled. Where to begin? It was never easy. "I am here about what happened with the undesirable yesterday when Yori saw you."

Confusion spread on the father's face, and he turned to Aki. Aki looked toward Tomi. "Is this because of that man?"

"What man?" the father asked, his voice piqued.

"The man I have mentioned before, Father. The one who moves dead animals in our ward. You have told me be nice to him."

"Oh, yes. We know him or of him."

"How?" Tomi's blood rose. These people were the unclean of society. People avoided them, as they should.

Her father hesitated and then spoke. "As Aki said, he removes dead animals in our ward. Years ago, my wife was in labor and needed a doctor. I was ill, and our cart was broken. He carried her to the doctor. Aki came later. He looks after Aki as he feels responsible."

Aki's mouth dropped open. "Mother rode on his cart?"

"We were grateful that night. I gave him two silk kosode. We have also sent other gifts to help him and his other children."

"I understand." Tomi grimaced under this. Removing dead animals was a necessary profession. Someone must do it. People should keep their distance, but Aki's family owed a life debt. "Is that everything?"

"His son now comes to our ward when we need his services. He is efficient and charges little."

Yori would find the story repulsive, but it was nothing. "Then it is duty for a debt, nothing more. I will explain to Yori. I have one more question."

"Yes?"

Tomi paused, considering his words. "The men who knocked you down. Did you know them?"

"I did not see their faces. I thought it was an accident."

"It may have been. It was just who did it that was a concern."

"Who was it?" Aki's father asked.

"Yori said they were weavers. I was wondering if you have contact with them. We suspect their activities. They produce much."

The father nodded. "There are many weavers these

days. The city is growing. People are moving into the city. There is a great need for cloth."

"These people are good with silk."

"The silkworms produce much," the father said. "The traders bring more from the barbarians. We know our weavers. Aki does, too."

Weavers. Silk thread. Could these weavers be the recipients of the thread that was stored in the shrine?

Confusion crossed Aki's face. "Is"—she hesitated— "Yori-sama upset with me?"

"Aki," her father said, his voice rising, "you can't use a samurai's first name."

"Don't judge her harshly," Tomi said. "Yori has no last name, at least that he will share with others."

The father nodded twice. Acceptance was status recognition but not a sign of belief.

"Should I avoid the man?"

Tomi opened his mouth to speak, but no words came out. Aki was intelligent as well as thoughtful. Watching her with his mother made him welcome her presence in his home. Watching her with her father supported that. Here he was questioning her for something trivial. She deserved better, but he had to do it.

"It is probably nothing, but do this for me."

The door slid open, and the brother reappeared. "Excuse me, Osamurai-sama. Father, we—"

"I can announce myself," a voice said with annoyance. "Good," the man said as he bowed toward Tomi, "the samurai is here. There is much to discuss."

Disgust flooded through Tomi. He had only seen this man in a distance. This was Aki's uncle. Riku the merchant, as Matsu called him.

Her adopted father.

Do this for me. Tomi's words echoed in her head. Of course, she would do it for him. He was her employer and a samurai.

He was also a man, and she was a woman. That required her to follow orders. Then there were his eyes. She would follow the man with those eyes. Those eyes had asked. Not ordered. Asked.

Nishioji stared down her uncle, who shrank in the samurai's presence. "You must be Aki's uncle. You appear happy to see me."

"I've heard much of your fair treatment of my daughter."

Uncle's words didn't match his tone. She glanced between them, Nishioji and her scheming uncle. The two had nothing in common.

The base of her neck tingled. They had *one* thing in common. Each had a scar on his cheek. Uncle's was fresh and deep. It would leave a permanent mark. Nishioji's was old, but the mark enhanced his visage. She doubted her uncle's scar would do the same.

"You speak like a man consumed in thought," Nishioji said.

Uncle's grin unsettled her stomach. "Aki has told you of her impending marriage, has she not?"

He would mention that. She did not wish to discuss this marriage in front of Nishioji. Uncle gave her no choice.

"She has. What of it?"

Her uncle's glance was like ice down her back. "I seek to arrange a first meeting between the families. Two days from now, with your permission."

The samurai glanced at her. Was that sadness in his eyes? He pursed his lips and turned back to her uncle. "Granted."

Nishioji lowered his head as if hiding his face. "I leave now. Good evening. Aki, make sure we speak tomorrow."

Aki acknowledged him. Nishioji switched back to his sandals and headed toward the street. The image of his scar remained in her mind. *How did he get it?*

"Aki, no one will approach that samurai on his way home." Her uncle sounded haughty. "You needn't worry."

"I am thinking of his mother," she lied. "I am fond of her."

"I'm certain she is of you, too," her uncle said. "What brought him here?"

"There was an incident with the eta," her father said.

"Him again?"

Him again? How did Uncle know? "He was kind to me. He was concerned about my welfare."

"Your father and his kindness," her uncle responded. "We should've been rid of him long ago. He cannot be allowed to impact Aki's new family."

My father's kindness? What did Uncle mean? The man saved Mother's life and Aki's. Was Uncle not grateful? Her father had taught her there was more to people. Her uncle could teach her nothing.

"I will speak to him," her father said.

"See that you do. And Aki."

"Yes, Uncle."

"About your concern for the samurai's mother. They are Kirishitan. Continue to do what you can to *understand* them better."

Aki imagined the street behind the closed door, imagining she could see Nishioji. Wishing she could tell him of her uncle's request for more information. "Yes, Uncle."

CHAPTER TWENTY-TWO

Last night's conversation with Aki and her family remained etched in Tomi's mind. A marriage. An undesirable that periodically shows and leaves. A different lifestyle from the one he knew.

What would the padre say?

And what would he say about the uncle? Tomi finally saw the man's scar. It was a deep cut. It would have taken something sharp to make it.

Tomi stared at the business under surveillance, a trading company but unfamiliar to him. Thankfully, it was warm. It would be dawn soon. He couldn't see the wisps from his breath. "What brought us here this morning?" Tomi asked Matsu, who stood nearby.

"A tip. Yori's brother. Possible swords. Ever since Yori requested his help, he has kept himself busy."

"Brothers can be like that." Tomi's thoughts drifted back to his old friends in Himeji. Their bond was strong. Tomi was an only child. He knew nothing of having siblings.

Tomi lifted his conical hat for a better view and brushed his back against the shop behind him. Two birds flew out from under the eaves. How had he not noticed that nest?

The business appeared mundane, nothing to excite. It reminded him of the time they had watched Aki's house, but that was a ruse. Yori's brother served elsewhere. His only connection was Yori. A nagging thought lingered within him.

"You have no brothers, Matsu, do you?"

His friend gave him a puzzled grin. "Have not seen my parents since I moved here last year. Just two sisters. Your mind is occupied. What is it?"

What is it indeed? "I hope this isn't a waste of time."

Men with heavy loads passed in front of them, their weighted footsteps crunching into the ground. Others came cleaning the streets while more doused the lanterns. A monk, a hat covering half his face, strode through and then took a post nearby.

"Cheer up," Matsu said. "Will soon get prayers to soothe your thoughts."

Tomi smiled when the man began chanting. "He is smoother than a sanshin," he said to Matsu. "That might relax you instead of your traditional habits."

Matsu's silence spoke the truth. He had no reply and changed the subject. "Talked with Aki about the eta?"

"I have." He exhaled sharply. "I also saw her uncle's wound."

"Think that's relevant?"

"I'll take anything I can get."

A dark figure moved into sight, his face covered in the shadows until he approached the front of the target. Realization dawned on Tomi.

"You're tense. What is it?" Matsu asked.

"That man."

"Riku the merchant. Saw him the morning we arrested the girl's father. Investigated him, remember?"

"He's Aki's uncle."

"Really? Then that scar is more than a coincidence."

The door opened. The uncle and the target greeted each

other, and then the man entered.

"He knows our target? What does it mean?"

"It means this is the family whose son Aki is to marry."

"This family? Then she may have some connection."

"I know this young woman and her family. They are honest. Hardworking."

"The uncle then? Like I said, there is something to the scar. Will he corrupt your Aki? What can you do?"

"What would you do?"

"One of my sisters is unmarried. Younger than Aki. Write my parents."

"That's not what I mean."

"Move on. That's what *I* mean."

No. It is not over. Something else has happened. What was it?

The light grew brighter. The day was starting. "Come, my friend. Morning is here, and the tip was to expect something pre-dawn. There is nothing more today. We have work to do before tomorrow."

Aki put away the ink and paper, then she sat down and examined her student's latest efforts. "You are improving," Aki said. "These are well-defined strokes."

The woman's cheeks glowed. "My young teacher is kind." She pushed her sleeves past her elbows. Aki pressed her lips tightly to maintain an even face at the display. Splotches and lesions, some filled with liquid while some had burst. The pus dotted the old woman's arms. Aki tried not to stare.

The woman's harsh cough told Aki she had failed.

"Look at me," the woman said. "I try to keep this from people. You cannot have been here these weeks, though, and not have seen it. I have leprosy."

Aki did not recognize the word. "What is that?"

"It's a skin disease that dots my arms and legs. It will someday cover my body. My skin will turn white as if I am living death and pieces of skin will fall away." She held up her left hand and showed the gnarled tips of the two smallest fingers. "It has already started."

"How does this happen?" Aki asked, staring at the woman's hand.

"I don't know, but my husband and Tomi care for me. They help me hide it from the public, at least while they can. One day I will be forced into a shelter."

The pronouncement drained her spirit. "Why would you be forced?"

"Because a sutra commands that people like me must live apart."

Aki's breath choked in her throat. "You follow a sutra?"

"Society does. It believes I did something wrong and that I'm being punished."

"And Kirishitan?"

"There are stories about believers being cured of this disease. At least I now have hope."

"Hope?" Aki straightened to look at her.

"The holy men make hospitals for people with my sickness."

"Hospitals?"

"A place where I can receive help. This is what Tsuneomi discovered when he fought for the regent three years ago in Kyushu. The regent wants to quiet the faith. Tsuneomi wants to spread it. He hopes to build a hospital here and cure me. Why am I an outcast if centuries ago the Empress Kōmyō bathed one such as me? How can I be unclean, if an empress could touch someone like me?"

Tears leaked from the edges of Aki's eyes. Nishioji was the most decent man she had ever met. She wiped her eyes with her sleeve and then picked up the woman's calligraphy. "Will you be saving this for later?"

The old woman nodded. "I plan to show it to Tsuneomi as soon as he comes home."

Sounds from outside caused Aki's pulse to race. The door slid open and Nishioji stood there. "Did I hear my name?"

Aki again dried her eyes.

"Nishioji-sama," Aki said, appearing to struggle with her composure. Her smile brought life to his day.

"You appear surprised."

"You told me last night that we would talk today. I did not expect you home early."

"Yes, but there is more work to do. What do you want to show me?"

"Your mother's latest effort." She nodded, as if asking permission to approach. "Do you wish to see?"

"Of course."

She walked toward him and handed him the papers, which he viewed with keen interest. "Mother, these are beautiful."

She blushed at the compliment. "It's been a good day. Aki and I went for a long walk. We had much time to *talk* this afternoon."

His mother's emphasis on the word 'talk' made him glance at her. "About what?"

She pulled down one of her sleeves and pointed to the lesions. "About this."

Aki looked away but finally faced him. "I noticed the splotches."

Drawing on the memory cut Tomi like a blade. "It started several years ago. It was nothing at first. Just a few things on the skin and numbness in her toes. The doctor said nothing and prescribed some root tea."

"Did it help?" She glanced between them.

"No," his mother said. "Found out later the tea came from the doctor's relative." She smiled. "Should have known. It was too expensive."

Aki laughed and Tomi's mood eased. He needed to

talk with her. "Mother, rest."

"I rest enough. I'm not an invalid, though I am hungry."

"I will take care of it," Aki said.

"I can do it. My son is here. You should return home."

Aki looked toward Nishioji for approval.

"You may go home," he said, "but we will talk outside. I need you here early tomorrow."

She nodded, and they headed to the door while his mother went to prepare food. Tomi recalled the joy cooking gave his mother. Something about Aki's presence brightened her spirits as much as his.

"My apologies, Nishioji-sama. I have intruded on your family's secret."

"It was unavoidable." His fingers grew numb as he rubbed them together. "Better you should know. Now that you do, you must never reveal it."

She didn't hesitate. "I will not say a word."

"I know." Tomi knew she could never lie to him. "Did my mother tell you anything else?"

"We talked more about your church. They build hospitals."

"It's more than that."

"You"—she paused and looked up the street as they started walking toward the watch—"you treat all people well. Does that have anything to do with your church?"

Tomi halted. "Is that what you think?"

"I do not know what to think."

"It teaches me things that made me want my life to be different."

"I think I understand."

Tomi stared into her eyes. "Would you like to learn more? You could visit the church with me."

He regretted his words but could not take them back. She nodded, as he had expected she would. He must not forget how she viewed him. She would never refuse a superior. If only she wanted it for herself and not out of duty.

Tomi turned away. How well did Aki know him? Could she tell what he was feeling?

How would she feel if she knew they were watching her future husband's family?

CHAPTER TWENTY-THREE

Tomi breathed on his fingers, hoping to warm them from the pre-morning chill. Yesterday's conversation with Aki remained in his mind. He'd asked her to join him at church, and she'd said yes. *Was it only because I made the request or because she was interested in learning more?*

"I thought it should be warmer by now," Yori said.

"Should be dawn soon," Matsu replied. "Was worse earlier this morning."

"Why us, anyway?" Yori asked. "The last time was a waste. Other officers could handle this duty."

"We serve as we're ordered," Tomi said.

"More will be here soon," Matsu added. "Remember—"

Tomi held out his hand to silence further conversation. Only the birds remained, along with a low but growing murmur. He pointed down a side street. Four men approached, bringing a large box.

Yori pressed close. "An odd route to use, unless you're trying to hide something."

Matsu gestured behind them, where two men appeared, porting another box on poles that rested on their shoulders. "A normal delivery?"

"Or maybe the ones over here have friends," Tomi said. "We wait."

Both groups continued their slow walk, appearing to approach each other.

"Being silent to not disturb?" Matsu asked. "Could be nothing."

"We'll see what happens," Tomi said. "Let's spread out. I'll approach alone from the front. Matsu, you come from the right. Yori, you from the left."

Yori and Matsu headed toward their positions. The delivery men stopped and set their cargo beside the target house. One of them, a wispy individual, wore a garment with a hood that hid his face. After a quick soft knock an older man appeared. Tomi endeavored to keep his steps silent.

The man stepped left and indicated the *kura*, the family warehouse on the side. A stocky man who had followed him barked at the others, and those waiting grunted in assent. Tomi glanced right and left, catching sight of both Yori and Matsu. This could just be a delivery. Time to find out.

"Good morning," Tomi said as he approached. "I didn't know shipments arrived at this early hour."

Several men tensed, glancing at each other. They then spread out in defense but remained within eyesight.

The leader, a stocky man, approached Tomi. "It is early for you, too. Why do you trouble us?"

"We've had reports of smuggling. I need to see your deliveries."

He crossed his arms over his chest. "What are you looking for?"

"That is not your concern."

"Our delivery is cotton and silk. I am curious. What is it you seek?"

Tomi knew the man was stalling, but it allowed Yori and Matsu to get closer without notice. "We're searching for jade, red agate, and other items."

A perplexed expression crossed the man's face. "Seems there would be a better use of your time. Those items are rare but of little value."

"You know a lot for a delivery man."

The man brought his hands together in a prayerful touch. "I am a devout man. Jade is important to temple priests. Red agate carries a similar appreciation. If I possessed any, I would donate it."

The man's tone suggested deception. "I see. You *are* devout."

"Yes. We have no such items in this box or anywhere else."

"I see." Tomi drew closer. "Then you won't mind if I review the contents."

His face tightened. "Allow me to open it for you."

The pitch in the man's voice changed with the final tone. Tomi viewed the others, making sure all were within sight. The man reached inside the box and opened it to show. "See. Silk."

"Allow me." Tomi stepped near them.

The man whirled, drawing a short sword from under his clothes. The other men did the same.

Tomi drew his own sword.

"You are outnumbered, Osamurai-sama."

One man on the end grunted and sank to his knees, then planted his face in the ground. Yori sped around and smiled. "He has friends."

The stocky one laughed. "This child is no threat."

Matsu appeared. "The child is not alone."

Swords clashed. Another delivery man dropped. The man in the hood stepped away from the battle and disappeared into the darkness. No time to chase. He had been near Yori. Hopefully, Yori saw his face.

Matsu made quick work of another man with a strike at the neck and shoulder. Tomi pressed his own opponent, striking him in the face with the hilt of his sword and knocking him to the ground.

One left standing.

The leader confronted Matsu but was knocked down. All three samurai held out their swords.

"Want to live?" Matsu asked.

A quick flick, and the leader's sword flew to the side. He held out his hands in a mock plea. "My life is yours."

Hurried footsteps approached. Their relief had arrived, younger men though older than Yori. One stepped forward. "Is everything well?"

"Check those on the ground. Lock away whoever's still alive," Tomi said."

The man nodded, his eyes conveying that he understood. Officers led away four men, including the proprietor who had not fought. One remained to guard the three bodies on the ground. Where was the undesirable when they needed him?

Yori tilted his gaze toward the ground and shook his head. "More dead. Why?"

Tomi glanced back and forth. "Good question. Whoever's doing this has many followers."

Matsu walked forward and knelt to arrange the clothing of one of the bodies. He motioned Tomi and Yori to come closer. Matsu looked at Tomi. "Do you recognize him?"

Tomi studied the man's face until comprehension dawned. "One of the people from the boat when we followed the shipment to the shrine."

"He wasn't on the ship when we searched it in port."

"Could they all be pirates?" Yori asked.

"Explains the smuggling," Matsu said, his brow furrowing. "Regent stifled piracy. Pirates need work."

"But what could be worth dying for?" Tomi tilted his head toward the storage room. "We should search the boxes and find out."

They pried the tops off the other boxes so Tomi could

rifle through them. One box contained silk thread, with items wrapped in paper. The other contained woven fabric, also with wrapped items.

Tomi opened one item.

Jade.

Hurried footsteps sounded from down the street as another group approached. Tomi recognized them but struggled to recall their names. More of the city defense force. They were all dressed in meager attire.

"Osamurai-sama," one of them said, "our apologies. We were busy elsewhere. We will see to the removal of the bodies."

Tomi grunted. "What has happened?"

"There has been an incident at another abandoned temple." He turned toward Yori. "Your brother is injured."

Yori turned pale. "How is he?"

"Alive, but Oeda says he will need time to recover."

"Take us to him now," Tomi ordered.

The lead man left an officer to oversee the corpses on the ground and motioned the remaining men to follow. They headed north and then turned toward the castle, stopping at an old temple that was now used for storage. More graffiti marked the outside.

He cannot save his legacy.

An unusual quote. One that nagged at Tomi. Most graffiti in Osaka rebelled against those in charge, a holdover of the siege that had eliminated the stronghold of the Buddhist sect previously here. The regent may control the city, but he didn't rule the hearts of the populace.

The lead man passed through the entrance and headed left. Holes dotted walls along the corridor, like the other places. Various stacks of items appeared undisturbed, except for a pair of legs that extended from behind a platform of oil barrels.

Yori's brother sat nearby with his back pressed against the wall. One man used strips of cloth to bandage him. Yori waved the man off and addressed the care himself. "How are you, brother?"

The man laughed like Matsu. "More embarrassed than hurt. What happened will heal. Allowing myself to be taken? That shame will last until I avenge it."

Tomi smiled to himself. Another pair of fortunate siblings. Yori and his brother were close, especially in appearance. In the dark, he might mistake one for the other.

The lead man issued more orders and then came back to Tomi. Tomi gestured toward the pair of legs. "Who is that?"

"A fire caller." The man pressed his lips together as if in serious thought.

"Never thought walking the streets at night to prevent fires was dangerous." Tomi stared at the body. "Until now."

"We believe he saw a lantern and came inside to investigate," an officer said. "Whoever was here was caught unaware."

The explanation makes sense.
Unfortunately, nothing else does.

"Arrested?" Riku said, pacing the floor as he did. "This is not good. What happened?"

"I arranged it," Wakizashi said. "Calm yourself. That proprietor has outlived his usefulness."

Riku kept his gaze down to avoid insult. "Why?"

"We needed a diversion. I only control so much, and my numbers are depleted. I need the police to think they have someone."

"Why are numbers thin?"

"The regent is drawing resources, planning for the impending battle with the Hōjō Clan. The men cannot disobey."

Riku could only nod. No one could disobey a direct order from the regent. "What does the arrest do?"

"It provides us a respite. We ship what jade we have

through other sources. Items left in the proprietor's shop will mark him as the leader. The police will ignore any protests of innocence."

"They will execute him." Riku allowed himself to stare at Wakizashi, knowing he might see it as a challenge. "My daughter is marrying into that family. If the father dies, the marriage will be delayed a year for mourning."

"Then you must hurry." Wakizashi's tone was an order. "Get it done. Has it not been three weeks since the birth of the servant's grandchild? Your daughter's service should be over. The samurai's servant should be returning."

Riku stroked his chin. He hadn't thought about that. "I will review it with my brother, but if he is executed too soon?"

"We buy the property and marry your daughter to the family when allowed. I'll provide the funds to acquire it."

That sounded good. "Understood."

"The police have limited numbers. The regent calls their men, too. They will concentrate on this business. We can regroup."

"Anything else?"

"Continue to press your niece to learn about the church here, though it may be pointless."

"Why?"

"Lord Eijiro has learned his love is not in Osaka. There is no reason to search further."

"Then why engage them?"

"Because I owe this Nishioji. Watching him lose his friends will be a fitting punishment for his crimes."

Riku bit his lower lip. "Then the more my niece learns, the better."

"Yes, after we are done with his friends, I will force him to take his own life out of shame."

Cancelled. The meeting with her future husband's family was cancelled.

Aki avoided Uncle's glare. His announcement was welcome, but she did not wish to appear happy. "What happened?"

"Did your samurai not tell you?" Uncle asked.

Nishioji? What does he have to do with it? "I have not seen him today."

Her uncle related details of the arrest of the father of the man Uncle planned for her to marry. The report of deaths left her shocked. Nishioji was a kind man. She had seen him angry, but he stayed his hand. "Nishioji-sama killed men this morning?"

Her uncle shrugged. "That's all I know."

Aki nodded and looked away. "I did not know any of this."

"Things will be acceptable soon."

Uncle sounds too sure of himself. He's hiding something.

"If I do not have to meet the man you want me to marry, then I should help Mother." She took a step to leave.

Her uncle cleared his throat. "Aki, not yet. Have you discussed the samurai's faith with him like I asked?"

Aki's chest ached as if she were being smothered with cloth. She took a deep breath, catching her father's sideways glance as she did. That caring look was always there. "We discussed it," she said. "He invited me to his church."

"He did?" Her uncle's words carried a hint of suspicion.

"Yes," Aki responded.

"What was your response?" Uncle approached like a snake wanting to strike.

Aki worked to moisten her dry throat. "I said I would go."

"Wonderful," Uncle said. "You've done what I asked. You are obeying me like my daughter."

A daughter. His daughter. The tone in Uncle's voice pricked her skin like a frozen needle. "I do not understand why you want me there."

"You're important to the samurai's mother. I want you to continue to be."

"What are you asking of me, Uncle?"

"The samurai's caregiver has been gone for a while. She must be returning soon."

Aki counted the days in her head. "It will be another week, I think."

Aki's father stepped between them. "We must delay the marriage, given the arrest."

"Delay?" Her uncle held a pause. "It's more urgent than ever."

Her heart sank into her stomach. "Why?"

"The arrest may lead to the father's execution. If that happens, the wedding will have to be delayed. Maybe for a year. We must hurry."

"I do not understand."

"We must complete the marriage now. The son will need you to run the business."

"That will not give me time to help here. The samurai's mother also has asked I teach her calligraphy."

"We can discuss that after you are settled. Teaching the samurai's mother is honorable, but we must get you married. You are my daughter. You will obey."

Uncle's daughter.

She must do everything he said.

CHAPTER TWENTY-FOUR

Aki brought Nishioji's mother some water. The day had been pleasant, but last night's discussion with her uncle remained in her mind. *After you are settled,* he had said. It meant that once she was married, Uncle had no intention of allowing her to serve the samurai.

"We go now. I will soon need to leave.

Aki's breath caught in her throat. Her uncle had encouraged her. She did not want to go for him.

She wanted to do it for Nishioji. "I am. Are you sure you want me to come?"

"You will be welcome."

Aki did her best to hide her feelings. She had passed the church Tomi had mentioned, but she had not given the place much thought.

The walk took twenty minutes. It felt like they had slowed to get here, as if Nishioji were cautious. The church came into view. It still resembled a Buddhist temple, as it had once been, except no statues at the front entrance. The building appeared beaten by wind and rain. She did not remember how it looked when she was a child, but it had been a temple.

Then she saw the entrance. The subtle arrangement of

wood and decorations on the front reminded her of the cross his mother wore and of criminals put to death. "Is that…your symbol?"

Nishioji nodded. "Yes, it's a cross. It differs from the practice here, but its purpose in that faraway land was the same."

"How long has this been a church?"

"It's the only place I have known since coming from Himeji. There was one here before. There was also a place for young men to study and become teachers. They were closed after the regent's edict three years ago. This place remained." He pointed to a small, thatched house across the street. "That place is where the padre lives."

"Padre? Is that a bateren?"

"The same. He is the priest of our faith."

The house appeared neat and well kept. "Just one?"

"One padre, but he has two helpers. One is a child. Just two rooms, and one for tea ceremony."

A stiff wind blew. Aki brought her hands together, doubting her hearing. "Tea ceremony?"

"Yes. All the padres practice it."

These men from afar had adopted one piece of Japan. "That would be interesting to see them do."

"Another day." He gestured to the building. "We should go inside."

Shame covered her face, and she looked away. She had asked too much. They walked toward the entrance. He straightened an askew door and slid it open. A few pairs of shoes had been placed on the left.

"How many will be here?" she asked.

"It appears busy." Tomi scratched his chin. "It's a special day. My mother would be here if she could. So would my father."

A special day and a reminder she needed to tell Nishioji about her uncle's pressure. What would he say?

A dog's bark broke her thoughts. Aki looked down and

saw a little white dog. It resembled the one that had followed the undesirable. Nishioji knelt and patted the dog's head. "I have missed you, my old friend. Where have you been? Did you follow me from Himeji?"

It responded with a tail wag that matched its bobbing. "Follow you from Himeji? You know this dog."

"I know a dog that looks like this one enough to be from the same litter. That one was a neighborhood dog, too. He stayed near the church in Himeji. It makes me think an angel is watching my steps."

"*Anjo?* I do not know that word."

Nishioji smiled at her, and her knees jellied. "A conversation for another time. A messenger from Heaven. The dog reminds me of home, either way."

The dog barked again. "Next time," Tomi said, "I'll bring you something to eat."

They entered and stepped onto the wooden floor. Lanterns lit walls on both sides. A cross greeted them and pointed the way.

"I do not understand why this is here."

"I will try to—"

"Nishioji-sama, I mean Tomasu-sama, you are here." A Japanese man dressed in a bright robe like a Buddhist monk strode forward, his smile wide. He was shorter than Nishioji and older but appeared as fit as the samurai. The enthusiasm on his face suggested great strength. "Padre will be pleased. He knows your schedule is difficult."

"It's good to see you, Hisa."

The man called Hisa glanced at Aki. "You've brought a guest."

Aki bowed low. This man had used Nishioji's first name, though the sound of it was strange. He must be of high rank. A low bow was a must. "My name is Aki," she uttered as she straightened. "I am Nishioji-sama's servant.

Comprehension dawned on the man's face. "Ah. You are the woman he hired while his mother's caregiver looks after her own daughter." The man's face radiated joy.

Aki's nervousness waned. "Yes."

The man turned to Nishioji. "How is your mother's caregiver?"

"All is well. A few more days, I think.

"Are there many here tonight?" Tomi asked.

"Eleven, so far, not including the two of you."

"We should pray for more to show."

"We will add your parents. Padre mentioned visiting them later this evening, to bless them with ashes."

The Buddhist-robed man left, walking with a bounce in his step. Aki stifled a chuckle. "Who is that?"

"His name is Hisa. He trained in Kyoto and is now here."

"He dresses like a Buddhist priest?"

"Some Japanese ones do. The foreign men wear black, the same as they do in their home countries."

"He called you by your first name. He must be important."

"No, he called me by my Kirishitan name. Outside, I am Tsuneomi or Tomi. In here," he looked down both halls, "I am Tomasu."

"Tomasu-sama? What is that?"

"A long story for later. Come."

They entered a room that appeared to have been the center of the temple but now had a table where the statue would have been. The smell of fresh tatami pierced the musty scent on the walls. A foreign man attired in black rushed toward them. He had a large nose, a bald head framed with a ring of hair, and a smile that matched the one named Hisa. He smelled of incense, and Aki was thankful for that. She had heard these foreigners do not bathe often.

"Tomasu-sama," the man said, performing a bow to which Nishioji reciprocated. "I didn't think you would make the service."

"I didn't expect to do so, but I bring a guest."

The foreign man looked at her. "Welcome, most welcome."

Aki froze. The man in black spoke her language, understandable though he accented the wrong syllables. "Thank you."

"It may be confusing. Try to follow as best as you can."

Aki did not know what to say, but something in the man's gaze held her. She nodded. He carried no malice. Not what she had heard about people who followed this new faith.

Nishioji guided her toward the center of the room. She glanced at the other people assembled, the gardener who dropped by Nishioji's house, the child whose parents owned a ryokan. Others there had also visited the samurai's mother.

This was a community. This is why they stopped by.

The room went quiet as the man in black headed to the front, accompanied by the one called Hisa and a boy about ten or eleven. The foreign man faced the cross, as if leading a group, and spoke in words she did not know. He turned to them and told a story she had heard from the samurai's mother, explaining it, and then back and forth with those strange words.

They went forward twice, once when the foreign man drew a black image on their foreheads and once when he gave them something to eat. None of it made sense, yet everyone smiled.

After it was over, people bid her well, rubbing the black lines on their foreheads into smudges that made them fade into their skin. Soon only she and Nishioji and the men from the church remained.

"Thank you for coming," the foreign man uttered.

Aki's throat constricted the way it had when she arrived. The man spoke her language, but the style made her pause. "It is new to me. I have learned much from Nishioji-sama and his mother."

"Stop by again," the one called Hisa added. "We will answer any questions."

Aki shook her head. "My time with Nishioji-sama's family is short. Then," She paused, considering what to say. "I have other family duties."

The Japanese cleric nodded. "I understand duty myself."

The foreign man looked at Nishioji. "Duty to family is important." He held out his hand to Nishioji, offering a small lacquer object. "Take this to your parents. Tell them we missed them."

"They hope to see you," Nishioji said. "Are you still coming this evening?"

"I have deliveries first. Is later acceptable?"

"Fine. It's dark, and I must see her home first."

"I will make the deliveries, Padre-sama," Hisa said.

The bateren handed the man two small circular containers. Hisa received them with reverence. What could be inside them?

"Later, Tomasu-sama," the padre said.

She and Nishioji left, heading back to her home, discussing the evening for the first few minutes. She peered repeatedly at his forehead. Nishioji continued to rub there. She needed to ask him about the caretaker's return but couldn't mention it.

"Why do you rub away the black?" she asked.

"Today's ceremony was important, but I must keep it secret."

"I see. You have duty, as well."

They cut left down a street where many of the houses looked worn, a poorer section of Osaka but a faster trip home. A fishy smell pervaded the cool air, punctuated by boisterous noise and the mewing of cats. People milled about, their eyes wide as they stepped back and allowed them to pass.

Nishioji glanced at her. "What's troubling you?"

She gasped. He had noticed her concern. "When does your mother's caretaker return?"

"A few days, I believe. Why?"

They moved toward another street, through the weaving section area. "My uncle is upset. Officers arrested the father of the match my uncle arranged. He says the marriage must happen now."

Nishioji stopped. His eyes misted. "I know of the arrest. I did not know this would force your marriage."

Her house came into view. Two blurry but familiar figures stood outside, her father and her uncle. They must be waiting. "I have little choice."

"I see."

The samurai rubbed his eye. Was he sad about her departure? Did he worry about her teaching his mother?

Her father and uncle hurried toward her. "Aki," her uncle said. "Have you told the samurai about the marriage?"

"She has mentioned it," Nishioji said, his tone as bitter as awful tea. Uncle's manner likely irritated him. "I will release her soon."

Soon. Nishioji turned and left, taking Aki's heart with him.

Padre Alvares stared at Tomi. "You are distant, my friend. Confession helps."

Tomi sat in the open-air space at the back of his house. Padre Alvares, who'd remembered his promise at church to come tonight, sat on his left, warm water in hand. He claimed tea kept him awake and never drank it late. "I'm not sure it will."

"Then tell me about her," he said as he leaned forward. "She has your interest."

Tomi gulped but knew not how to reply.

"Tomasu-sama, what is it? Do you need a friend to listen?"

Tomi looked away. "I do not know."

"Tell me what's troubling you." Alvares pulled closer. "I promise secrecy either way."

Tomi wondered how to begin. Maybe with the ending. "We arrested the father of the man she is promised to marry."

"Marry, she—"

"Her uncle adopted her to marry her off and gain an heir. The man's father is a criminal."

"That doesn't make him a criminal."

"No, but with the arrest, her uncle now presses for the marriage to be immediate, in case the father is executed."

Alvares nodded. "The required time of mourning. I understand. When does her service to you end?"

"My mother's caregiver should return soon. It is almost twenty days since the birth of her granddaughter."

"You wish to keep the young woman, if you can."

"She teaches my mother calligraphy. We plan to have lessons. I'd be able to see her. Now learning she—"

"Will leave a void in your heart. You must trust to God. He will reveal his plan in time.

"It's difficult."

The padre smiled. "It often is, but I'll be here when you need me. One question. Is the arrest related to the group that persecutes us?"

"I don't know. I only know that officers have been injured and killed and that the group likes jade and graffiti."

Alvares tilted his head. "Graffiti?"

"Yes, written words that make fun of the regent. *He does not produce children, but he has opportunity.*"

The padre laughed.

Tomi stared at him. "Why is that funny?"

"When your *kampaku*, Toyotomi, built the castle, he gave some of my fellow missionaries a tour. We saw many women and thought they were the regent's wives. We learned later they were his wife's servants."

Tomi laughed. "I understand."

"The young woman you brought today. Maybe she will come to church to learn more. Maintain your faith. I will pray for your investigation. I will pray that God moves the young woman."

Tomi nodded. His feelings for Aki were as strong as his desire to find the anti-Christian group. Something nagged at him. Could the family have some connection to the smuggling that Aki didn't know? Her uncle?

What would I do if Aki knew?

I would do my duty.

He glanced at the clock. "It is late. You should get some sleep."

"Do you still want confession?" Alvares asked.

"I have trouble pronouncing the first words."

Padre smiled. "That is good enough. We will continue."

"You look troubled, daughter," Aki's father said. "Perhaps you should sleep."

It had been over two hours since Nishioji had left. Uncle had also departed after getting the information he wanted from the samurai. Father had left with Uncle and returned a short while ago. While he was gone, she'd helped Genta count their wares and review the day. "Yes, Father."

Aki rose and said good night then headed to the back, glancing at her father and brother without a word. She wished she could talk to Mother. Could she do so without Father seeing? Not likely. He had told her to go to sleep.

She took a few minutes to unroll her bedding and then pulled out her sleep kosode. The nights grew cold in this corner of the house, but it was silent if you did not need to be near the hearth. When it was warmer, her brothers would evict her for privacy, though the room could be split by a screen for the same reason. They also used the outside storeroom. Ogin sometimes kept her company when she was mad at Shuji or wanted to complain about Sadayo.

The door slid open. Her mother entered and sat next to the bedding, like she knew Aki was troubled. "How are you?"

Aki was right. Mother's tone implied concern. "I am well, Mother."

"Do not lie to me."

Aki smiled. "I do not lie, Mother. My health is well," she said with emphasis. "I am just troubled."

"I could tell by your voice when your uncle was here. When you're bothered, you slow the way you talk."

Aki stared at her mother. Her youthful appearance lied about her age and wisdom. Mother had married younger than Aki was now.

Aki was fortunate Mother was here at all. Her sibling had told her the story. Mother almost died in childbirth. Her siblings mentioned it, but her parents never discussed it.

Genta knew something. Always a joke about a visit from demons before Aki came into the world. Aki owed her mother a debt more than any of her siblings. "You always know me best, Mother."

"Is it your uncle or the samurai?"

"Can it be both?"

"You don't want to marry your uncle's choice, as there's someone you want to marry."

Mother always knew. "He is a good man."

"Now I know you mean the samurai. Because he's a Kirishitan?"

"It has nothing to do with that, or maybe it does."

"What do you mean?"

"I do not know what I mean."

Mother beamed at her. "You understand both men. How do you see them?"

"This samurai cares for those beneath him," Aki said. "Uncle has no love for anyone but uncle. Why do we listen to him?"

Her mother's expression grew somber. "Duty and debt

are tough discussions."

"Will it end with my marriage?"

Her mother sighed. "That is my hope. You don't care for uncle's choice?"

She hadn't considered that. She did not know the young man. "I do not care for Uncle. I have not thought about his choice"

"But you care for the samurai?"

Her gut tightened. "What makes you say that?"

"I know you," Mother said. "Your passion shows for certain things. You enjoy helping his mother, do you not?"

"I do." The tension within her disappeared. Aki recalled where she read to the woman, helped her with her calligraphy, and walked with her.

And listened to her. There was truth in her words and her struggle. She had passed her goodness to her son. She wanted to learn about this woman and care for the samurai.

"Mother, you are right."

"Of course I am," she said as she laughed. "What do you want to do?"

Aki thought for a minute. "I must ask Nishioji-sama to make a direct request to Uncle for calligraphy and make it permanent. Also ask if there is any other thing I could do when the caregiver returns."

"You would still go home every day to your new family."

"But maybe Uncle's choice might disagree and seek someone else."

Father's voice called out, and then he stepped inside. The look on his face did not bear joy. "Good, you are awake."

"What is it, Father?"

"Uncle is here. He saw the family. The mother is deciding things while the father is under arrest. The wedding will be in ten days."

"Ten days?" Mother asked.

"Yes, there is much to do."

Ten days. There is not enough time.

Aki yawned. Her parents left her to get dressed. She twice dropped her kosode before putting it on.

Was there anyone she could ask for help? She would ask Nishioji and his mother. She could talk with the foreign man at Nishioji's church.

The foreign man? The thought made her pause.

In trying to escape Uncle, she was seeking the samurai's church. She was doing what Uncle wanted. He would press it again, anyway. Could she get closer without getting close to these people?

Nishioji would never forgive her if he knew.

CHAPTER TWENTY-FIVE

"How many days until the marriage?" Wakizashi asked.

"Eight," Riku said, his stomach churning. He hadn't eaten this morning, thinking it was dark and he would have time to later. He more feared keeping Wakizashi waiting. He pulled at his coat but remained uncomfortable. Wakizashi's expression appeared different from before. Something had changed in him. "Are you troubled?"

Wakizashi eyed him with a flat smile. "I didn't expect you to notice. Yes, Lord Eijiro has received news that changes things for him, but our plan remains the same."

"Then I will make sure the marriage happens on schedule."

"Ensure it does."

"What about the Kirishitan group?" He rubbed the back of his neck. Was this no longer a problem? "Do you still want my daughter to visit the church?"

Wakizashi smiled as his gaze drilled into Riku. "Yes. I have plans for this Nishioji. Has anything happened?"

Riku bit his lip. "She visited and met a few people."

"Good. See that she goes again. This Nishioji will certainly enjoy her interest."

###

Tomi finished his morning prayer and chatted with his father. He had to leave early for the sake brewery. The land transfer was finally expected to be approved, and there was much work to do his father had told him. Moonlight streamed in from the cracked windows on the side. His father opened the door to leave.

Hisa stood there waiting, his face tense.

"What brings you here so early?" his father asked.

"I need to see Tomasu-sama. It is urgent."

His father nodded, inviting him in and leaving with a smile. The man appeared flustered. He rarely came to Tomi's house.

"What is it, Hisa?"

"My apologies for disturbing you so early."

Tomi stared into his face, red with the remaining rivulets of tears. "What happened?"

"One of our members has died."

"Who?"

"The lantern maker's family. The wife passed."

"Where's Padre?"

"He is at the family's house… To perform the final blessing."

Tomi nodded. He had visited them once before. The daughter brought a gift to welcome Tomi's family when they arrived in Osaka. "I'll visit them, too."

"That will mean much to them."

"How is Padre?"

"Shaken."

"I will visit him, too."

"That will warm his spirits. Bring your servant, if you can. Her presence elated him. It was only her first time, but I see happiness in his face when new people inquire about the way."

Tomi hoped Aki would choose to join one day, but he wanted her to do it on her own. Was an errand too much to ask? She would do whatever he ordered. "It's too early to think that, but I'll send her today."

"That would be most helpful."

After Hisa hurried off, Tomi thought hard. His mother could inform Aki. She was more independent than Tomi gave her credit for being sometimes, and Aki's presence buoyed her spirits even more. The usual caregiver was skilled and took care of many things, but with Aki his mother was the happiest he had seen her.

Visit the church, Nishioji's mother had said.

She was doing what her uncle wanted. He had pushed her two nights ago to join Nishioji at the church.

Now the samurai's mother sent her there on an errand.

She was doing Nishioji's bidding. Unfortunately, she was also doing her uncle's. What would Nishioji say?

He would be within his rights to kill her.

Death was preferable to being Uncle's daughter.

She turned right, stopping for a second as the eta appeared in the distance. Was he avoiding the main street to avoid people? Did he smile in her direction? It was hard to tell.

Aki reached the church and found the bateren working outside, his young shadow nearby following his orders.

"Bateren?"

The man turned and smiled. "Ah, the caretaker of Tomasu-sama's mother. Welcome."

Aki stopped. Hearing the samurai addressed by the name that sounded like his first name still startled her. "It is good to see you."

His stiff bow made her laugh. "You, too. How is she this morning?"

"Very well today. She is up and around."

"I understand you help her with her calligraphy."

"Yes. She continues to improve."

"Praise be to God."

He paused and looked at her. Did he sense what was

on her mind? Was there a way to serve the samurai without doing her uncle's bidding? "I am here at Nishioji-sama's request."

"Hisa told me you would be coming."

"Nishioji-sama asked that I see if there is anything I can do for you."

"My main request is that Tomasu visit the family. I have a letter for you to take to him. I will get it." He looked toward the boy. "Kazu."

The boy ran over and listened to the foreign man's instructions, then hurried inside. The man studied her again.

Yes, he understood her feelings. "Do you wish to talk?" he asked.

"It is a simple request. Would there be a chance to teach calligraphy at this church?"

His gaze lit like fire. "A class for children? We do that at other churches. Would that be good?"

Aki had not expected that answer, but it made sense. The members of the group were likely not rich and could not do individual lessons.

Groups of people passed along the road, most carrying loads and all in a hurry. Did they notice Aki at the church? Did they know it was a church?

Could she teach children?

It was Uncle's orders to spend more time here. It would keep her busy and away from the man he wanted her to marry. "Yes, I think so."

"Great We'll discuss more later." He looked back toward the building. "Where is Kazu?"

He motioned for her to wait, saying he would return, and then entered the building. She studied the building, examining in the daylight what she could not see at night. The place was older than she had thought, as if it had once been in poor shape. Many spots appeared repaired. Certain sections looked new. The members took care of this place.

She walked around to the other side, checking out the

rest of the building. Where was the bateren?

Strong hands grabbed her shoulders and pulled her from behind. She fell to the ground and tried to pull away, seeing her attacker's angry face.

From the left, a blur appeared and knocked the man to the ground.

The eta.

Aki screamed. The attacker rose and struck the undesirable. He fought back, but the attacker knocked him to the ground.

The door opened. Out came the padre, his assistant, the boy, and another man.

The attacker spat on the man and fled.

Aki and the padre moved toward the man.

He was unconscious on the ground.

"Go, Hisa," the padre yelled.

"Go where?" the man responded.

"To the other house we use for visitors. One man there has medical training."

The one called Hisa nodded and took off at a run.

She and the padre returned to the man on the ground, who now stirred. Blood trickled from his forehead and ran across his cheek. Aki gagged but kept it down. "What about a doctor nearby?"

The man she did not recognize knelt on the other side of eta. "He is unclean. No doctor nearby will treat him."

The unknown man had a mustache and thin beard that offset his wide frame. She searched her mind but could not recall ever seeing him before. "This man saved my life. Can no one help him?"

Kazu appeared, holding a bucket and a wet cloth. He handed it to the bateren, who applied it to the wounded man's face. The man's eyes kept opening and closing, glancing at her when they did. "You are safe. I am relieved."

The man's gaze moved her, as if they shared a connection from what happened when she was born. His smell still bothered her, but his presence no longer did. Aki took the cloth from Kazu, dipped it into the water, and applied it to the growing bump on his head. The man's smile grew.

"We need to let him rest," the bateren said. "We will take him to the residence. Help me."

The foreign man and the bearded one picked the eta up as Kazu ran across the street and opened the door. "Come with us," the foreign man said. She waited at the door for a few minutes until the two men returned.

"He'll be fine." The man's expression was one of pain as he tried to avoid looking at her. "You must return home." He pointed to the bearded man. "He will escort you back to the samurai's residence."

Aki nodded and looked at man, who gestured they should leave. She knew the bateren was right.

Yet the feeling burning within her told her that she belonged here, too.

"What happened?" Tomi asked, his voice on edge. Hisa had found him after fetching the doctor. He'd wanted to rush home, but Oeda had kept him busy, and he could not disobey. His supervisor had other ideas.

Aki only shook her head. "I have thought about it again and again. The man attacked from behind. Then the undesirable got hurt, and I remember little else."

Tomi cursed himself. "He didn't get far. The undesirable must have hurt him. We caught him. He's in jail."

"Who was he?"

"A pirate. We encountered him before, but he got away."

"Why did he attack me?"

A good question. "I don't know, but you are safe."

"Thanks to that man."

That is the other question. "Why was he there? He may

have helped your mother the night you were born, but there is more to this."

Aki had no answer, but Tomi knew who might. A piece of the story was missing. "We'll go to your house."

Aki nodded, surprise across her face. "I can make it home. The man was caught, you said."

"I want to talk to your father. As soon as my father returns, we'll leave."

"I understand."

The rest of the afternoon was short. Aki helped his mother prepare dinner, something she enjoyed but hesitated to do. She remained in good spirits, the best he had seen.

His father arrived an hour later, tired but relieved to be home, and Tomi and Aki set out. Tomi couldn't ignore the feeling in his stomach. They may have found Aki's attacker, but was she safe? While he walked into town, his mind darted toward every movement of those around him. Usually, he preferred quieter streets, but staying in the open and among light crowds was better.

They soon reached Aki's house, closed for the moment. The eldest brother and his wife were outside, their attention drawn to the samurai. The brother rushed over and bowed. "Osamurai-sama."

"Fetch your father. Immediately."

The brother hurried away and returned soon with Aki's father. Tomi expected him to leave, but the eldest son remained in the background, the look on his face one of pique.

"How may I serve you?" Aki's father asked.

Aki related the incident. Her father's face showed parental concern. The eldest son continued to eavesdrop. There was an unspoken truth here. What was it?

"I hope the man recovers from his injuries."

"He will, but it will be slow."

Aki gasped.

He'd kept that information from her, as he didn't want

her to worry.

"What do you ask of me?"

"There is more to the relationship with this man than you have told me."

The father sighed. "Will you come in for tea? It is a long story."

Tomi looked at the sky to gauge the time. "Yes."

"Genta, bring the three of us tea."

"The three of you?" the brother's lips quivered.

"Yes, make it four. Have your mother join us."

The brother's reaction showed he knew the story, too. Only Aki appeared confused.

The father led them inside, offering them a seat near the floor hearth. The mother set trays as the brother brought out the cups and tea. "Genta," the father said, "leave us."

He bowed and exited hastily. His hand quivered as he closed the door.

The father nodded and asked permission to begin. "There is more to the story with the man. Years ago, your mother nearly died in childbirth. We needed to take her to the doctor. I was ill that night and could do nothing to help. The eta assisted us."

"I know that already." He gestured toward Aki and her mother. "He saved both their lives."

"No. He saved Aki's mother that night. He also saved the life of Aki's sister, Hoshi."

"Hoshi? He saved Hoshi?" The tone in Aki's voice matched Tomi's confusion. "Then why does he follow me?"

The man looked at Aki with years of love and care.

"Because he's your father."

CHAPTER TWENTY-SIX

Riku opened the door. His mouth dropped open. "Tantō? Why are you here?"

"I bring word from Wakizashi. We've taken the necessary steps to preserve the marriage."

The edge in Tantō's voice cut through an early evening filled with distant, unintelligible sounds, yet it paled next to that odd grin and deadly gaze. Riku lived near the castle grounds, a privilege afforded by his position among the merchants. This meant those in charge could find him if needed. "Preserve. How?"

"We sent a man to watch the church, knowing you would send your adopted daughter there. He faked an attack and allowed himself to be caught. He's now in jail and will protect the cloth merchant until his son marries your daughter."

"After that?"

"After that, we will let justice commence. You've been a faithful servant. Make this happen soon."

Tantō departed in the direction of the castle. Usually, Riku could see the reflection of the golden sculptures at the castle's top, but there was scant moonlight now, so they were in shadow.

Riku watched Tantō disappear into the darkness.

His intimidation remained.

"My father?" Aki stared at the floor. *An undesirable. One of the unclean.* How could her family even look at her? How could Nishioji?

"Don't lower your head, my child," her father said. "We are not ashamed of you."

"I understand that, but am I really your child?"

He reached across and grabbed her hand. "You are not my blood, but you are my daughter. More than you will ever be your uncle's."

Her mother smiled at her. "You are part of our family."

Aki's skin tingled, and she drummed her fingers against her leg to help her think. "Why did he bring me here?"

"Your real mother died giving birth to you," her father said. "The man brought you to us when you were born, saying he couldn't care for a baby. He asked that we raise you as our own, as payment of the debt for saving your mother and Hoshi's life."

The news hit her hard

Her real mother, her eta mother, was dead.

She was the daughter of an eta.

She was unclean. *An undesirable.*

This explained much. She'd always wondered why she didn't resemble her mother and why her calligraphy skills were not the same as her sisters. It made sense now.

She was not one of them. Instead, she was an outcast.

Would the samurai even allow her in his house now? "Is he still at the house across from the church?"

Tomi grunted. "I received word they would try to get him home today or tomorrow. I don't know."

"Where would they take him?" Aki asked.

"The main eta neighborhood is southwest of the city," her father said. "Beyond the pleasure district. He lives there."

The eta village, where I belong.
They should take me there and leave me.

Nishioji rose and said his goodbyes, staring at Aki. "I have time tomorrow after the morning. Come by the house first. We will go to the church to find out about your father."

Come to the house? How could he still welcome her?

He must have no choice. For now, she was allowed until it became untenable in his mind. He still needed to help his mother until the caregiver returned. After that, she would never visit him again.

She may have gotten her wish. Uncle must know. If she made it public, it would end the marriage.

It might also require her parents to disown her. Who would want to do business with a merchant whose daughter was an undesirable?

###

"An undesirable. So?" Matsu asked. "My thoughts are always on a *yūjo*. That's one class above an undesirable. You know that. That's why the wards are next to each other. Samurai much higher than us spend time in my favorite district."

Tomi stared at his friend but didn't know what to say. He'd only last night learned the truth of Aki's background. He'd apprised Yori of the latest, gladdened to find that his brother, Yaesu, was improving, but he'd thought of little else since. Matsu was right. The main village of undesirables was beyond the ward of the prostitutes. Did this mean Aki was beneath them?

He could not see it. She was a girl loyal to family and worked well with his mother, but what if the others in his ward discovered her identity? "I'm not high-ranking, but I can't have someone of unclean status in my house."

"Yes, you can."

"Why?"

"Admit it. To me and yourself. She means something

to you."

"Yes, she is special. I have never met anyone like her."

"Soon she'll be gone." Matsu crossed his arms over his chest. "Promised to another already. She will be married soon."

"It's more complicated than that."

"This is Osaka, not the capital. Nothing here is complicated."

Tomi stared at the outer wall of the police building, as much a prison for him as it was for the criminals he brought here. Having Aki in his life would alter his status if everyone knew, but he'd never met anyone like her. Never would again. "There's nothing I can do but accept her place in life."

"New woman where I listen to music. She's untrained in the arts but might appeal to you."

Tomi shook his head. "*You* enjoy her."

"My heart belongs to my sanshin player."

Tomi sighed. If only Matsu would see that thing differently?

"Nishioji-sama," a nervous voice said. Tomi glanced at the young man who had interrupted him and Matsu. Another transfer from the city defense force to offset the loss of people. "What is it?"

"Oeda-sama requests you both in his office."

Tomi grunted at him in dismissal, and then he and Matsu headed to the front. The young officer opened the door for them. They turned left, crossed the main area, and moved right. Oeda's door was open. He was placing incense on his brother's shrine. They waited for an appropriate moment. "Oeda-sama."

"Come in and close the door behind you," he said without a glance.

Tomi and Matsu complied, waiting while Oeda prayed. He ordered them to sit in front of his desk while he took a seat behind it.

"We have a connection."

Tomi and Matsu glanced at each other then looked at Oeda. "What do you mean?"

"Kenkō once said it was better to play backgammon not to lose than to try to win. We've been chasing these smugglers slowly, trying not to lose. I decided to ignore him for once and try to win."

"What did you do?" Matsu asked.

"I hid one of the new officers away, and then I put him in jail. It was risky. There are dangerous people in there, and he is untrained."

"What happened?" Tomi asked.

"The wholesaler we arrested a few days ago and the man who attacked your caregiver. They talked. They know each other. Two people connected to that girl."

"She's innocent," Tomi said, a fire rising within him. "She has nothing to do with any of this."

"Not knowingly, but she is part of it. Possibly just a stone on a go board, but she is part of someone's strategy. How much longer will she be with you?"

"A few more days. My regular caretaker should return soon. The girl is planning a marriage."

"To the son of the wholesaler, correct?"

Footfalls behind him slowed. Was someone listening at the door? Tomi waited before answering. "Yes."

Oeda's eyes sparkled, and he leaned forward. "That explains it. The man who attacked her wanted to be arrested. He is in jail to protect the wholesaler, at least until the wedding occurs."

"Why would he do that?" Matsu asked.

"If the man dies in prison," Tomi said, "the wedding will be delayed."

"Then what happens?" Matsu asked.

"Either they speed up the wedding, or they have an alternative strategy," Tomi said.

"I agree," Oeda said. "We need to be ready."

"What about your officer in jail?" Matsu asked.

"I'll leave him there for now and withdraw him when it's time to *review* his case. No one will be wiser."

The aroma of incense filled Tomi's nose. "Did you burn more than usual today?"

"Yes, I was inspired. Even in death, I feel my brother is with us."

Death. How close had Aki come to being killed? If not for the undesirable, she would be dead.

The man had saved her life. Or had he?

"What is it, Tomi?" Matsu asked.

"Do you have an idea?"

The incense irritated his eyes, but he didn't know why. "What if the attack was planned?"

"You think the eta knows more?" Oeda asked.

"I don't know," Tomi answered. "His injuries are real."

"How about your caregiver?" Oeda asked.

"She is fine. She plans to check on him today. I will go with her."

"Go now," Oeda said. "Both of you. See if he's there before you take your caregiver there."

"*Hai.*"

"One more thing," Oeda said as he grabbed an envelope on his desk. "A couple of camphor sticks. If you must visit *that* neighborhood, you will need them to erase the foul scent. Your mother will enjoy them, too."

Tomi and Matsu left and then exited the building. A brisk wind chilled their faces as they headed south down the main road. Dark clouds billowed above. A storm was coming. They needed to hurry.

Some minutes later, they reached the church and the small house across the street. Hisa answered the door. "To—," he began and then glanced at Matsu. "Nishioji-sama. What brings you here?"

"I'm here to see the…man who was hurt. Where are he

and the padre?"

Hisa tilted his head down, his voice somber. "He went home. He was not well, but he insisted. Kazu and I took him there last night."

"What's wrong?" Matsu asked. "Something else?"

Hisa glanced between Tomi and Matsu. "The baker has fallen ill, just like the lantern maker's wife. Padre has gone to see his condition."

Tomi sighed. Was this a coincidence? Or were his fellow Christians being attacked? How was it happening?

"Thank you, Hisa." The air continued to sting. "Where's Kazu?"

"With the padre. Why?"

"Making sure he's not on the roof. I'll see you soon."

They took their leave and headed back to the road. "Where to now?" Matsu asked.

"To my house. To talk with Aki. She should see her father."

Light drops fell. Tomi expected more rain, but it held off. They hurried home and found his own father resting, the door to the covered area open to allow in the fresh air.

"Father, you're early."

"Another delay in our new building," he said. "The brewery owner is upset."

Not surprising. Osaka Administration remains slow. The machi-bugyo, whoever he is, must approve all land decisions, but he's busy helping the regent. "It will happen, Father."

"He upped his offer to two barrels of sake."

"Father, there is nothing I can do."

"Tomi," Matsu said, "we should at least try."

Tomi shook his head. His friend was incorrigible.

"Tsuneomi, you're early, as well." His mother's voice called from beyond the door. His mother was the only one who ever used his full first name, except for Matsu when he wanted to emphasize a point.

Tomi found his mother sitting outside, looking the best he'd seen her in a while. She was teaching Aki, pointing out things about nature and the skies. It reminded him of when he was a boy and lessons that did not take. His mother looked at him and then behind him. "Matsubara-sama, so nice to see you."

"You, too." For once, Tomi had almost forgotten the effect Matsu had on his mother. They shared a love of nature.

"What brings you home so early?"

"Aki"—he paused and held back on saying father— "the man who saved you."

"He is still at the church?"

"I was just there. He's home, but you should see him."

Aki's gaze fell to the floor. She knew what that meant. A trip to the eta village. "When do I go?"

"I'll take you there. We leave now."

CHAPTER TWENTY-SEVEN

"I am sorry about what happened to the people at your church," Aki said to Nishioji. "I hope the ill person gets better."

The samurai had said little along the long walk, and she had kept to her own thoughts. One death, two near deaths, and they were his friends.

"We will support them however we can," he said.

Support them. Her uncle had asked her to get close to the Christians. She had already asked about teaching at the church, if only to keep her from her future husband.

She now understood her request was wrong. What would Nishioji say?

The eta village came into view. She had always known its location but never had a reason to visit.

They reached the entrance of the district. The presence of a samurai drew attention immediately. "Where is his house?" Aki asked.

"Close, I think. Hisa gave me a general idea when we talked to him earlier."

There were shops but much tighter and smaller than in the city, essentially a larger community shrunk. Of course, the merchants willing to sell to them would be few. People nearby talked in hushed whispers, unwilling to stare at the samurai.

A child of maybe ten darted down one side of the street, out of the row and toward what appeared to be houses.

"This way," Nishioji said, following the same direction of the child.

A few minutes later, the child returned, a solitary woman trailing behind him. She was older than Aki, both striking and similar. She had a subtle beauty, though most would only see her unclean status.

"Have you seen that woman before?" Nishioji asked her.

"I have not." She searched her memory. "I have seen undesirables…" She hesitated at the word and then accepted its implication. "I have seen them in the neighborhood, but I only know the old man."

The woman reached the two of them and shooed the young boy away as she studied Aki. "You came."

"Who are you?"

"One who knows who you are. Come with me."

They followed the woman and soon reached a row of residences that were poorly made. Another minute later they saw sturdier dwellings. The woman went to one and told Aki to announce herself.

Aki paused at the door and couldn't speak.

The old man was here. Correction, her *father* was here. She was the lowest of society. An outcast.

Her presence in the home where she grew up would defile even her parents. She was no longer the daughter of a cloth merchant but the daughter of a dead animal mover. *An undesirable from a family of undesirables.*

She took a deep breath. "*Gomen kudasai*," she called out.

After she heard a few shuffled steps inside, the door slid open.

A young man, though older than she was, stood before her. She had seen him in her own ward doing the work the older man used to do.

This must be her brother, maybe a little different, but with a beard showing strands of gray. Being an outcast must take years off one's life.

"I did not think you would come," he said.

Aki swallowed hard. "I wanted to visit him. Is something wrong?"

Another woman came into view from behind the man, her stomach greatly extended. She was due soon. "You don't believe you belong here. It shows on your face."

She looked at Nishioji for support. His nod gave her confidence.

"A lie is a rude way to greet family."

The woman behind her gasped. "Being blood does not make one family, going beyond blood does."

She glanced around at the three of them. "I owe a debt I cannot repay. Our"—the word hung on her tongue like a bitter daikon radish—"mother died for me." She bowed. "My name is Aki."

The woman from behind came around, her eyes open wide. "I am Shio."

Recognition struck Aki hard. "You are my elder sister?"

"Yes."

"You were named after *salt*?"

"I arrived at New Year's. Mother and Father always called me that, saying that my arrival chased away demons and brought them luck." She laughed. "It's silly, but it cheers me."

Shio's tone dampened Aki's spirits. Her life was not easy, but her father had money for comforts. Could this family do the same?

"I am honored to meet you, older sister."

Her eyes contained a mixture of disgust and distrust.

"Most might feel shame." She gestured to the man in the door. "This is Hachi, your brother."

"Hachi? Number eight? You have seven brothers?"

Ha laughed. "No. My name is Hachiro. Two bees stung Father the day I was born. He took it as a sign. Calls me Hachi as a nickname." He pointed to the pregnant woman. "This is my wife."

"Honored to meet you all. Congratulations on your child."

"Congratulate me when it's born. There is danger until then."

Aki inhaled sharply. "I understand. The three of you are worried."

Hachi sighed. "The injury was more severe than he told us."

"May I speak with him?"

Hachi waved for her to enter.

"Do you want me to come with you?" Nishioji asked.

He would step into an eta's house to support her, but she did not want to taint him. There was no one like him. "I should do this alone."

Aki stepped across the dirt genkan and onto the wood, what there was of it. A light stench filled her nostrils, either sickness or rot. There looked like there were rooms on both the left and right beyond the entryway. A doorway in the back led to the outside.

To what?

Shio pointed toward the left side. "There."

She opened the door and stepped inside the room. The old man lay on the floor on straw bedding. She bowed. "Father?"

He turned and his lips curled into a weak smile that accented his sallow cheeks. "Aki? My child, you are here."

"You know my name?" She approached him and sank to her knees. "Was that the name you chose for me at birth?"

"It suited you. You were born under a clear autumn

sky. Your time with us was short but bright."

"I am moved by your comments," she said, pausing on the last word, "Father."

He lifted his hand and patted the top of hers. His touch felt weak, as if he had little strength. "To hear that word from you gladdens my heart. I never thought I would."

Aki pressed her lips together. She never imagined saying it to anyone else. "Why did you not keep me?"

"Your mother was a wonderful woman. You look just like her. When she died, I realized I could not care for an infant and your siblings. There was no family to send you to and no one close willing to adopt you. I asked a favor of the silk merchant. He agreed."

"You carted my adopted mother to a doctor to save her and my sister. Why could no doctor save my birth mother?"

"Because she's unclean," Hachi's wife answered. "We had no doctor in this village then and none now. That is why you should save your congratulations until I have the baby."

"No doctor?"

A tear streamed down his face. "I tried to get help when it was time for you to be born. I even went to the doctor who saved your other mother."

"What happened?"

More tears ran down his face. "He refused to treat her."

Aki rubbed her chest, but a growing tightness remained. Her birth mother had given her life to give Aki life. Another debt she could not repay. Her father closed his eyes. Aki squeezed his hand. He smiled and squeezed back.

A light tap touched her shoulder. Shio urged her to rise. "That's it for the moment. He'll need to rest. Come with me."

Aki rose and followed Shio out. Shio closed the door behind herself but left a crack so they could hear a voice from inside.

Her family stood before her. "No doctor will treat him."

"There is one," Hachi said. "He's not a doctor. He's one of those *banjin*, the foreign barbarians in black cloth. There's an empty house nearby. Some of them hide there and do what they can."

People from Nishioji's church. "These men will visit here?"

"Yes, but they can do little." Shio's gaze narrowed. "Just like you."

Aki's hands fluttered. "What do you mean?"

"Why didn't you come before?" Her words came in a huff.

Aki bit her lip. The veiled accusation of not caring struck her hard. "I did not know."

"He watched you every week from afar. Do you understand that?"

"I saw him often. Usually in the morning. He always wore a smile."

"Of course he did. You resemble our mother. He often talks about his beautiful daughter, the child who never came home. When he dropped you off, he should have left you alone."

The words smacked like a firm slap. "I would have come if I had known. How can I convince you?"

Shio leaned forward. "By accepting your responsibility."

"My responsibility?"

"Look at us," Shio said. "Look at what you have done. You are responsible for our mother's death, and you may have killed our father."

She was a baby, yet her mother was dead because of her, and her father was now near death, having protected her. "I will do my duty."

"If you cannot, then don't come back."

The words shook Aki like thunder. She glanced back where her new father was resting. Did he feel that way? He had followed her all her life. Now he was like this.

So much hiding of the truth. Family hid her true birth. She hid the samurai's secrets. She hid her uncle's request.

No. Those things were different. Some things were done for love and loyalty.

What Uncle had asked her to do was out of greed.

"I will return to see how he is," Aki said. *If I am able to return at all.*

Aki stepped out the door and back to the street. Tomi waited near the side. He'd heard every word through the walls but wished to keep it to himself for now.

"How is he?" he asked.

"He is not well. I spoke with his"—she took a deep breath—"my brother and sister. They believe he does not have much time left."

"Are *you* feeling well?" he asked.

Her face held back tears like the clouds above held rain. Which would break first? "I am fine."

The two of them started their walk back, keeping a brisk pace. People in the street stared as they passed. He mentioned the need for haste, but she remained distracted. They left the village, eyed as they did by the residents, and then crossed the river. Aki turned to glimpse behind her.

"What is it?" Tomi asked.

"I made a promise. I need to keep it."

"I heard."

Her lips thinned out. "How much?"

"All of it. Your birth father lives in a nice place for this village, but the walls are thin."

"I wondered about that."

Nishioji smiled. "I asked Yori to investigate his past. The man shows up too much for a coincidence. He's successful, as successful as many merchants. It may be from him you got your business skills."

"Yes, and now I likely cannot serve my older brother."

"Because of what your siblings said?"

Aki again appeared to struggle with tears. "They blame me for the death of their mother, my mother, and that their father, my father, is dying."

"You are not the cause of your mother's death. You had nothing to do with the attack on you. They cannot blame you for this."

The sky grew darker, a combination of lateness of the day and an impending storm. He would get her home soon. She needed rest. "My sister told me what your church does for people. There are also houses they use. Did you know about that?"

He did but had never asked. "I know there are houses they use. I don't know where they are."

"They looked after...my father." She exhaled softly. The words must not come easy. "I see why you like them."

"It is more. If you wish, you can visit again."

Apprehension crossed her face. Should he have asked her to visit again? Duty would compel her to go. Did something trouble her? "I know."

They continued to walk, saying little else. Her family business came into distant view.

"Nishioji-sama?" she said in a rising tone. "I must apologize."

He stopped and looked at her, perplexed. "For what?"

Aki could not return his gaze. Her whole body trembled, but she finally spoke. "I have not been truthful with you."

The words soured him. "What have you done?"

"I enjoy the stories your mother tells me, but my uncle pressured me to learn more about your church. He wanted me to learn everything I could about your beliefs. I do not understand why it is important. Only that I was to report back to him."

Anger rose within him. This? From Aki? "Both your father and uncle?" He gritted his teeth.

"Only my uncle. My father disapproved but remained

quiet because he is the younger brother."

"He could have come on his own. There is no need for secrecy."

"Uncle believed I would be welcomed more." Her tears flowed over her face. Her body closed itself in shame.

"You think to gain forgiveness through tears?"

"I have lied to the most decent person I have ever known." She bowed low. "My actions are unforgiveable."

Tomi tapped the hilt of his sword and then jerked his fingers away. He was within his right to kill her for this betrayal, but he would never do it. To even touch his sword at this time was a betrayal of his own beliefs. What would Iesu say? What would the padre say?

He should talk with the padre as soon as possible.

"Live with your shame," he said. "Go back to your father. Whichever one, I don't care. Don't return to my house."

Tomi turned, hearing Aki fall on her knees and cry in the street as he walked away.

Part of Aki was relieved to be home. Another part wondered if she could call it home anymore.

When she saw Tomi's fingers brush the handle of his sword, her heart had raced. A quick death would be merciful. Shame often meant ending one's life. He had commanded she live with hers. She had done the right thing. Now she must admit it again.

She walked in the door. Uncle was here again. He smiled like a merchant who used faulty weights. "Hello, Aki. I have been waiting for you." Uncle's voice grated against her skin like coarse thread. "Is there any word? Is the caretaker back yet? Your wedding is in a few days."

Tears welled in her eyes, but she would not cry in front of him. Marrying Uncle's choice would be punishment enough for her duplicity. "I admitted you wanted me to learn about the church. He ended my employment."

Uncle's expression dropped. "Why did you do that?"

"I have met no one like him," she said. "I could not lie to him anymore."

For once, Uncle's face softened. Like the time she had tended to his wound. She had touched a part of him "I know, Aki." Uncle's breaths came in gasps. "I know what it means to love someone."

Did Uncle sound contrite? "Then why do you do this to me?"

"Because I must. One day you will understand. I haven't been good to you. But once you are married, you will see. It will be better." His words choked him. "It will be better for the family."

"I want my life to mean more, Uncle."

Tears appeared to moisten his eyes. "The adoption is complete, but I hope you'll soon call me Father. We must hurry. Prepare for the wedding. I'll make the arrangements."

Flushed, Uncle turned toward her father. "I need to leave." He said goodbye and headed out the door.

"You told the samurai?"

"Yes, Father."

"You may not be my blood, but I'm proud to call you my daughter."

Aki's heart warmed. There was one place she could call home, at least until Uncle forced her to live elsewhere.

"What is troubling him? I have never seen Uncle like that."

"Sometimes I forget his past. Your uncle was once in love, too. He never talks about it, and I don't think about it."

"Uncle was in love?"

"Yes." Her father sighed, and his gaze softened. "Many years ago. She was a kind woman and made him happy, but she died young. Uncle never wanted to remarry."

Uncle once in love and forever alone. She was all he had left.

CHAPTER TWENTY-EIGHT

"Betrayed you?" Matsu shook his head. "Never expected that."

Tomi took the kettle from the hearth and poured the man warm barley water. His friend's visit this morning was welcome, though his habits remained strange. Matsu preferred cool drinks in summer. Most people drank warm ones when it was hot. Another reason Matsu differed from anyone else.

"What will you do?" Matsu asked.

"We should restart the investigation. The family *may be* connected."

"Don't mean that," Matsu said. "Would be fruitless."

"We've found nothing. This doesn't mean nothing is there."

"Searching for a demon is pointless if you only look in the wrong forest. Don't let anger guide you. Have you forgotten the advice you gave Yori?"

"What advice?"

"When we arrested the father, Aki defended him. She did it for love and duty. You explained this to Yori."

Tomi shook his head at Matsu. Before, he'd only used Aki's name to annoy Tomi. Now he mentioned it in her defense. "Love? Are you saying that she did this out of love?"

"Yes. This girl would do anything for family."

"Then why tell me about it?"

"Because of love. For you."

Tomi's father passed through the room, and Tomi went silent until he left. "Have you had *sake* this morning?"

Matsu sighed and sipped his drink. "Women have eyed you for years, but you acknowledged none of them. The samurai in Himeji were glad you moved. Tired of being ignored by the more attractive women on the mistress's staff."

Now Matsu was trying to needle him. Unfortunately, it was working. "What's your point?"

"Aki is the first woman you've ever acknowledged."

"She used it against me."

"Not married." Matsu's voice carried reproval. "Some choose duty to family over service to liege. You could take her life, state she lied to you in the paperwork, and have it approved. But do not doubt her actions."

Tomi pressed his fingers against his forehead, but his thoughts remained confused.

"Looks at you the same way. With love."

Tomi glowered at him. "That is one joke too much."

"It is not a joke," his mother's voice called out.

His mother entered the room, her strength growing with each step, and a light burning in her eyes. "She made a mistake."

"Mother, it is more than that."

"I like this girl. I know you do, too. She would be welcome in our family."

"Mother, she's unclean."

She pulled up her sleeves and pointed to her lesions. "Have you forgotten? I'm as unclean as she."

"If you could go to the hospital south, I would take you there."

"That will not happen. We are here. If I am discovered here, officials will force me to live in a separate village, one next to people like Aki."

Tomi's resolve teetered. He'd never seen his mother like this. Despite her anger, she was alive and healthy. "She lied about her interests."

She neared and looked up at him. "As I said, she made a mistake. Just as that scar on your cheek shows you once did. Have you forgotten?"

He ran his finger along the line on his cheek. "I've never forgotten."

"What next?" Matsu asked

Tomi rubbed his chin. "We need to check the uncle again."

Matsu nodded. "Agreed. What do we do?"

"You find Aki and bring her back," his mother said. "Forgive and accept her."

"Mother, I will find Aki. First, though, we must find Yori. There's much to discuss with him."

"Then what?" Matsu asked.

"Then we visit Aki's uncle."

Aki went over the numbers again. With nowhere to go this morning, she had talked with her father and Genta. Genta was improving, but she knew she would always be needed. Nishioji was right. She gained her business skills from her birth father, or her birth father had made her ready to learn what her father could teach her.

The business was closed today. Father had posted a sign thanking customers for allowing them a day of rest. It had been a busy morning.

Aki had eaten little. She could not forgive herself for what she had done to Nishioji.

No. Nishioji-sama. She did not have the right to even think about him without his title.

Her mother entered and set three small trays near them.

"Eat," she said.

Aki nibbled at the rice. It was the best she could do. There was no one who could help her.

No, someone could.

The bateren. The foreigner in black at the church.

"Father, with your permission, I—"

The bell at the door interrupted her thoughts, and Father held his hand out to make her pause. Genta soon entered the room. "Aki, a woman is here for you."

Aki hurried to the door, wondering who it might be. She froze at the entrance.

Shio.

The woman's long hair was tied on the side in a green braid that accented the left side of her face. Her outer cotton kosode was nicer than the simple coat she wore yesterday, as if she was trying to avoid being seen as an undesirable by others. In other words, by looking like Aki.

"Shio, is something wrong?"

Her father came behind her. "Aki, who is here?"

"Father, this is Shio. My sister."

Her father bowed. "I remain indebted to your father. I should send more gifts, but it would not be sufficient."

"Another day," she said, her voice almost quiet.

Is she surprised to receive respect from Father?

"Aki, you must come with me now."

The urgency in her voice implied bad news. "I will. What has happened?"

"Father is much worse today. He asks for you. We worry he may not survive."

"Aki, earlier you were going to say something."

"I wanted to visit the church. Nishioji-sama is angry, and I owe the church an apology."

"Wait then." Her father hurried inside and returned a minute later with two kosode, one for Aki and one for Shio.

"I do not need this," Shio said.

"It could get cold, and in case you and Aki are

delayed."

Shio acquiesced. It was now a gift. No one would buy it after Shio had worn it. Her sister nodded and said nothing more, except to say Aki should follow her.

###

Riku used a cloth to wipe his eyes. All those years ago gone in an instant. He and his wife had wanted a large family. Then she had died, and everything had changed. Aki was his last chance for a family, but she didn't want him.

Because of the way he had treated his brother's family over the years, he understood Aki's hesitation.

A call from the door disturbed Riku's notes.

He'd hurried home from his brother's house after hearing Aki's news, shutting the shop and sending employees home so he could plan the wedding. They could change the date and make it in fewer days. Once married, there was no need to worry about the merchant in jail. Every day was a risk.

Why could he not listen to what his brother wanted? What Aki wanted?

What if he could delay it instead? The merchant would die in jail, then the wedding would be postponed. Maybe he could change so Aki would accept him.

No. He had to do what Wakizashi said, or Wakizashi would kill him.

The call from the door came again, delaying him. Whoever was here, Riku hoped it would be quick. He slid open his door.

A monk in gray stood there, his face hidden by the low brim of his hat.

"Bless this house," the monk said. "Invite me in to bless this house."

Just what he needed. Another monk begging for funds. Couldn't he just chant on the street corners like the others? "I don't need you to bless this house."

He closed the door. A few seconds later, the call came

again.

The monk had remained in place. "Bless this house. Invite me in to bless this house."

Riku sighed. Monks that blessed houses were always persistent. Allow the man to do his blessing, give him a few coins, and get back to work. "Come in," Riku said.

He motioned for the man to enter and then shut the door behind him. "We should start in the back and then come forward," the monk said in a gravelly voice.

"Follow me," Riku said.

He headed to the back, hearing the flutter of cloth sliding behind him. Metal pressed against his neck. "Turn," a familiar voice said.

Riku complied, his heart in his throat. "Tantō? Why are you here?"

"Making sure the wedding is proceeding. The girl no longer works for the samurai."

He studied Wakizashi's underling, wondering where he obtained his information. "We can," he paused, "we can move the wedding up."

"Why the hesitation?"

"My niece is a good girl. She works hard. She does not want to be my daughter. I want to give her a chance to accept me. Let's postpone. It will work better. Can we give her a little more time?"

"There is no more time, Riku. Why do you delay? Has something happened with the adoption?"

"No. The adoption is complete and legal. Just a little more time."

The man looked at him with eyes that shifted between brown and gray, as if his whole body were a sword. "There is none. Have you made plans?"

Riku turned. "Yes, my notes are on my desk."

"Then you must be turning against us, merchant."

"It's not that. It's—"

"If you must bare your soul, confess to one of those

insufferable bateren. I have no interest in hearing it."

"Tantō. There are other possibilities."

"Yes, there are. The adoption is complete. That offers us a second possibility. Your brother would do anything to protect *his* daughter."

A sharp jab flooded his neck. He raised his hand to press against the pain but could not stop the blood draining down his arm.

"It gratifies me to know that mine will be the last face you see."

Riku's head swam. He crashed onto the tatami.

It had taken longer than expected to find Yori and tell him to locate Aki, but they knew Yori would be fine. Yori's brother continued to mend, and Yori desired to get back to his duties, even if it meant finding the girl and watching over her.

The walk to the higher status garment district, the area for those who served the castle and nearby inhabitants, had been quick. The uncle's position in the community provided benefits. He led groups, got to dispense justice in neighborhoods, and lived near the outskirts of Osaka Castle. Granted, the castle was so large, most people felt like they lived near it.

They arrived at the door and then scanned the sides. No activity. Matsu reached to open the door.

A coppery smell hit Tomi. Tomi stayed Matsu's hand.

With a nod, they both drew their swords and opened the door.

The putrid smell of death assaulted them.

 Aki's uncle lay unmoving on the floor, his blood soaking the tatami and seeping into the wood cracks. Tomi and Matsu checked the other rooms but found them empty. The storefront was closed and unoccupied. They returned to the body. Tomi ran his fingertip along the cut on the man's cheek, the one Aki had mentioned. It wasn't definitive, but it resembled a cut from a blade.

"He has not been dead long," Tomi said.

"What next?"

"I will stay here. You get Oeda and bring him and others back."

"Anything else?"

"Pray. I am worried about Aki."

"Yori will find her."

CHAPTER TWENTY-NINE

For the second time in as many days, Aki crossed the neighborhood border into the district. People turned toward her and Shio. Their being together indicated there was a connection, though what it was remained unknown. They had spoken little on the walk over. Shio was worried and likely blamed Aki for the situation.

They headed toward the house. On her second time here, Aki again took in the differences. Yesterday, she had noticed the lack of similar stores. Today, it was the narrow streets, which were tighter than the city but felt the same otherwise. They soon reached the house and stopped out front.

Shio paused at the entrance and looked at Aki. "Thank you for coming."

"Why would I not come?"

"You could have said no."

"He is my father. He saved my life. My debt exceeds all else."

They opened the door. Aki tilted her head at the familiar face. "Hisa-sama?"

He smiled back at her. "Ah, it is good to see you again."

"You are here to look in on him?"

The man nodded. "I arrived a few minutes ago. He was hurt at our church, and we are responsible for his health."

"Is he better?" Shio asked.

"Come see for yourself."

They entered the room and saw Hachi, who was standing back. Another foreign man in black was kneeling and talking with her father. He appeared to be a doctor, or at least he knew medicine.

"There is hope?" Shio asked.

"Yes," the kneeling man said, "but he rest. He could worsen. Best leave alone. I will come again."

Aki pressed her lips together at the man's broken Japanese. The man spoke to Hisa, then said his goodbyes and left.

Aki knelt beside her father and grabbed his hand. "Father, I am here," she whispered.

The man grinned and then drifted to sleep.

"A fitful night," Shio whispered. "He is exhausted."

She glanced at Hachi. "Where is your wife?"

"Sleeping as well. Best to leave her alone, too."

They closed the door and went into the entryway. Hisa followed.

"I made you come for nothing," Shio said to Aki.

"I promised I would be here, and I wanted to keep my promise."

Shio and Hachi eyed her, possibly with a look of appreciation. "If he needs to sleep," Shio said, "then you should go home. If you stay, you will return home when it's dark."

"I will walk with her," Hisa said.

Aki glanced over. "I want to go to the church and visit with the bateren."

"Is something amiss?"

"No," she said, not wanting to explain. "I just have questions."

"I will answer what I can, though Padre-sama knows more. His Japanese is also much better than the man who was here, too."

If only Aki was ready to ask questions.

"Any ideas?" Oeda asked in Tomi and Matsu's direction.

Much of the afternoon had passed since the Oeda's arrival. Two officers searched the house and made notes. Tomi had tried to help but remained distracted about Aki. "None. Have you found anything curious or interesting?"

"The men are still searching. One odd thing. Did he have eye problems?"

"Eye problems?" The mention of it stirred Tomi's memory. "I do not know of any."

"An officer found this." Oeda held out his hand and showed him an eye patch. "Does this mean anything?"

Tomi's heart raced. He motioned Oeda to join him outside. Matsu followed them. "That has been found in other cities. It is associated with the anti-Kirishitan group. Check if it has two pieces. There are sometimes messages inside."

Oeda examined it and found a tiny piece of paper. "I don't understand it."

"What does it say?"

He showed it to them.

得計錬者

An unfamiliar grouping of four kanji. Together they made little sense. It was likely a word pun, impossible to understand the meaning unless you choose the correct pronunciation. "Does this mean your caregiver is in trouble?"

Tomi pursed his lips. "I hope not. We sent Yori to her house to find her and make sure she is safe. I don't know if he has located her yet."

"Yori is resourceful. He will perform his duty. When

we finish, I will let you search."

Tomi nodded and returned to work. A nudge from Matsu drew him aside. "What is it?"

"Could the uncle be the one in charge? A disagreement?"

He recalled the face of the dead man. "If he was, then who gave him the scar?"

"Welcome, Aki," the bateren said. "I am surprised to see you here alone."

Aki nodded. "I am also surprised, but I needed to see you."

The man's face broadened, like a teacher educating an eager pupil, though the ring of red hair that circled his head made her nervous. She knew of people with red strands that they buried under their black locks, but nothing like this man's head. Only demons had this much red hair.

"You stare at me as if you are frightened. Does my appearance trouble you?"

"I have only heard stories of the *banjin*." She blanched at her use of the word. She did not think it rude, but this man was not a barbarian. "This is my first time to be this close to someone like you."

She was close enough to glimpse his eyes. They bore a strange shade of brown. At least they were not blue. Childhood stories of the red-haired, blue-eyed demons kept her cool on muggy nights but had also kept her awake.

The priest chuckled. "I know. With red hair, I resemble the monsters used to frighten children to behave. It makes me laugh. How can I help you?"

Aki sighed. "If I tell you something, will you keep it to yourself?"

The bateren laughed. "At the cost of my eternal soul. It is required of all like me."

"Very well. How do I ask forgiveness?"

The bateren steepled his fingers. "First, ask yourself

why you are seeking for forgiveness? Is it for something you did to Tomasu?"

Aki took a deep breath. "It is for something I did to all of you."

She told the man everything about her uncle, her father, and how she had broken Nishioji-sama's trust.

"You tried to apologize?" he asked.

"I did. He has been a decent man toward me and my family. I lied to him and his mother. I worry about her. Now he wants nothing to do with me."

"I see."

"Can you have him forgive me?"

"Forgiveness must come from him. He must choose on his own."

"Has he mentioned anything to you about what happened?"

"I cannot break the secrecy of what he has told me, either."

"Then what should I do?"

"Give it time. Tomasu-sama does not hold to his anger."

"He may have another reason."

The bateren eyed her with a kind gaze. "What do you mean?"

Aki steeled her nerves. "I am one of the unclean."

The priest's gaze grew wide. "I did not know. The same as the man who saved your life."

"I am his daughter. I just learned I was adopted at birth. Even if Nishioji forgives me, he cannot have anything to do with me. It will shame him and his family."

The padre shook his head. "There is no shame in this."

"We are the lowest of society."

"You remain welcome in my presence. I accept your apology."

"Why do you serve undesirables?"

"Our Savior sought the outcasts in society to send his

message. He told us to seek the hungry, the thirsty, the stranger, the naked, the sick, and those in prison. We are commanded to help the least of our brethren."

Aki nodded. "What should I do now?"

"Do you know how to pray?"

"Is it like the way we pray to the Buddhist gods?"

"Not quite." The man motioned her to the front, pointing at what looked to be the focal display. She remembered it from her previous visit. "That is our Savior. You can do this when you are alone and in silence. Make your needs known. He will hear you."

Aki looked at the man on the cross. So much pain. So much terror. Yet Nishioji-sama's mother carried a cross for comfort. "This is different."

"You can ask for blessings."

"I do not deserve to ask a favor."

The priest nodded. "Then ask that His will be done. There is no greater request."

"I will need to think. I will ask when I get home."

"Think quickly, please," he said with a light laugh. "I want a calligraphy class to offer children."

Aki smiled. This *was* a friendly place. "I should return home. I have been gone most of the day."

"Very well. Hisa will take you there."

Hisa was on the other side of the room, sweeping the floor and talking with the boy. When the bateren called his name, he hustled to her.

"Are you ready to go home?"

"You have been too kind to me today."

"It's my duty. We should go now."

The two of them stepped outside. Darkness was growing. It was indeed getting late in the day.

A yell from the side made Aki freeze. Yori, the young samurai, appeared from nowhere, his sword drawn.

Hisa drew a short sword from within his coat and pressed it to her ribs. "Hold." He then drew a dagger and threw it at the young samurai. It struck him high in the chest. He dropped his sword and sank to his knees.

"Move with me now. One scream and you'll join your uncle in death."

CHAPTER THIRTY

Tomi and Matsu headed to Aki's home. He wanted to check on his mother but knew she was safe. Hopefully Aki was, too.

He slid the door open. Arai stood in view, the eldest brother at his side. Officers had notified the family about the uncle. They were here to ask questions.

"Where's Aki?" Tomi asked.

The brother looked stunned. "I do not know."

"No one else has been here," Arai answered.

Aki's father appeared behind them.

"Where's Aki?" Tomi thundered.

"She went to visit her father. She planned to stop at your church on the way home."

"Why did she go see her father?"

"Her sister came by. Her father's health worsened. He may not make it."

Tomi swallowed hard. The man who saved her life was dying. She did her duty as a daughter. He had pushed her away when he should have protected her.

"Why would she go to the church?"

"I do not know."

He nodded. "We will find her. Send a message to the

church if she comes home. They will find me."

"Is she in danger?" her father asked.

"Certain she's fine," Matsu said. "Let us know."

They left, hearing the door close behind them as they stepped into the street.

"Calm down," Matsu urged. "We'll find her. Visit your church first. Go from there."

Tomi nodded but didn't reply. A minute later, he saw a familiar face running toward him.

"Kazu," he yelled.

The boy rushed to Tomi and bowed low to both men. "Nishioji-sama, I found you."

"What has happened?"

"At the church. Your young samurai friend is hurt. The girl is gone."

"What happened?"

"Hisa. Hisa took her. He hurt your friend."

Hisa.

If he kills Aki, it will be my fault. Mother was right. "How'd you find me, Kazu?" Tomi asked.

"Padre-sama sent me to your house. Your mother told me to come here."

"What do we do?" Matsu said.

"We head to the church. If Hisa can defeat Yori, then all of Aki's family is in danger. We must do this ourselves."

The two broke into a run toward the church with Kazu trailing behind. Tomi cursed himself. The enemy had been in his midst all along.

Dead. Her uncle was dead.

When Hisa had mentioned it, he'd told her not to scream.

It was unnecessary. It took all her strength to move.

Hisa jerked her arms behind her and tied her to a post. "Why are you doing this? Nishioji-sama trusted you."

"He placed his faith in the wrong gods."

Aki pulled against her bonds, but the ropes cut into her wrists. "He will stop you."

The man from the church tightened her bonds, which pressed her arms against her sides.

"*Itai!*" Aki said. The ropes bit into her skin, tightening like a weaver's loom. She tried to scrunch her face, hoping to fight the pain.

"That's enough from you."

Another man approached. "Tantō, she's our guest. Nishioji will find us unless he's foolish. And if he is, you will find him later, despondent." He pointed to Aki. "No more outbursts from you. Women should learn their place. Learn yours."

Aki pressed her lips together tightly. She had to wait for Nishioji-sama. Hopefully, he would be here soon.

The run to the church hadn't taken long, but to Tomi it had seemed like hours. Once there, he headed to the house. Padre Alvares greeted him at the door. "Tomasu-sama, come in. Both of you."

Yori lay on the floor, awake and alert. The wound on his chest had been cauterized. Splotches of blood dotted his clothes, including a point near the shoulder that had absorbed more. A doctor worked on him. Yori remained calm, just like his brother.

"I failed," Yori said. "I thought I would surprise him, but he was too quick."

"How did you know?" Matsu asked.

"I had seen him before. When I watched that small shrine where the smugglers stored the silk threads, I saw him. When he appeared here, I knew he was part of the group you are looking for."

"He had us all fooled," the padre said. "To think anyone touched by God would be a traitor. He joined my brethren in Kyoto over three years ago. They spoke well of him. He asked to be transferred here to support our efforts in Osaka."

"An Akechi Mitsuhide among us," Tomi said. "Sorry, Padre-sama, you—"

"I know the name of the man who betrayed the regent's predecessor."

"You've learned much."

"I've had reason to learn."

Tomi felt a glimmer of hope. He would save it for another time.

"Transferred?" Matsu asked. "Requested to come here? Is that common?"

"Yes. I have letters. Do you need them?"

"Yes," Tomi said. "It might prove useful for the investigation."

"They are on my desk at the church. I will fetch them for you."

"Let's do that later. We need to figure out where he took her."

Alvares pointed to the other side of the room. "He slept over there. That closet contains his belongings. Search them."

Tomi and Matsu pulled everything from the closet. Alvares confirmed they had it all. Both men searched through his things.

Matsu found the eyepatch. "Look."

"Open it."

Matsu split the halves and found a piece of paper. Shaking his head, he passed it to Tomi. Just like the uncle, but this time in foreign letters. Unintelligible.

"Padre-sama"—he handed the paper to him—"does this mean anything to you?"

"It's Latin."

"The words of the church," Tomi said to Matsu, seeing his confusion. "What does it say?"

"It says *ecclesia*."

"How do you say it again?" Tomi asked.

"Ecclesia," the padre said.

Tomi mulled the word over. "Is it possible?"

"What?" Matsu asked.

"That group of four kanji that we saw at Aki's uncle's house. '*Ekerenshiya*' is a possible pronunciation. Padresama, would you say the word again?"

"Ecclesia."

"Sounds the same to me," Matsu said. "What does the word mean?"

The padre grunted. "It refers to church, but this is the only church in the area."

"Could it mean," Yori called out with strained breath, "something else?"

Alvares looked at the books on a nearby table. He opened one and thumbed through it. "There is an older meaning. It just means 'place to meet'.."

Tomi thought hard. Why did that sound familiar?

Again, right in my midst. "I know where they are."

"Where?" Matsu asked

"The building my father's sake company is trying to buy. It used to be a meeting place."

"The one with all the kingfishers?"

"Always with the birds."

Matsu smiled. "Show them to you after this is done."

"It must be a trap," Yori said.

"I know," Tomi said, "but I have no choice. Doctor, how is he?

The doctor bowed. "I have stopped the bleeding. He needs to rest."

"I will care for him," Alvares said.

"Yori, we'll return soon."

Alvares gestured to Tomi and Matsu to lower their heads and then uttered a few words he didn't understand. He had blessed them both. It was up to them now.

Tomi stepped outside and crossed the road. It was a clear night with a scant moon, but the wind had whipped up and was now blustery. Any guards would be concerned more with staying warm than staying focused. Better for their approach.

A low bark drew Tomi's attention. The small white dog stared at him.

Yes, my friend, I will bring her home.

Time to go.

CHAPTER THIRTY-ONE

The two of them left at a full sprint. Nothing mattered until they got close. At last, they reached their target alley, knowing the temple was down and off on its own.

A pause and press on his arm drew Tomi's attention. Matsu wanted him to hold, suggesting they should move to the side.

Tomi joined him, hiding in the shadows of a nearby awning. They slid into darkness.

"What is it?" Tomi asked. "What are you seeing?"

"Your bateren gave me a Kirishitan blessing?"

"It's appropriate."

"Too loud," Matsu whispered, mimicking a tight mouth with closed hands. "Know you're worried. Keep your voice low. Look down the street."

"What?"

"The lanterns that line the street in the middle. Lit. These are usually not lit."

Tomi scratched his chin. "Could be a change." He paused. "Or they're expecting us." He searched for shapes in the dark. Matsu grunted in agreement. "Let's try from the rear."

Tomi shook his head. "That may be watched as well."

"How then?" Matsu asked.

"Away from the river. We stay on this side and this corner, out of eyesight of the temple itself."

"Out of view? Out of sight?"

Tomi peered into the distance. "Exactly."

They doubled back two streets, planning to pass behind. A few people strolled about, a mixture of common thieves and scrap hunters. Glances their way turned to lowered stares as the people moved from them. Rows of fields lay further out. The darkness grew, and the streetlights faded.

Tomi crossed over the darkened street and then crouched down. Stray movements in the small grove drew his attention.

He motioned to Matsu, who nodded. Matsu circled the grove, while Tomi moved forward stealthily.

The man came into view, walking with his right hand on his two swords. A ronin. He would be good.

Larger noises came from Matsu's position.

The man turned.

Matsu emerged, sword drawn, and sliced him across the chest.

The man's eyes rolled up and he fell on his side on the ground.

"That's one," Matsu said. "Think there are any more?"

"No. I believe he was there to guard the rear. Likely, the lights guard the front. Now how to get in?"

Tomi scanned the wall, which was partially blocked by a tree.

A tree.

Tomi and Matsu each climbed, resting on separate large branches. Tomi surveyed the grounds in the moonlight. A figure paused at the opposite edge, mirroring someone on the other side.

"What do you think, Matsu?"

"Two guards outside the building. If we take one, the

other will notice."

"One of us should circle to the other side. We jump simultaneously."

"Agreed." Matsu responded

"Will we be able to see each other?"

"Jump when you hear my signal. I'll take the one on the far side."

"Why?"

"You're bigger. More chance to notice. Besides, I'm faster. Once in, we come in from opposite sides."

Tomi took his position and waited. Matsu's bird call broke the silence.

Now.

Tomi leapt to the ground below and knocked the guard against the wall. The man turned and drew his sword.

He couldn't have been much older than Yori.

Tomi drew his sword, sidestepped, and slashed across under the young man's chin.

The young man dropped his sword and pressed his hands on his neck to stop the flow of blood. He tried to call out, but nothing sounded. Instead, he fell to the ground.

Tomi cursed under his breath. Someone poisoned by Hisa. His youth had surprised Tomi. Tomi was fortunate. He hated to kill, but his hesitation could have cost Aki her life.

He had to find her now.

"Why did you kill my uncle?" Aki directed her question to the two men in front of her.

The one from the church stepped forward. "He had second thoughts. He wanted to give you more time. We have no more time."

"He grew a conscience," the older one added, "and became useless."

The older one tied a rag around her mouth. "Now no marriage will happen at all. Pity. But at least you have one use. To bring Nishioji here."

Tomi entered from his side and searched the rooms. Lanterns lit the walls, but the place was empty. The scent reminded him of Oeda's office as much as a temple. Two guards were within the wall. One outside. There should be more men here.

Or not. Many had died. On the boat. In the smuggling. Were these men the only ones left?

Aki was in more danger than ever. If only he could talk to Matsu, but the benefit of this approach in coming from each side meant one of them might get through to save Aki.

A creaking board and then a click sounded from the left.

Tomi ducked, drawing his weapon and looking up. A man with gleaming eyes brought his sword down. Tomi brought his up to deflect. The clang resonated through the hall. Whoever it was now knew Tomi was here.

"Worried, Kirishitan? You should be. The master wants to eliminate you himself."

Comprehension dawned. Another one from that delivery of silk threads. "He will get his chance," Tomi said.

When Tomi pushed forward, the man lost his footing. He pressed his advantage, slicing him on the arm and then across the chest.

"Kirishitan," he called out and then thudded to the floor.

Kirishitan? Aki repeated the word in her head. Did someone say it? The clanging was loud, and that meant fighting. Nishioji-sama must be here.

"He's coming," the older man said. "He is in for a surprise."

The door slid open with a flash of blue.

Hisa swung his sword, sliced down and brought red.

Matsu-sama.

They traded three quick strikes. Matsu-sama cut Hisa's leg. Hisa slashed Matsu-sama's chest and stomach. Matsu sank to his knees and then fell forward. Hisa was injured but standing.

"Well done, Tantō. Better than I hoped," the older man said. "Only one left." He stepped back and into the shadows. "I'm going to enjoy this."

Tomi slid each door open and stepped back, expecting someone to charge. When no one came, he checked and moved on.

The next scene took his breath.

Matsu lay on the floor, injured and barely moving. His sword lay at his side, a tribute to his last fight. Aki was tied to a wall, a cloth in her mouth to prevent her from warning him.

Hisa held his long sword up, ready to fight. His smug expression showed his true self. "Welcome, Tomasu." He sneered as he pronounced his Baptismal name. "You have made me wait."

His former friend moved to the side, showing a small limp as he favored one leg. Matsu had inflicted damage.

Tomi took a deep breath. Would the injury give him an advantage?

Hisa assumed a fighting stance. Tomi countered.

"Why did you betray us?" Tomi asked.

"My true master bade me study and pretend to be one of you. He knew the time would come when having someone inside your accursed sect would be beneficial."

"We have done you no harm."

"Enough talk."

The two circled. Tomi struck. Hisa parried. Blade met blade. Hisa swung around and tried to surprise him.

Pain crossed Hisa's face. He couldn't lift his katana high enough.

Tomi pressed forward, slashed Hisa's wrist, and then

sliced his neck.

Life drained from Hisa's face. He dropped his sword.

Tomi looked at Aki. Her eyes told him to stay back.

Another man stepped out of the shadows, blocking Aki from his view.

"Well done, *Tomasu*, well done."

Tomi stared at the new person who mocked his name. "Who are you?"

"My name is Wakizashi. We met once before in battle. I doubt you remember."

Remember? The man before him was a stranger, but something about him Tomi knew.

What was it Goto said before he died? The attacker looked familiar.

Tomi's body froze in astonishment.

"Impossible," he said. "You're dead!"

CHAPTER THIRTY-TWO

"You know me now, I see," the man said. "Do you remember me from Negoro-ji, or are the faces you slaughtered then a blur?"

"Many brave warrior monks died in that battle. The faces haunt me even now."

"They should. I would have died then, too, but for my younger brother. A man you know well."

Oeda. Even without the picture on the shrine in Oeda's office, the family resemblance to the constable was clear. No wonder the smugglers were always ahead of them. Oeda must have kept his brother informed or felt he had no choice as the younger brother. Anger barreled through Tomi like a waterfall. Yori injured. Matsu dying.

He glanced at Aki. Her life depended on him, too. "This explains why your brother's shrine is not at his house."

"I've never liked his wife. She knows I'm alive. It's why she wouldn't allow it."

"Why do you hate my faith?"

"Because of a Kirishitan, a worthy ruler of this country died. One who can take his place seeks revenge."

"Who is that?"

"Defeat me, and I will tell you. Lose to me, and your god can tell you. Either way, you will learn soon. *Saru*, the monkey Hideyoshi himself, will learn when he is toppled."

A plot against the regent. If only he could get that to Uji. He glanced down. Matsu moved a bit. Perhaps there was still time to save him.

Wakizashi advanced and swung hard with a horizontal strike.

Tomi ducked and rolled left. He swung up and then turned. After two more parries, the man smiled. He was trying to goad Tomi, but Tomi would have none of it. Too much was at stake.

Tomi glanced at Aki. Wakizashi charged, slipping through and cutting Tomi's cheek.

Tomi stepped back out and struck a defensive posture.

"That was careless, Nishioji. I expected more. After I am finished with you, the woman will survive for my enjoyment for a while."

Anger boiled within him. Tomi pressed. Wakizashi's leer taunted him and pulled him forward.

Back him up and right.

Tomi shifted left and forced Wakizashi to match. *A little more. A little more.*

Wakizashi hit Matsu's leg. He dropped his guard. His balance teetered. Tomi shoved him toward the floor. Wakizashi held up his sword as he fell.

Tomi swung down at the hilt with all his might.

Wakizashi's sword fell to the ground. Blood dripped from his fingers. Tomi reversed and struck the man's face and arm.

It was over.

Tomi knocked the sword away and put his own blade against Wakizashi's neck. The blood ran from his shoulder. "Now talk. Fulfill your bargain."

"On one condition." Wakizashi reached his knees and then sat on the backs of his feet. He removed his short sword and scabbard from his sash and placed it on the ground.

"Permit me the honor?"

"I'm not stopping you."

"I need a *kaishakunin*."

Serve as his second? Allow the man to slit his own stomach for honor and then cut off his head. No. There must be another way. There were reasons to kill, but none to justify this.

"I cannot." *God would never forgive me for serving as a second.*

"Deny me honor, and you will not know."

What could Tomi do? Could he face judgement?

Serving as a second would be an act of mercy. Like breaking legs to speed the death of the condemned. He had no choice.

"Talk first. Why were you collecting jade?"

"We send the jade to China. There is a new warlord. The jade buys him power and respect. He sends silk and silk thread, skirting the laws, as payment. We sell the excess and fund our operations."

"Who is Eijiro?"

The man tilted his head. "You have learned some things. He is someone close to the Regent. To find him, follow the tea leaves. To stop him, you must find his wife, his missing Kirishitan wife."

"A woman named Iri?"

Wakizashi's eyes opened wide, and he nodded in respect. "She is in the capital. Lord Eijiro does not know where."

Tomi signaled his affirmation. Wakizashi opened his kosode and bared his belly while Tomi sliced Aki's bonds, telling her to stay against the wall. He stepped behind Wakizashi and raised his katana. There was no water to purify the blade, but the man did not deserve full honors.

Wakizashi withdrew his short sword.

Matsu stirred, lunged at Wakizashi, and stabbed him

in the chest.

The man gurgled. Matsu withdrew his blade and struck again.

Wakizashi fell forward.

"Matsu," Tomi's voice rose, "you still have life."

"Yes," he said, "but I don't have much time."

Tomi and Aki hastened to Matsu.

"I thought you near dead," Tomi said.

"I will be soon." He coughed and sputtered. "I have learned much about you since we came to Osaka. I saw your conflict. Your faith does not let you take a life. I knew killing him, even in mercy, would be against your beliefs."

Tomi patted his shoulder. "There is still time."

He grabbed Tomi's hand. "There is none."

He stared into his friend's eyes. "Yes, there is. Accept what I have accepted. He awaits you."

Matsu smiled and coughed up blood. "Nishioji no Tsuneomi, I must decline one last time. Worry not, my friend. See each other again. Your God is love and sacrifice. Today, for the two of you," He grabbed Aki's hand and placed it in Tomi's, "I do both."

"What can I do for you?"

He handed his swords to Tomi. "Take these to the sanshin player. Tell her I would have said yes."

Matsu's body went limp and ceased to move.

CHAPTER THIRTY-THREE

Kyoto, Japan. Three days later.

"So Wakizashi is dead?" Eijiro asked, his breath slow and deliberate, as he stared at his two compatriots, Akagi and Fukuhara.

"Yes, sir," Akagi said. The thin samurai's swarthy grin portrayed his rough upbringing. "Nishioji killed him. That is all we know. Tantō is dead, too."

"Tantō, as well? I will miss his written musings. *Saru* needs his failures brought to his face. What about Wakizashi's worthless brother?"

"His brother resigned his position and plans to take the tonsure. Should I have him killed?"

"I would not silence a new Buddhist priest. We have other tasks for now. Come closer."

The two men drew nearer. They were obedient servants and had performed well in searching for Iri. A letter from the empress had arrived. The report was hard to believe. His beloved Iri was hiding in the capital.

All this time, you were here, my love. Hiding so close. How could I not have detected your presence?

"The Empress's letter has pleased you, has it not, my lord?" Akagi asked.

"Immensely, but there is much to do."

"What next?" Fukuhara asked.

Eijiro stroked his chin. "Mobilize our remaining followers. Check the local nunneries."

"You no longer believe her to be with Kirishitan?"

"She is likely still with them.

"Is there a divorce nunnery?"

"Not here in the capital, but she is somewhere. We will find her."

Akagi and Fukuhara bowed low and hurried away. Eijiro smiled to himself and then turned to the window, looking out at the lamps burning on the streets of the city. Tonight, they lacked a moon. Darkness was the best time to search.

Iri, my love, we will be together soon, and we will make this nation as it should be.

Osaka, Japan. Five days later.

Aki looked at the church with less trepidation than she had in the past. Two samurai stood at the entrance, supposedly standing guard. An important guest, Nishioji had said, but that Aki could meet her another day.

It had been over a week since Matsubara's death. The funeral was held yesterday. A debt she could never repay. She would clean his grave regularly along with the woman who had cried and played the sanshin.

Nishioji had eyed her strangely when she mentioned her plans to him but said he understood.

Aki walked around the grounds. Kazu was hard at work.

The bateren returned. "We are excited about your class. I expect people here before the next hour."

"You should be ready for the children by then," Nishioji called out.

Aki watched the handsome samurai approach. "What

should we do until then?"

"Always time to discuss your wedding," the bateren said.

"If she has time," Nishioji said.

Aki smiled but kept to herself. For once, time felt ample. The adoption had been official. Her uncle had become her father. Since uncle had no heirs, his property passed down to Aki by law. Genta could run one shop. She could run the other, though Shuji would do sales. She could do the finances on both with Shio's help. She and Shio apparently had much in common.

Her father was also as happy as she had ever seen him. Both fathers were. "I have time to talk."

"Must we wait the standard mourning time?" Nishioji asked.

"My uncle died because he cared for how I felt. I still detest him, but since I now have his properties, I should honor him."

"We should honor her uncle," the bateren said. "It will give her time to learn more about us."

"Maybe by then," Aki said, feeling her cheeks warm, "I can use your Kirishitan name in your presence."

He leaned in, brushed his lips on her cheek, and then whispered in her ear. "When we're alone, you may."

EPILOGUE

Two weeks later

"You're about to become a rich man," Ujihiro said.

"I don't know about that," Tomi said, standing on the steps of the Justice Building. "Aki is busy with her uncle's property. My new position occupies all my time. Were you hoping to see the wedding soon?"

"I will make the trip on that day." He lowered his voice. "I received your last report. We need to talk."

"We can go to my office." Tomi was not accustomed to saying that yet. After the revelation about his brother, Constable Oeda resigned and took the tonsure. Tomi was promoted to fill his role.

"Actually, I wish to pay my respects to an old friend first."

Nishioji motioned for Ujihiro to follow him. They headed west several blocks and crossed the main road, reaching a temple in the earliest stages of repair. "This is the place where it all happened."

"Why here?" Uji asked.

"We have a new cemetery for those killed serving the people." Five graves dotted the fresh landscape. They walked to the most prominent place. There lay Matsu's grave."

"You think Matsu wants to be here?" Uji asked.

"A request from Oeda. After becoming a monk, he is taking over the place where Matsu died. Oeda says he will make it respectable again."

"How did they maintain this building so long?"

"A person in the Administration Building was keeping the building from being transferred with the help of someone at the castle. That person has since taken his own life. We do not know who at the castle was involved."

"How are you handling your new role?" Ujihiro asked.

"With Yori's help," Tomi grimaced. "His family got approved for a new name, so he is now my assistant. Oeda did many things. One day I may visit Matsu just to ask Oeda questions."

"What is the update?"

Tomi related the news of the plot against Hideyoshi, the finding of the eyepatches, Wakizashi's reference to tea, and the search for a woman in Kyoto. "What does this mean?"

"No idea, but we need to get word to my brother, Toshi. He could use help. Any suggestions?"

"Is there a divorce nunnery in the capital?" Tomi asked.

"I've only heard of the one in Kamakura. If there is one in the capital, it may take a woman to find it."

"I know a sanshin-playing former *yūjo* who wants revenge."

"May be a good idea," Uji said "How about your. . .padre? Will he help?"

"What happened with Hisa has made him wary. I will ask. I'm certain he will find a way."

"We will need to stay close. Let me know when the wedding day comes."

AUTHOR'S HISTORICAL NOTES

Thank you for reading *The Samurai's Soul*. This is a work of fiction, and some liberties have been taken. Overall, I've endeavored to make the story as historically accurate as possible, but there are likely errors. Please email me with any mistakes you find.

For those offended by the term "eta", I apologize. I endeavored to use it as little as possible. I learned about Japan's "undesirables" when I went there in the early 90s on the JET program, a government program that places native language speakers in Japan's public school system. One of the things we learned during training was never to ask students where they lived in town. This is because the stigma from long ago remained. The challenges for this group became more poignant when I started teaching. My supervisor at the junior high school where I worked often wore an odd medallion. I later learned it was an anti-defamation symbol and that he worked to promote acceptance of this marginalized group. It's one of the things I remember most about him.

I worked with maps of Osaka under Hideyoshi, trying to fill-in what was there (e.g. the pleasure district and undesirables' village) and subtract what wasn't (e.g. canals completed after 1590) and created a makeshift map. In January 2025, a long-time Osaka resident and volunteer at the Osaka History Museum reviewed my map and made corrections. I got the pleasure district correct, placing it south of what is today Namba. However, I had the main undesirables' village in Nakajima (modern-day Nakanoshima). My guide said it was beyond the pleasure district. I took his word for it and modified my manuscript.

Time during the day is measured in roughly two-hour increments and Chinese zodiac references. The increments are as follows.

Rat: 11:00 PM – 1:00 AM	Horse: 11:00 AM - 1:00 PM
Ox: 1:00 AM – 3:00 AM	Ram: 1:00 PM – 3:00 PM
Tiger: 3:00 AM – 5:00 AM	Monkey: 3:00 PM – 5:00 PM
Rabbit: 5:00 AM – 7:00 AM	Rooster: 5:00 PM - 7:00 PM
Dragon: 7:00 AM – 9:00 AM	Dog: 7:00 PM – 9:00 PM
Snake: 9:00 AM – 11:00 AM	Boar: 9:00 PM – 11:00 PM

To meet at the "hour of the snake" meant to meet at the middle of the two-hour period or 10:00 a.m. The hours before and after the middle were broken up into 15-minute increments which allowed people to further specify time. Some people would divide them into 30-minute divisions.

A complete list of historical details will be available for separate download. (Check my website for more information.) Key elements are listed below.

Hideyoshi's Anti-Christian Edicts – In July of 1587, Toyotomi Hideyoshi issued edicts ordering the Jesuits out of the country within twenty days. The Jesuits stalled for time, citing it was the wrong time of year to sail back to Macao. Hideyoshi also needed the Jesuits for foreign trade. When the time came, only a small number of missionaries left Japan.

Lunar New Year – The Lunar New Year in the book is February 4 on the Gregorian (modern-day) calendar, though sources differ by a day. Jesuit missionaries in Japan used the Gregorian calendar. However, to adapt to the culture, the Jesuits celebrated High Mass on significant local holidays such as the Lunar New Year.

Clothing – The word "kimono" is not used in this book as the term has not yet entered the Japanese language.

Osaka Castle – Modern-day Osaka Castle is white. The Osaka Castle built by Hideyoshi in the 1580s was black. There are paintings online if the reader is interested.

The use of "-sama" – In 1590, the term "-sama", an honorary form of address, is in use. However, the better known "-san" has not entered the language.

Sanshin – Sanshin is the 16th century name for the shamisen. It means "three strings". The instrument reached the Ryukyu Island chain in the early to mid-16th century and central Japan later.

Rich man and poor man story – The story is called *The King of Farts* and can be found with an online search.

The term "constable" – The word used for this position is *yoriki* while the word for officer is *doshin*. These terms are appropriate beginning in the 17th century but debatable for the 16th century. I deferred to the term "constable" as it appeared in books on Japanese history.

New Administration Building – Hideyoshi initiated a massive building spree in Osaka in the 1580s. I do not know that he built such a building. However, when he took control of Nagasaki from the Jesuits in 1587, his first action was to order a new Administration Building be built.

Smallpox – Smallpox was common in Japan. The nation endured several epidemics over the centuries. Those who had survived the disease could be identified by pock marks on their faces.

Shitennōji incense – A priest at Shitennōji informed the author that the temple uses various grades of camphor. It has been used as incense in Japan for centuries.

Odawara – In 1590, only one clan, the Hōjō, still challenged Hideyoshi's rule. The final battle, The Siege of Odawara, began in May 1590. Hideyoshi's forces departed Kyoto at the beginning of the third lunar month. The story assumes preparations have begun in Kyoto.

Ryukyu – A group of islands that stretches south from Kyushu, the southernmost of Japan's four main islands. This group includes Okinawa.

Ishida Mitsunari – An advisor to Hideyoshi, Mitsunari was one of the most powerful men in Japan. However, he was known for his administrative skills as opposed to his battle prowess.

Medieval Japanese birthing practices – Per NHK,

Japan's educational network, women were kept awake and seated for seven days after the birth to protect against health issues and demons. Luis Frois, a sixteenth-century Jesuit missionary in Japan, stated that Japanese women remain seated for twenty days after birth.

Cotton – Cotton was a growing industry in the late 16th century, and land outside Osaka was shifting to it. The one challenge was that it required four times the fertilizer other goods did.

Church in Osaka – The church and seminary in Osaka were both destroyed following Hideyoshi's expulsion order in 1587, and Masses were celebrated in the homes of wealthy benefactors. The mission is fictitious; however, creating church buildings from old Buddhist temples was common.

The pronunciation of Alvares – Though modern Japanese has ways to approximate a "v" sound, such lettering didn't exist in the 16th century. Tomi hears a "b" sound in Alvares's name.

The pronunciation of Osaka – In modern Japanese, Osaka is pronounced with an "s" sound. In the 16th century, it was pronounced with a "z" sound. A Japanese speaker would have used a light "z" sound. A Portuguese speaker would have used a heavy "z" sound, as Tomi notices.

The Kamakura Divorce Nunnery – The divorce nunnery in Kamakura is more synonymous with the Tokugawa Era (1603 – 1868), but the temple itself predates it. Supposedly, women would throw their shoes over a wall and then request asylum in the nunnery.

Calling out at the front door – Knocking on the door is not a custom in this period. Some would even open another person's door and then call out inside the house.

Jōdo Shinshū – The Jōdo Shinshū (or "True Pure Land Sect" in English) had a temple called Ishiyama Honganji (also written as "Hongan-ji"). The temple inspired economic growth in Osaka; however, in 1570, Oda

Nobunaga laid siege to it due to its strategic location. The siege lasted until 1580, when the temple was burned.

Scrawled writing – Graffiti was not uncommon in Japan, but it could get one executed. I chose "scrawled writing" as the term "graffiti" doesn't fit the story.

Harima jade – After Hideyoshi placed Takayama Ukon in control of Harima Province, Ukon destroyed Buddhist temples, sent jade to Osaka, and converted much of the populace to Christianity. Ukon was exiled from Japan in 1614 and martyred in The Philippines in 1615.

Rice storage – In later years, provinces would store rice in Osaka and create futures contracts to satisfy taxes. In 1590, the practice of storing rice in Osaka is in its infancy.

The regent controls Osaka – Certain districts were under direct control of Hideyoshi vs. having a daimyo in charge of the area. Osaka was one such place. Nagasaki was another.

Associate in China – The associate in China is a Ming Dynasty rebel.

Four-character kanji riddle – The term *eccelsia* would have likely been uttered with a Portuguese pronunciation. It had one kanji translation in this time: 恵化連舎. This would have been pronounced as both エケレンシヤ (ekerenshiya) and エケレンシャ (ekerensha). The contraction "sha" for "shiya" would have been been verbal only, as the written contraction form did not exist in 1590. The kanji grouping of 得計錬者 is meant to be a joke by Hisa.

ACKNOWLEDGMENTS

The voice was heard a second time: "What God has
purified you are not to call unclean."
- Acts 10:15. The New American Bible

This story was initially inspired by the quote above. Having Aki be from society's undesirables was part of the story from Day One. Giving Tomi's mother leprosy came later. I originally started with the quote that comes from the Revised Standard Version, Second Catholic Edition. There the quote reads: *And the voice came to him again a second time, "What God has cleansed, you must not call common."* This is my current Bible and the source used for Tomi's quote to Matsu on the question about his philosopher. However, I couldn't get the word "unclean" out of my head, so I posted the NAB version from the Bible I read as a teenager.

The Samurai's Soul has been rewritten about eight times. Occasionally, I wanted to ignore the story, but Tomi's time in Osaka needed to be told. I spent two years in Sakai, just south of the city of Osaka, and love the area, so I wanted an Osaka-based story.

There are many people who deserve thanks for their assistance in this novel. I hope I don't forget anyone. Please forgive me if I do. Also note that any mistakes made in historical and other details are completely the author's fault.

Thank you to Dr. Sachi Schmidt-Hori, Associate Professor in Japanese Literature & Culture at Dartmouth College. One of Dr. Schmidt-Hori's specialties is pre-17th century Japanese linguistics. She corrected my impressions on how my characters would hear a Portuguese accent and created the four-kanji puzzle that Tomi and Matsu discover.

Thank you to Riki Ohkanda and Doris Newsom for providing a beta review of my complete story and letting me know where my heroine was both anachronistic and disconnected.

Thank you to author Charles Kowalski, who writes a few decades after me. He reviewed the final draft for errors and made suggestions.

Thank you to authors Lydia Kang and Lindi Peterson for reviews and insights of the early chapters. Lydia Kang, who is a medical doctor, also reviewed medical issues related to a deleted prologue that shows how Aki's biological and adopted families came together. The prologue will be released separately with complete historical details.

Thank you to Dr. Mary Elizabeth Berry, Professor of History Emerita at Berkeley for pointing me in the right direction for research on late 16th century Osaka.

Thank you to author John Kang and RVA Katana in Richmond, Virginia, for allowing me to use a picture of one of the swords from their website on the cover.

Thank you to Thiago Guilhon, former co-worker and fellow Japanophile. A native of Brazil who spent a few years in Japan, Thiago introduced me to the challenges Portuguese speakers have with the Japanese language. Thank you to the Portuguese embassy in Tokyo for documenting these challenges.

Thank you to Chuchu Wang, current co-worker, who assisted with questions I had about Chinese history.

Thank you to Dr. John Nicholson of the University of Geogia Department of Classics, Amy Smoler of the University of Georgia Department of Linguistics, and Fr. Augustine Tran, former vicar at my church, for assisting me with my Latin research and questions.

Thank you to Eriko Miyagawa, Co-Executive Producer of *Shōgun*, who answered questions on the dialogue process and directed me to additional resources.

Thank you to Carlos Rosario, Costume Designer on *Shōgun*, whose posted about the wardrobe on social media after each episode in the ten-part series and answered every question fans had. While there wasn't a direct discussion related to my book, I learned things that improved my descriptions.

Thank you to Dean Eilertson, Property Master on *Shōgun*, for answering questions about the crosses and rosaries worn by some of the characters in the series.

Thank you to Ryuta Kato, translator behind the scenes on *Shōgun*, for answering questions I had about the language used in the series.

Thank you to wife's cousin, Mina Goami, who spent a day with me touring Osaka to help me confirm some historical details. Thank you to the docent at the Osaka History Museum, who reviewed my Osaka map and answered Osaka history questions. I cannot find your name in my notes, but I know that you were a retired Kubota engineer.

Thank you to Yuki Sekiya from the Japanese Midwives Association (JMA) for her explanation on the historical role of midwives in Japan, and to author Teresa Roman, who with her prior experience in helping deliver babies under her real name, made some background suggestions.

Thank you to Ciara Knight, who did the development edit on this book.

Thank you to Mary Marvella Barfield for the copy edit on this book.

Thank to you my writer's group, Georgia Romance Writers. The opportunities and support you provide are amazing.

Thank you to historians in my bibliography for your books on Japanese history. Again, all historical or technical mistakes in this book are the fault of the author.

Lastly, thank you to my wife, Motoyo, and my sons, Andrew and Christopher, for putting up with my writing-related obsessions.

BIBLIOGRAPHY

The list below suggests references for further reading.

Berry, Mary Elizabeth – *Hideyoshi*. Published 1982 by The Council on East Asian Studies Harvard University.

Boxer, C. R. – *The Christian Century in Japan 1549-1650*. Published 1951 by University of California Press and Cambridge University Press.

Burns, Susan L. – *Kingdom of the Sick: A History of Leprosy and Japan*. Published 2019 by University of Hawaii Press.

Cooper, Michael S.J. (Editor) – *They Came to Japan: An Anthology of European Reports on Japan, 1543 – 1640*. Reprinted 1995 by the Center for Japanese Studies, The University of Michigan.

Elison, George – *Deus Destroyed: The Image of Christianity in Early Modern Japan*. Published 1988 by Council on East Asian Studies Harvard University.

Hauser, William B. – *Economic Institutional Change in Tokugawa Japan; Osaka and the Kinai Cotton Trade*. Published 1974 by Cambridge University Press.

Hideyoshi and Osaka Castle; A look into its history and mystery. Published 1988 by the City of Osaka and the Osaka Tourist Association.

Kenkō (also Yoshida Kenkō) – *Essays in Idleness; The Tsurezuregusa of Kenkō*. Translated and with a preface by Donald Keene. Published 1967 by Columbia University Press.

McLain, James L. & Wakita, Osamu (Editors) – *Osaka, the merchant's capital of early modern Japan*. Published 1999 by Cornell University Press.

Tales of Tears and Laughter; Short Fiction of Medieval Japan. Translated by Virginia Skord. Published 1991 by University of Hawaii Press.

ABOUT THE AUTHOR

Walt Mussell lives in the Atlanta area with his wife. He works for a well-known corporation and writes in his spare time. Walt writes historical novels with a focus on Japan, an interest he gained during the four years he lived there. He is working on his next book, *The Samurai's Strength*, which takes place in Kyoto (early 1591). Outside of writing, his favorite activity is trying to keep up with his kids. As both are college graduates, this is proving difficult.

You can follow Walt on Instagram, TikTok, and Threads as @authorwaltmussell, on X as @wmussell, and as Walt Mussell on YouTube. Please check out his Japanese history videos. Please sign up for his Substack newsletter *The Chrysanthemum and the Cross* and visit his website www.waltmussell.com. Please contact him via his website or at authorwaltmussell@yahoo.com.

Walt offers lectures, both virtual and in person, on *Japan's Christian Century* and *St. Paul Miki and His Companions*. He is available to speak on other topics related to Japan's Christian Century. Please reach out to him via his website or the email address above.